THE STUDENT

Philmore Butts

ISBN: 978-1-962231-39-8 (Hardback Edition)
ISBN: 978-1-962231-40-4 (Paperback Edition)
ISBN: 978-1-962231-41-1 (EPUB)

Published by: Crosswords Noble House
Cover Design by: Crosswords Noble House
Interior Design by: Crosswords Noble House

This biography is a work of non-fiction. The events described within are true to the best of the author's knowledge. Names, characters, places, and incidents either are the product of the author's experience or are used fictitiously. Any resemblance to actual events or locales or persons, living or dead, is entirely coincidental.

Book Ordering Information:
Crosswords Noble House
165 Broadway Suite 23rd Floor,
New York, NY 10006, USA

info@crosswordsnoblehouse.com
www.crosswordsnoblehouse.com
(646) 825-3389 | Ext. 1102

Printed in the United States of America

CHAPTER
ONE

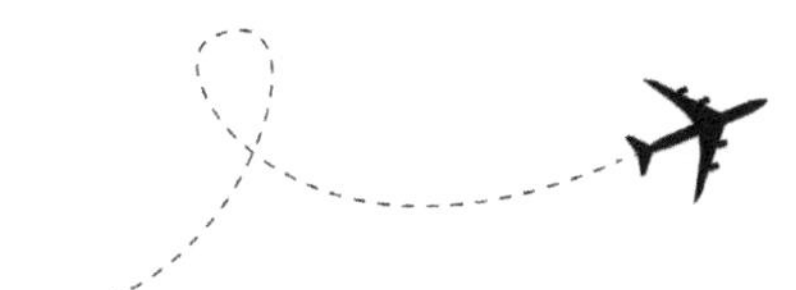

High school life is crazy when everyone's goal is to get laid. It appears as though the media had turned everyone into sex crazed zombie's. I'm not a homosexual, nor have I ever considered becoming one. My associates believe that I'm queer, because they've never seen me with any one of the opposite sex. They would often leave humorous 'queer' notes on my locker and on my desk, but I didn't let it bother me.

I dated a girl named Carla in my freshman year, but we had to go our separate ways once we became juniors. She and I had a lot in common and it all fell apart once she realized that there were feelings for an old boyfriend. It cannot be said that I've been celibate since my junior year, but the mere fact that I was committed to my textbooks left me open for all sorts of criticisms.

The criticisms don't bother me, because I consider myself to be as much of a man as my dad. He was the only one who believed that I was destined to become a doctor. My dad was a "player" in his day, but once he decided to make a life with my mom, he put his old ways behind him. They supported one-another while my dad was in med. school, but once she became pregnant with my sister, Krystal, and my brother James, the commitment was made. However, my mom was always busy heading the law firm that she received as an inheritance.

Before we moved into this incredibly large home, I was fortunate enough to have lived in some of the most affluent cities in the America. By the time my parents had decided to make this our permanent home, I had decided what career field was most appealing to me. For years I wanted to study law, but once my grandmother died of ovarian cancer, the decision for my dad to move to Chicago became easier to make, along with my decision to become a gynecologist. It was my dad's idea for me to attend Lake Forest Academy high school and excel in science courses, because he believed that these courses would benefit me in the future.

I attended a prestigious private school in a suburban area, and by my dad being a reputable physician, he made sure that I attended the proper classes. My classmates think I'm weird, while others knew that I was focused. I was striving for something. The academic scholarship was the break that I needed, because it's the beginning of greater things to come. Interestingly enough, I was chosen to receive the scholarship.

I would like to be the first to admit that I didn't have sex a lot during high school, but I did manage to get my groove on from time-to-time. Sex was something that I indulged in when I wasn't trying to make the grades. However, making the grades was always primary. Leaving my junior high girlfriend behind was difficult for me, because she was my first, but I've managed to adjust to these 'windy city' girls. After all, I was striving for a scholarship to med. school and I wasn't trying to establish anything permanent with anyone.

It didn't make sense to me as to why everyone

was interested in the person I was doing, but I guess that's the part about growing up that my grandparents tried to explain to me. When I wasn't studying or trying to bust my balls, I was busy shooting basketball. The school coach often asked me to come to varsity tryouts, but receiving a sports scholarship wasn't of interest to me.

It was obvious that the jocks had all the girls, but by the end of the semester many of the jocks were strung out on drugs and the girls were overweight, single mothers. I believed that I was hassled because my game was different from others. The goal was to earn the grades and eliminate all distractions. Overall, I wanted to be just like my dad, because my sister and brother had made a commitment to become lawyers, so it was only fair for me to follow in my fathers footsteps.

All of my life my dad's work in his field gave him so much joy. If I can manage to be as helpful to others and find joy in it, I would feel successful, also. After all, I've got to put forth my best, because I've only wanted to become a physician for about two years. My grandmother's passing was the spark of my medical interest. 'To think that someday I will be able to call my self Dr. Harris,' brought about a certain joy within me, because I wanted to help others. My mom always said that anyone could be nothing, but that it took even more to become something. Those words have been my guiding force since grade school.

I was out of school for three months and I couldn't wait to move out of state and get a real taste of campus life. Through months of research, I decided to attend a university in Michigan. I had considered attending a nearby university, but I believed that an out-of-state university would be a better choice. The city of Ann Arbor was known as a 'college town' and I was eager to move away from Chicago. My mom has family in Michigan and her older sister had opened her doors and welcomed me inside, so I was set.

We hadn't seen each other since my freshman year, but I can remember that my aunt Joyce was a sweet person. She and her family lived in a Detroit suburb called Southfield. It didn't boast the elite homes that I was accustomed too, but they were nice. My aunt is a hairstylist who owns and operates a salon in Detroit, and my uncle Ray works as an engineer for one of the 'big three' car companies nearby. Uncle Ray was preparing to retire in the spring and he was hoping that he and I and my cousins could get together and spend some time on his boat. He has always enjoyed fishing, but I wasn't very fond of spending my time on a boat fishing for something that I wasn't going to eat.

Aunt Joyce and uncle Ray have three sons that aren't much older than I am. What makes us different is the fact that they're criminals. The oldest son takes care of his seven children with drug money; the second son is a junkie and the baby-boy is on probation for attempt murder. All of that doesn't matter, because we didn't have a perfect family. It will just be good to see them, because several years have gone by and things have changed considerably. This will be an opportunity to reconnect with my family and unwind. However, I was looking forward to attending one of the strip parties that my cousin Ray would throw every season, because I've heard that they are outrageous.

I had planned to leave on the last Saturday in August, and I was overjoyed with anticipation. My mom had to be in the office for an early meeting, and my dad was gone before I awakened. Mom came into my room to say her last words to me with tears in her eyes. "Well, this is the big day. Your father and I put something in your bank account for a rainy day, because we know that you have got to survive," she said. Mom sat on the side of the bed and wiped her tears as I clutched my pillow. "Mom, do anything, but please don't cry. I'm going away to school, not war," I said. "Michigan is four-and-a-half hours away and you and dad can come and visit anytime. However, I'll probably be back before you guys make it there. After all, the holidays are quickly approaching, and you know that I'll be looking forward to seeing everyone. I may need you and dad to come up and visit a-lot, because I'm going to miss those Sunday dinners." She and I laughed over that remark, as I sat up and embraced her.

Wiping away the tears, she said, "I'm not crying because you're leaving for school, but it's because I'm going to miss seeing you. When I come home from work, I've always known that you were going to be home to greet me. Your dad is here, but it's not the same. I place my faith in God and I know that you're going to be okay. Although, while you're in Michigan, I'll appreciate it if you would call your aunt, and your cousins." She then gave me a hug and kiss before leaving the room.

The look on my mom's face was all that I could remember, as I thought about what the girls were like in Michigan. When I spoke with my aunt, she assured me that my cousins would introduce me to the 'right' girls. What my aunt didn't know was that I could find my own girls, and I heard that Michigan has a lot of them. There's a young pussy, black pussy, white pussy, several kinds of pussy, seeking attention and physical contact in Michigan. The more I drove, the more excited I became. After-all, there is nothing like fresh, out of state booty. I had $35,000 in my bank account, I'm four hours from home and I have family in the same state. Filled with joy, I drove at the steady speed of 90 mph and it seemed like I wasn't getting there fast enough. Once I saw the sign that read 'Welcome to Michigan,' a different kind of feeling came over me. It was a feeling of elation. An overwhelming excitement.

When I arrived onto the campus, there were people coming from everywhere. They were white, black, Chinese, all kinds of people, of many origins. The women looked hot and I could only imagine the things that I would experience before my education was complete. Standing 6'4, weighing 190 lbs., an athletic build...Adam Harris was now ready to face the world as a freshman from Chi-town. Ready to conquer the 'Big D.'

I didn't know anyone and no one knew me. Everything from this point was going to be a new experience. With money in the bank and my classes/ supplies paid for, I only had to concern myself with meals and clothes. My car was paid for and I had unlimited minutes on my cellphone. I was about to begin living like a "black prince." Therefore, I unpacked and took a stroll around campus and through the neighborhood. Every girl I saw was more attractive than the last. The shops and eateries were crowded with individuals running up tabs on their parents credit cards.

This town reminded me of Key West, because it had such narrow streets. As I stared at the buildings and nearby homes, I saw a woman run past me that was so damn gorgeous that I wanted to run next to her. The black hair was done in a ponytail, she wore spandex shorts and had one of the firmest behinds of everyone woman on the street. 'If I could somehow run into her again, I would make her my own private joy,' I thought. "Well, if it's meant to be, it will be," I whispered while staring over my shoulder.

However, I couldn't be rude and ignore all of the other pretty faces that were nearby. Seeing a group of people at an arcade really caught my attention, so I walked inside. Video games are favorites of mine and this was a great opportunity to play some games and meet a few friendly faces. Once inside, I noticed that the games that I was interested in were all taken. All of the cute girls were with someone, so I wandered back onto the street and made my way toward the dorms.

The first class I attended was Anatomy and I heard that the teacher was so attractive that I wouldn't be able to take my eyes off of her, although from a distance the instructor did look familiar. Her name was Miss Daly and she stood 5'5 with shoulder length black hair that was so dark that it looked like it was washed in black ink. It held a glimmering shine. Someone pointed her out to me before class started and I was impressed. She had skin that appeared to be as soft a baby's butt.

Miss Daly appeared to be in her twenties, but that didn't matter to me if the vibes were right. Besides, I've always had a thing for older women. When she entered the room, half the guys stared while the others sat there like mummies. From her small waist to her petite feet, she was definitely a "ten." Looking as if she was desperate for attention. 'Judging from her size, I'll bet that her vagina is as tight as a hat band,' I thought with a smile. However, as attractive as she was, I would love to make her acquaintance.

As the weeks went by, I focused on my grades and less time thinking about Miss Daly. I aced everything she threw my way. However, acing her assignments was only the beginning. Miss Daly tried to come across as someone with an education from Harvard or Berkeley, because she put a lot of effort into making her assignments as difficult as possible. Her efforts were a waste of time, because when you got it, you've got it. The assignments were teasers and I actually got a big laugh out of them. It was at this point that I was grateful for having paid attention in my science classes during those four years of high school. However, it wasn't long before other students were coming to me for help and I believe that's what upset her the most. It was as if Miss Daly taught the class, and I would come behind her and add clarity to what she had previously discussed.

While studying in the library one Saturday afternoon, I looked up from my text and she was standing over me. Miss Daly wore a pair of body hugging, designer denim jeans and jacket. Her hair was done in a ponytail and she wore designer sandals. It then dawned on me that she was the girl that ran past as I walked across the campus. "Am I keeping you from your studies," she asked? I shook my head as I sat back in my chair trying to believe what I was seeing. Slowly, she removed her jacket and placed it over her forearm, giving me a chance to take a glance at her toned thighs. While she spoke, I stared at Miss Daly's crotch, surprised that the woman whom I wanted to meet was actually my instructor. This felt like a grade school crush, but she was attractive and there's nothing wrong with doing a little daydreaming.

It wasn't long after she started speaking that Miss Daly invited me to lunch. Spontaneously, I shouted "Yes!" I sat there startled as Miss Daly walked around the library, waiting patiently for me to gather my things. 'The guys from home wouldn't believe this was happening to a guy like me after a month of being in a new environment,' I thought. There wasn't a clue in my mind as to what was going to take place today, but as long as she and I were together, it really didn't matter. I was game for whatever.
Miss Daly and I drove to a small family restaurant that was unfamiliar to me, but the area was decent. It was along a street filled with old homes that probably

dated back to the early thirties and forties. The place only held six tables and three booths. We seated ourselves at one of the booths and I tried to make my way toward her as she got comfortable. Miss Daly sat down and slid her body toward mine and surprised me because I wasn't sure if she'd want to sit so close. Mature for my age, I had to play the part. Miss Daly smelled so good that I wished that she would sit on my lap. However, I'll be patient and let nature work things out.

We talked over lunch and it was amazing how much we had in common. I became more interested with her every time she spoke. This woman wore a smile that brightened the room, and melted my heart. Miss Daly was a "dime" piece and she knew it. My grandfather used to tell me that if I could make a woman smile or laugh, then I'd probably have a chance with her. Miss Daly laughed so much that her panties should have been damp.

I talked about my ambitions and she grew more interested in the fact that I had a goal, than the fact that I was a young student who was moderately attractive. Miss Daly waved for the waitress and within a few seconds the bill was placed on the table. As I reached for the receipt, she placed her hand on top of mine. "I'll take care of this," I said. Miss Daly slowly ran her hand across mine as she removed hers. "Would you like to come back to my place and watch a movie or something? I have some wine in the fridge and a lovely Futon sofa that reclines," she said. "Yeah, that sounds good," I replied. I then got up from the table and approached the register, scratching my head as I thought about her proposal. 'Hell, yeah, I was up for a movie, the reclining Futon and the drink,' I thought while reaching for my wallet.

Before leaving the restaurant, I went to the restroom. As I stood before the urinal, I began imagining what could eventually happen between Miss Daly and I. There was the desire to hold her, kiss her and do any and everything possible. I was so engulfed in the thought that I wasn't aware that I had finished using the restroom. It wasn't until I noticed others coming into the room that it occurred to me that I was finish, and had been so for at least minute.

Miss Daly had rose to her feet and began putting her jacket on when I arrived to the table. Taking her purse from the table, she brushed up against me several times as she left the tip, took the mints and fondled through the mess on the table. I knew that it was all apart of her plan for me to feel her body against mine and vice verse. She walked in front of me and the sight was very pleasant. "Slow down," I yelled as she waved her flag in front of me. "I want to see it move in slow motion!" Miss Daly slowed her pace as we exited the restaurant. Watching her walk in-front of me was a pleasant treat as my mind continued to wander.

Once outside, the thunder roared in the distance as we both looked toward heaven. "We better hurry if we're going to beat this storm," she said. The restaurant wasn't far from the university, but it was much closer to her home. We arrived at her place within minutes, and the neighborhood was lined with detached condos. I was eager to see her place and when I saw the garage door of one residence open, I knew we were there.

We entered the home from the garage entrance and she quickly told me to make myself at home. I went into the living room and was amazed that she had white carpet throughout the house. "Take your shoes off, Adam, before you walk through the house," she yelled. The shoes were quickly removed and left at the side door. There were pictures on the walls and mantle of people who resembled her. I figured those were the family pictures and the others were of Miss Daly and her girls. Funny, I didn't see a man's picture anyplace in the room. Just as I was admiring a painting on the wall, Miss Daly called for me to join her downstairs.

Once downstairs, I was impressed by how it was decorated. There was a full bar that accented the large screen television. The floor was tiled with throw rugs covering sections of the floor. She fixed our drinks while I searched for a movie. It had been years since I had seen the movie 'Face Off,' so I slipped it into the DVD player and began watching the credits. We sat on the sofa and talked for hours as we watched TV and listened to the storm. The movie was worth watching again, but I was surprised to find out that the movie was given to Miss Daly as a gift and that she had never watched it.

We shared a glass of wine and talked about our future plans as the movie was no-longer holding our attention. This was a moment worth savoring. Miss

Daly felt good sitting next to me with her legs stretched across mine. "What do you do for sex, Miss Daly," I asked? She was stunned by the question. "I manage," she replied. Running her fingers through her hair, Miss Daly leaned back on the sofa in a seductive pose. "Why did you ask that question, Adam?" "I was just curious, because you are an extremely attractive woman and I just know that someone has to be hitting your switches. Hell, I would," I said while setting my glass down.

Miss Daly laughed and said, "I've noticed you watching me in class. It feels like you're undressing me with your eyes." I placed my hand on her thigh and asked, "How does my undressing you with my eye's make you feel?" She took a sip from her glass and said that it makes her feel giddy. "It's not every day that a student undresses me," she remarked. "Does it make you horny being undressed by a student," I asked in a soft tone? Before Miss Daly could reply, I pulled her close to me and planted a kiss on her lips. Miss Daly was so eager to kiss me that she forced her tongue into my mouth.

I "French" kissed her, sucked her earlobes and running my tongue along her neck, listened to her moan. Like a wild woman, she groped my body as I squeezed her breast. "I think we need to slow down, Adam. This is too sudden," she said nervously. It took all that she had inside of herself to push me away, because her face was flushed and her nipples stood out like pencil erasers. "Well, my erection doesn't get any harder than this," I replied. Miss Daly sat quietly for a few minutes, looking as if she was lost in thought.

'This young guy is so hot, and he has me feeling hot for him. A teacher shouldn't be interested in her student, but the timing sure feels right,' she thought. I toyed with the television remote while she ran her fingers through her hair. Miss Daly then pulled me closer to her and resumed the kiss that we started.

This woman then pushed me away and began to undress, and within seconds she was completely nude. 'Boy, what a sight,' I thought to myself as Miss Daly fell onto the Futon sofa and placed one hand between her legs, as she fondled her breast with the other. Slowly, I began to undress. There was the fear that she was going to have second thoughts before I was completely naked, but the thought passed when I saw Miss Daly rubbing her clitoris. 'I hope this doesn't interfere with our professional relationship,' I thought while staring at her smooth body.

Miss Daly had the largest clitoris I had ever seen. It looked like a swollen finger. "Are you sure that you want to do this, because I don't want to pressure you into doing something that you'll regret," I asked? Standing before her with a stiff erection, Miss Daly leaned forward and took every inch of me into her mouth. Standing 9inches taller than Miss Daly offered me a real sight as I watched her gulp down as much pipe as she could. This woman's throat was deep. This teacher sucked like a pro, and I was mesmerized as she rolled her tongue across the head. I placed my hand on top of her head as I stood there with my eyes closed, taking in the moment. The sound of her wet mouth was all I needed to hear as the thunder roared in the background.

As I ran my tongue along his stiff shaft, my mouth was so hot that it felt like my saliva was boiling. With his hand on top of my head, Adam steadied my strokes. Burning with desire, I wanted to eat him alive as I held his penis in my hand. His firm hands groped my body as his charisma intellectually drew me closer, putting me on the brink of self destruction, as I was unaware how long I could hold out. It had been over a year since I claimed celibacy and I knew that this was going to be mind blowing. 'I hope that he's not a sucker in the bedroom. Judging from his athletic build, I certainly hoped that he wasn't a dud. I hope we're not going too far,' she thought.

Pushing Miss Daly down onto the sofa, I put on a condom and climbed on top of her as she parted her warm thighs. Taking my rigid penis in her hand, I slid it into her gaping hole. Miss Daly's eyes rolled up into her head as I went deeper. Without hesitation, I began riding her as the sound of thunder and the flash of lightening enhanced the moment. Miss Daly squirmed and moaned as I made my way into her, and within minutes she came repeatedly.

As her body shook uncontrollably, I continued forcing my penis inside her womb. "Just lie still as I push the juices back up into you," I said while riding her. Miss Daly then turned me onto my back and began riding me. Yelling as if someone was killing her, she bucked like a girl riding a horse without a saddle. While up inside of Miss Daly, I fondled her breast and placed my fingers in her mouth. I noticed that doing this only intensified the moment as sticky cream ran down her thighs.

Lying on my back, I filled the condom with sperm, as I could not hold out any longer. As I caught my breath, Miss Daly kept grinding her pelvis onto mine as the feeling of me being inside of her was overwhelming. Afterwards, she broke her Futon down to a bed and it was on between us. What Miss Daly didn't know was that drinking prevents me from ejaculating, which meant that she was in for some long, hard strokes. 'This teacher has my head spinning,' I thought while admiring her voluptuous figure.

The fact that I had only climaxed once seemed to excite Miss Daly, as we screwed for hours, while it stormed outside. "I love stormy sex," she said as I gave her more of my manhood. The more I gave, the more she wanted. Miss Daly came hard and before I could withdraw my penis, like a mad woman, she put her arms around my shoulders and pulled me closer to her. I laid there with my penis in her for two, maybe three minutes before I could continue stroking her kitty.

With my back arched and Miss Daly writhing beneath me, I came so hard that it felt as if the condom was going to burst. "Shoot that hot load in me," she cried. To my surprise, that's exactly what I did as the condom could not hold out for another round. Miss Daly yelled as I grind my pelvis onto hers. "Don't stop, Adam," she repeated over and over. Miss Daly managed to get me onto my back, and she laid on top of me, holding me with a firm grip. "I felt you come inside of me. It may not have been on purpose, but it felt good," Miss Daly said while laughing. "I must have come seven times, because every time you spanked me, I got more excited. I'll bet you didn't expect anything like this to happen," she said.

Once she freed me from he grip, Miss Daly opened up wider than her legs. Within 45 minutes I had relived her entire life. It seemed as if she didn't want to stop talking. However, she did stop talking long enough to give me some head, which lead to more sex. We screwed the entire day away and I can say that I enjoyed every stroke. It also felt good to take a break from my studies to release some stress. I just pray that my sperm doesn't make a positive connection and we be joined together for life. Sexually satisfied, we got out of bed and showered together. She washed my body and I washed hers as we took time to fondle one-another. I didn't have a clue about what it was like to be in love with someone, but I can surely say that this woman had all the right moves to hook a man.

As we drove to the dorm, Miss Daly spent her time talking about how good she felt. "I have never been freaked like that. I've never been with a man your size. I mean, your rod was tickling my insides, and once I came, I knew I was hooked on your hot passion," she said. Listening to her, I was becoming concerned about our professional relationship, because judging from her expression, I don't think she's going to do much to hide the fact that she likes me.

The conversation was beginning to make me a little nervous because things had the potential to get out of control, and I didn't want either one of us to get hurt. She may not want anything else to do with me or maybe I'll lose interest in her, but that was only wishful thinking on my part. After two days of hot passion, Miss Daly was probably looking forward to a repeat performance. 'I knew that I was hoping for one,' Adam thought to himself.

At the dormitory, I leaped out of the car and she yelled, "Can't a girl get a kiss or was the sex that bad?" I didn't want anyone to see us, so I got back into the car and we kissed passionately. Resting my hand on her thighs and kissing the base of her neck, she moaned deeply. Miss Daly writhed in her seat as I shoved my tongue down her throat. "Come home with me, Adam! I don't want you to leave me," she begged. I didn't want to believe what I was hearing. Without saying a word, I was hoping that my silence was giving her second thoughts about my returning to her home...today.

Suddenly, Ms. Daly's hand found my crotch and she began to unzip my pants. It wasn't long before she was giving me head in front of the dormitory. 'Thank God for tinted windows,' I thought. Once Miss Daly came up for air, she asked, "Do you still have to leave or should I keep sucking until you change your mind?" I placed my hand on her head and guided her mouth back into position. With my seat reclined, I felt myself losing control, and just as Miss Daly removed her lips, she gave my rod two strokes with her hand and I blew up. Holding my penis steady, I shot my sperm on her dashboard. She squeezed every drop of juice from my penis. "That was great, Miss Daly, but I still have to leave," I said as I put my penis away and zipped my pants. "When will I see you again," she asked with a sad look in her eyes? I replied, "We'll see each other in class tomorrow."

As she drove away from the dorm, Miss Daly smiled as she reflected on the events that took place between she and Adam. 'This man is fantastic. No one could have ever told me that I would fall for a younger man. I could almost imagine falling for someone closer to my age, maybe another instructor or someone who works for the institution. Although, Adam Harris is going to be my new choice for a mate. I had no plans of sleeping with him when I invited him to lunch, but I'm glad that it happened. Never has anyone ever made love to me all night long, and not complain about being tired. Hell, this may lead to something positive. However, I feel somewhat ashamed because of the way things have developed, but I just can't help myself right now. Adam is attractive, athletic, hung like a horse and very charming. This guy has ambition and oh, I can't forget his brilliance.' Engulfed in her thoughts, Miss Daly nearly ran her car into the car in front of her. Caught off guard, she slammed on her brakes, causing the car behind her to slam on their brakes to avoid an accident.

Miss Daly pulled over to the side of the road to gain her composure as the possibility of an accident scared her. Frightened, she immediately burst into a cold sweat. Miss Daly hadn't smoked a cigarette in months, but returning to the thoughts of her and Adam, she withdrew a cigarette from her glove compartment and lit it. Slowly, she took a drag from the lit cigarette and sighed. "I have got to get this man into my life," she whispered to herself. Ms. Daly continued smoking as she pulled away from the roadside curb. Regaining her composure, she managed to keep up with the other cars as her mind stayed fixated on the day before.

CHAPTER
TWO

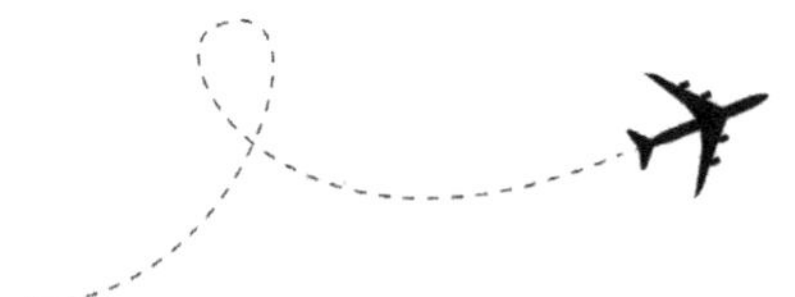

The next four weeks were as exciting as the first day Ms. Daly and I had gotten together. She would have me to hang around after class so that she could give me head, and I was loving it. On certain occasions Miss Daly and I would get busy on the lab tables, and that's what I called chemistry. It was apparent to me that things were getting out of hand, but we both found it difficult to say "Stop." Our time together didn't interfere with my studies, but it was putting a dent in our professional lives.

Miss Daly and I were no longer viewing each other in comparison to the rolls we played, but as sexual partners. She and I were getting too involved and I knew that it wasn't going to be long before someone noticed something. It would devastate her co-workers if they knew what was going on, but she's the one who needs to get a grip on things. Some of the other students called me "teachers pet" because she's always giving me class perks. However, I was cautious about anyone finding out how I earned those perks. While others were trying to stay on her good-side, I managed to stay inside of her.

We had sex so often that I often asked myself when she'd have time for a monthly cycle. The time she refused was done because her parents were staying the night and she couldn't get away. Since they've been gone, she's made up for the lost time with hot sex and several trinkets. When she purchased the white gold bracelet with my name encrusted with diamonds, and matching his/her white gold necklaces, I knew that I had messed up. Miss Daly was hooked and not even aware of it. I could see that her behavior toward me was changing, but I tried to remain optimistic about things. She was going from jealousy to possession.

My plans shifted from going to study groups to hanging out at her place. It always amazed me that no matter how often we got together, she always wanted more. There was a time when she caught me without a condom in class, and I shot a load into her womb. Screwing with a condom is okay, but that hot flesh connection was even better. However, I was aware of the possible consequences and I hoped that it wouldn't come to that.

Miss Daly hadn't been seen for weeks and she hadn't been to work in several days and I hadn't bothered calling. This was the day before Thanksgiving break was to begin and I was preparing to drive home. A white guy named Greg was riding with me and we had agreed to meet at my room between 2–2:30 p.m.. Suddenly there was a knock at my door and I yelled for them to come in as I finished shaving. There was a second knock and I opened the door and greeted Miss Daly standing there in a trench coat. Wearing a smirk, I was surprised to see her, especially looking so attractive. Judging from the expression on her face, I couldn't tell if she were there to be sociable or because she needed some pre-holiday attention.

I closed the door and she stood behind me, staring at me through the mirror. Unbuttoning her jacket, Miss Daly took a seat on the bed and crossed her legs. "I see you're packed and ready to go," she said. Trimming my beard, I said, "Yeah, it's almost that time." Miss Daly sighed and said, "Adam, I'm pregnant!" My eyes widen and my mouth dropped. Before I could say a word, she told me that she was going to keep the baby and that I didn't have to be worried about anything.

Standing there with shaving cream on my face, I asked, "What do you mean by I don't have to be worried? You're talking about a living, breathing human being coming into this world. This is a fine time to tell me. How long have you known," I asked? "I just found out this morning. I bought a pregnancy test and it showed that I was pregnant. However, I will know for certain when I see my doctor next week," she replied. With a look of surprise on my face, I asked, "Are you prepared to have an abortion?" Miss Daly uncrossed her legs and said, "I'm having this baby with you or without you, Adam. I don't believe in abortions, and I'm surprised that you would suggest that I have one. Aren't you proud to know that I'm having your child," she asked? Confused, I nodded my head as my thoughts ran wild.

"I've thought about it, Adam, and I think this is best for both of us. I'm against abortions and because this is my first pregnancy, I'm excited and this means a lot to me. It must have occurred the time we did it in class without protection or the day that the condom broke. For two weeks I've been deciding how I was going to tell you that it may be pregnant, but I've also been afraid to find out the truth for myself. Afraid to find out, I've just been dealing with mild morning sickness. Of course I blamed the sickness on something else, like a virus or something. One side of my brain is saying to keep it and the other side is saying not to. "What can I do to help," Adam asked with a blank expression on his face.

With a calm reply, "Buy some 'Pampers' and give me a little something-something when you have the time," she said. Adam stood next to Miss Daly, smiled, and took her by the hand, and getting up from the bed, held her in his arms. "It's going to be okay and if you need anything just give me a call." Without words, we began undressing. Miss Daly and I made out in the room for the remainder of her visit, and the sex felt good. On her knee's, I banged her doggy style until she collapsed onto the bed. I couldn't believe that I was sexing it up with the woman who just recently told me that she was going to have my baby. Most men who didn't want to have the baby would have freaked out, but I believe that time is the greatest story teller. While catching my breath, she hit me with another issue. Miss Daly told me that she was offered a job in Chicago and that she wanted me to relocate to a school there.

Angrily, I said, "If I wanted to attend school in Illinois then I would have remained there. I'm not leaving this university to please you, nor for the baby. Aside from all of the sex, I'm about my education," I told her. Furious, she said, "I don't think of what we do as making-out, it's more like making love and now that a baby is involved, you need to think about making some changes in your life," she shouted. I laughed at her statement and said, "Fucking-is-fucking and that's what we do. We are good friends," he said with a straight face. "Why are we good friends," she asked?   Adam replied, "I have sex with my good-friends, I don't have sex with my friends."

Miss Daly leaped off of the bed and began getting dressed; not saying two words to me. She approached the door and said, "Think about my offer, and don't worry about the baby. Oh, by the way, my name is Lisa, so when someone asks what your baby's mother name is, you don't have to tell them Miss Daly. Upset, Lisa stormed out of the room and slammed the door and I sighed in relief. Suddenly, there was a knock at the door and I yelled for them to wait a minute. I slipped on a robe and opened the door to find Greg standing there with a smile on his face. A musky aroma filled the air and as Greg entered the room he said, "It smells like you've been banging some booty!" We laughed as he sat down and began fingering through my magazine collection. I turned the television on and left the room to go and shower.

It was surprising that I didn't drown from all of the water that I ingested as I stood underneath the shower head with my mouth open, in shock. I couldn't believe that she actually wanted to keep this child. 'Hell, it's difficult for me to believe that she's actually pregnant. What was I thinking when I got with her in class? The incident that occurred when the rubber broke was out of my control, but damn, she still didn't have to make this decision. A baby! How was I going to break this to my mom? Dad probably won't care much, but it will shock him. Just think, me a dad. What in the world have I done,' he thought.

I guess it could have been worse because I could have impregnated someone with no education or plans for the future. Although she had some positive things going on for herself, I'm not one-hundred percent sure that she would have been my first choice to be the mother of my kid. Well, God knows what's best and if it's his will, then I'll be satisfied with it. It then occurred to me that I was suppose to be getting ready to leave and I couldn't stop staring at the shower stall walls. I believe that it would be a good idea for me to get this shower over with before Greg begins to think that I'm not serious about leaving.

The days flew by and the holiday break was over and Greg and I were on our way back to campus. Greg fought with his girlfriend during the break, so he spent the entire ride sleeping off his anger. I was exhausted because I spent every day with a different girl. I had slept with them before, but when I returned home they remained eager to give it up again. At this point, the last thing I wanted to see was a naked woman, but I knew Miss Daly would be waiting for me. We hadn't spoken to each other during the holiday break and I was hoping that this was a good sign, because her pregnancy had me baffled during the entire break. There were a lot of questions going through my mind at this point.

When Greg awakened, we were at the dormitory. I went my way and Greg went his way, so tired that we damn near crawled through the front doors. To my surprise, I found a note for each day I was gone underneath my door. The letters were from Miss Daly and I was in no mood to read them. In my current state, I opted to climb into bed and get some sleep. Although exhausted, I found it difficult to sleep because the phone continued ringing. Suddenly, there was a knock at my door to alert me that the phone call was for me. It was a land-line phone that was only meant for emergencies, and those who didn't have a cell phone. I practically knew whom it was calling, so I pretended to be asleep.

The next morning, after coming out of the shower, the dorm-hall phone rang several times. I don't usually answer this phone, but I thought what could it hurt to answer it this one time. Believe-it-or-not, it was Lisa and she was breathing like a rabid dog. "We missed you every day that you were gone," she said. "My thoughts have been of you. At night when my thighs are trembling, I think of you and I together. I even thought about the last time I gave you head and you screamed because it felt good to you." I quickly interrupted her. "Miss Daly, this is cute, but it's going to have to wait. I'm getting ready for class and I need to dry off," I said impatiently. Miss Daly sat quietly on the phone. "Hello" I screamed! Softly, she asked, "Well, can I come over and help you dry off?" I grinned and said, "I'll catch you later, Lisa Daly." Quickly, I hanged up the phone and laughed as I returned to my room.

After my first class, I found myself walking behind Miss Daly as she entered the administration office. The number to the administration office is saved in my cell phone, so I decided to fight fire with fire. I entered the restroom a few feet from the office and I called and asked for Miss Daly. Lisa took the phone receiver and before she could speak, I began breathing heavily into the phone. "I'm standing her holding my fat rod and picturing your lips around it. There is also an image of you taking this penis doggy-style. You know how much you love that, and you know how much you've been missing it. Your love nest got wet when you heard my voice this morning. Now, picture yourself sucking this pipe," I said. Before she could speak, I ended the call. As I crept out of the restroom, Miss Daly was exiting the administration office with her arms folded across her chest as she shook her head, looking dazed. She began clapping her hands and shaking her head more, while laughing loudly. I couldn't believe that this woman was going to have my baby and here we are playing games on the phone.

Later that evening, Lisa dismissed class and asked me to stay behind for a few moments. She locked the door and took me in-back of the biology lab and began kissing me wildly. Lisa forced my back against the wall, and freeing my member, she began sucking. After a stressful day, this was great. Miss Daly, or should I say, Lisa, not only wanted to suck my rod, but she also wanted to jerk on it. It was just a matter of time before she was going to receive a mouth full of sperm. My eyes rolled up in my head as she sucked harder and harder. There was no denying that she knew how to give head, but this time Lisa acted like someone who had no intentions of stopping.

Eventually, I stopped fighting and just rested my back against the wall until she decided that she was ready to give me a break. Lisa stopped sucking, and lifting her skirt, she turned around and removed her thong. 'A thong in the winter time,' I thought to myself. "I want you to ride this pregnant love tunnel, Adam. Tell me how it feels?" She and I had intercourse in school once before, but this time felt more comfortable for both of us. Lisa climbed on top of the table in a doggy-style position, and pulling her close to me, I began riding her from behind, smacking her firm cheeks. Lisa bit the sleeve of her lab jacket to prevent herself from screaming. Having sex in the biology lab was more exciting than anything else we had tried.

There was a fifteen minute break between her classes and we managed to screw until the last minute was over. She and I came together in a matter of minutes. The sight of her grinding her round rear-end onto my torso kept me stimulated as I rubbed Lisa's smooth globes. Neither one of us wanted to stop, because the hole felt good, and time was not on our side. Lisa ran to the restroom while I sneaked out of the back exit. I had to laugh to myself when I saw Lisa walking ahead of me with a wet rear-end and sperm running down her leg. 'I love Michigan,' I thought to myself as I hurried to the library.

As I stood at the vending machine, Lisa approached me and whispered, "I hope to see you later." I gave her a quick nod as she hurried to her next class. This was part of her new plan to get me to change my mind about moving to Chicago and attending school there, but I didn't see any possibility of that happening. I understand that she's overwhelmed about what we share and I know that she's pregnant, but this is a sexual thing. It's too early for me to put feelings into this thing we share, because this may only be a bridge that I'm crossing.

Lisa and I exchanged information about when and where we were going to meet between classes. However, I didn't want to be bothered, so I purposely stood her up. For the first time during her pregnancy, I actually felt sick. I returned to my room before going to shower. Once in the shower, I could hear my cell phone ringing inside of my robe pocket. At that moment I began throwing-up.

I quickly cleaned myself up and began drying off. After I was done, I went to my room to discover a long voice message from you-know-who. The message said: "If you don't want to be bothered with me, then just say so. You're acting like I asked you to kill the president or something. Look, I apologize for being rude, but I don't believe you're feeling me. We would be great together. We're in similar career fields and I know that we could make it work. No matter what school you decide to attend, I will give you all of my support. Also, I don't want you to worry about the baby until you get yourself together financially. I can take care of its needs. I just want you to be apart of our lives. We can be a family and I know that you would be a great father. If I didn't think you were going to be a good father, then I would have made a different decision. This is my first time being pregnant and I'm excited and I hope that you will become excited at some point. Call me or I'll call you," she said.

Calling is exactly what she did. Lisa called me at least seven times, leaving a message each time she called. At this point, Lisa was beginning to piss-me-off. The sister does have some positive things going on for herself, but damn. She's hooked-on-phonics and unaware of the trouble she could be making for both of us. Lisa couldn't see beyond the sex and that was not a good sign. To further complicate things, she wants to go through with having this baby. The school policy forbids instructor/student relationships outside or inside the work place. Maybe I did put the sex on thick, but that's the only way I know to do it. What happened is, she fooled me, because I thought she could handle the 'depth.' However, instead of handling the 'depth', she's more ready to settle down and brag to her friends about the good sex that she has at home, and the wonderful family life that she was hoping for.

Sitting quietly, I realized that 'these past weeks have been a living mess,' I thought to myself as I reminisced on how Miss Daly has been reacting lately. It's like she's following me around. The woman has me dodging her when I'm at the school and it's really becoming a problem. I'm looking over my shoulder just to get to my car. 'If pregnancy has to be like this, then what will it be like once the baby is here,' I thought. To make things worst, I attended a party and this woman showed up in a disguise. She stood out at the party, wearing a pair of jeans and a midriff top. Her stomach hasn't begun to show so she was able to play it off. The lights were flashing in my eyes, and her voice didn't sound the same as I explained my interest in her. To make a long story short, we found ourselves at a hotel called 'Best Western,' and once inside the room, she blew my mind. After that occurrence, I've been trying to stay away from her. It was a Christmas party and the surprise was too much for me to bare.

Angrily, I had sex with her until her brains accepted this form of reeducation. I flipped her so much that if someone were listening, they would have thought that she was being raped. However, pregnant sex is still considered the best-by-far. "I want you to stop playing these games with me," I whispered as I gave her harder thrusts. To get my point across to her, I spanked Lisa's rear and turned her in all sorts of awkward positions. We left the hotel and I had the privilege of watching her cry all the way to the dorm.

"It seems like we're drifting further apart. Maybe things would be different if I hadn't told you that I was pregnant. On top of that, I want you to leave with me and you're behaving like I'm some sort of criminal. It was never my plan to fall for one of my students, but it happened. I just want you to care for me the same way that I care for you," she said. I sat with my arms folded, as I could not believe what had just taken place. I'm not referring to the sex, but the whole disguise thing was a complete shock for me. The reality of me not changing my mind was becoming a bit too much for her. I could see that she was going to keep playing dirty and me not changing my mind was only going to make things worse. I laughed to myself and thought, 'These are the disruptions that I tried to avoid during high school, especially the baby part.'

That morning I rose early and got on the highway. It was two days before Christmas and I was eager to get home. Lisa had no idea that I was going to be leaving the day after the party and I didn't bother informing her of my plans. I felt like a heel, but it was my way of dealing with this situation. Several times my phone rang as I sat there thinking things over. There was no denying that I was attracted to her, but things are appearing to be going faster than we both imagined. At this point, she would be extremely upset if I walked away from her and began sharing myself with someone else. After all, what she really want is for me to acknowledge my child and have a relationship with him/her, or them. Once I reached the Illinois border I called Miss Daly to get the low-down on what she's doing for the holiday.

Lisa answered the phone in a dry-tone. It sounded like she had been crying. "I was calling to see how you were doing, or to find out what you were doing," I said. Miss Daly cleared her throat and replied, "I was just sitting here wondering where you were and why weren't you answering your phone. My first thought was that maybe he's laid up with some girl. My next thought was that you didn't want to be bothered, with me," she said. "I'm not laid up with some girl nor am I still upset with you. Although, that stunt you pulled at the party the other night really changed my perception of you. Was the sex so good that you felt like it was necessary to put me in that situation? How would you feel if I were to do that to you," Adam asked?

"I want to apologize for my actions, but you don't realize how much I love you and that sleeping around isn't fair to me. There are always going to be other girls, but I want you to realize that I'm the one who's willing to share all that I have with you, and carry your child. If I thought that having anal sex would keep you in my life, I'd do it. Right now, my emotions are all screwed up and it's because I'm loving you that much," she said. Lisa never said that she loved me during sex, so to hear her say it now was startling. "Listen, I'm close to my home, so I'm going to get off of the phone." Miss Daly interrupted me and asked, "Were you going to tell me that you were in Chicago or was I supposed to guess?" She began crying as I tried to explain and before I knew it, Lisa had hung up the phone.

I called Lisa several times during the holiday break and she discussed all the great things she had planned for me when I return to school. Being at home gave me a chance to think about some things and share them with Lisa, but she didn't totally agree with my plans. However, we managed to laugh and be friends despite the fact that I was still against moving back home. Ms. Daly said that she understood where I was coming from, but I didn't believe that for a second. She was only agreeing with me because she hoped that it would change my mind about leaving and the baby. However, I had to give her an 'A' for effort, because I was beginning to understand what she was trying to do. My best advice was for Lisa to pray about it, because I had expressed how I felt and it was out of my control.

To my surprise, it's unbelievable how time has flown by and this is the last day with Miss Daly as an instructor, and I can finally let my hair down. This day symbolized her being able to focus on her career and the remaining time before her due date. Lisa knew that I hadn't considered her invitation and that was bothering her more than anything else. If I were to give her a direct answer, then she would be okay. Saying "No" is as direct as I can be, but I need to try something else, because she's not getting it.

Lisa saw us as a couple and that was pushing things too far, but I did enjoy doing 'couple' things like taking walks and going to the doctor's office with her. We knew some things about each other but it was not enough to build a strong relationship. There's always the possibility for us to have something special, but now wasn't the time. First, I had to concern myself with my education. Although, I still had to address this baby issue before she makes a bigger concern out of it. To make matters worse, I haven't discussed anything with my parents.

Miss Daly phoned me while I was cleaning up this semester's mess. She invited me to dinner and I accepted. I told her to give me an hour to get prepared and that I'd meet her out in the front of the dorm. "Please hurry Adam, because the baby is getting hungry," she replied. Although I was eager to get out of the dorm, I knew what would take place after dinner. This was the opportunity to enjoy her summer and she was ready to pull out all stops. Lisa liked pregnant sex as much as I did.

While I killed time, some of my friends from home called me to discuss the local gossip and latest happenings, so I ceased from rushing as I thought that it would be better to make her wait awhile. My friends and I talked for fifteen or twenty minutes and the rest of my time was spent lying on the bed reading my 'Daily Word' booklet and talking with the Lord. If I were going to face what I feared I was going to face, a daily prayer was exactly what I needed. Although I looked forward to a peaceful evening, there were no guarantees.

Lisa wore some hot outfit that damn near made my mouth water. She had her hair done in a ponytail that accented the shorts she wore. This woman's pregnant body was banging and I did everything possible to disguise the fact that she had me turned on the moment I saw her. There aren't a lot of women who can still remain attractive once they become pregnant. The truck she drove had been waxed and she looked sexier than ever sitting behind the wheel. She had that mother-to-be glow about her.

Once inside the passenger seat, Miss Daly sped away. "Are you ready for some summer fun," she asked? I nodded my head and said, "I'm ready for whatever, because after all, I'm a guest in this town. By the way, you're looking 'hot' today, baby." Shocked, Lisa's mouth hang open as she said, "This is my first time hearing you refer to me as baby, Mr. Harris." I then surprised her again when I rubbed her stomach and began talking to the baby. Gently, she placed her hand on my thigh. "If you're not careful, Lisa, you may find me up inside of you, knocking a hole in my baby's head." I then placed my hand on her thigh and rubbed gently. "If I were to stop this car and jump your bones, then you would say that I'm wrong," she remarked. From that point on we talked and laughed as we discussed our summer plans.

Miss Daly pulled into a restaurant called 'Red Lobster' and we sat in the car and appeared to be counting the other cars as she wanted an idea of how crowded they were. "Order whatever you want when we get inside, because this is a celebration," Lisa said. "Are we celebrating," I asked as we got out of the car? "We're celebrating the beginning of a new semester and the end of and old one. We've also got to celebrate a successful pregnancy and a happy future," she replied. When we walked into the restaurant, it didn't appear to be as crowded as it looked from the outside. The waitress led us to our seats and Lisa practically insisted that I sit next to her. "I want you to rub my belly and see if you can feel the baby kicking," she said jokingly. At this point I was starting to get excited because the gynecologist said that things were going okay and I was feeling differently about the pregnancy. I could feel the baby kicking and I was well pleased.

I was beginning to enjoy my time with Adam more than ever. We were still having intimate moments without having sex. He and I held each other closely and often fell asleep in one another' arms. Adam was preparing meals for me and making sure that I made it to my scheduled appointments. This man was spoiling me rottenly and I loved every minute of it. We had breakfast in bed, and we continued taking our usual walks. There were times when I couldn't have intercourse with him, but I made up for the difference. He didn't like 'head' as much as he liked intercourse, but he wouldn't turn me away. What bothered me was that seeing him as often as I did developed a closeness between us that would bring tears to my eyes. 'Boy, I want this guy to leave with me so badly that I could scream.' I thought. "How will I manage in Chicago with a baby and a lover that I hate leaving behind," I asked myself?

CHAPTER
THREE

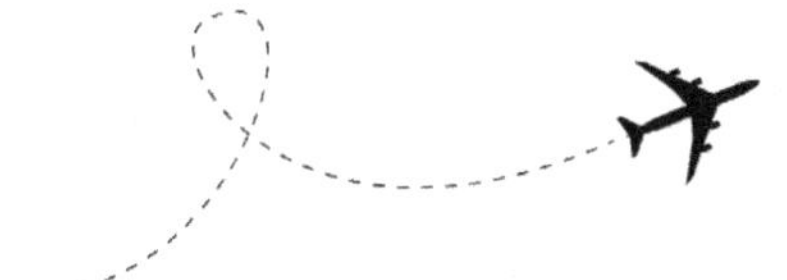

Lisa and I spent all of our time together for the remainder of the week, but this was Saturday and I was going to let my hair down for a while. I rose early, filled my gas tank and traveled toward Detroit. Eager to visit my family in Southfield, I raced down the highway. My aunt Joyce worked at the shop on Saturday's, but my cousin Eric was home and I knew that he would have something planned for the day. Nervously, I traveled this unknown highway growing more secure as I followed the arrows pointing me in the right direction. At one point I had to get onto an expressway called the 'Southfield' freeway, and from there it was smooth sailing. The expressway ended on Southfield road, and the house was only a few blocks away.

The home was easy to find, because it set in the middle of the block, with a circular driveway. Eric's car was parked in the driveway and music was blaring out of the house. I grinned as I walked up on the porch and knocked on the door, only to be greeted by a girl whom I had never seen before. "Damn, what's your name," I asked as she let me into the house? "I'm Stacy, and I'll be hanging out for awhile. Came to see Eric? He's downstairs with my girl, but you're welcome to come down and join us," she said.

I followed her down into the basement only to find Eric lying between some girls legs running his tongue along her neck. "What's up, 'E'," I shouted? Eric climbed off of the girl and approached me with open arms. "How's life, cousin? I'm glad you made it, because Stacey is a little bored. Hey, do you want to hit this "bud", because it's the bomb," he said. "I just say no to drugs," I replied. "Well, this is Angela and we're going upstairs to do a little mattress dancing, so keep this girl entertained. She's been smoking, so do what you have to do to keep her calm," he said with a grin.

Stacey and I remained in the basement watching television and talking. We were watching a sports show and once a commercial came on, Stacey turned the television volume down and turned the radio volume up. Stacey's eye's were squinted as she danced like someone from a strip club. She had a nice rear end that was accented by her flat stomach and firm thighs. "Do you have a girlfriend, Adam," she asked? "I haven't been in Michigan long enough to have a girlfriend. Although, not having a girlfriend has nothing to do with the show that you're giving me," I said.

Stacey got on her knee's and shook her butt like someone from a 'Luke' video. Suddenly, my nature started to rise. I got up from the bar stool, walked over to Stacey and smacked her booty cheeks. "Ooh, smack it again, daddy," she whispered. I began smacking her butt continuously. Once the song was over and the game was back on television, she turned the radio off and turned up the television volume.

"Give me a little something-something, daddy. Do you think you can handle all of this?" I removed my tee-shirt and shorts as she fell to her knee's and began her job. Stacey had full lips and she gave "head" better than Lisa. This girl would make a lollipop so happy. Taking her head into my hands,

I began stroking her mouth with a slow rhythm. She managed to keep up with the pace of my strokes and it surprised me. Stacey sucked as it she was waiting for me to unleash my load into her mouth. The strokes stopped and I took her by the hand and lead her into the bedroom that was off of the laundry room. We entered the room and she lit the blunt and took several drags before lying down and spreading her legs.

Penetrating her womb coincided with the coughing that she was already doing. I held her arms down and began riding within the folds of her sopping wet flesh. This girl's body was so hot that her wetness practically drenched my member. "Give it to me Adam, ooh, yeah," she repeated several times as I gave her all that I had. My strokes were long and hard, and her screams came after each moan. Placing her hand on my butt, Stacey steadied my strokes. "That's it! I want to come all over this pipe. Keep giving it to me. Oh, yeah, here it comes," she cried. Stacey's thighs bucked as she rode me for all that it was worth. No one could have told me that getting sex on a sunny Saturday would be this easy.

The more Stacey smoked, the more we got it on in the basement. It was as if the "weed" made her horny. She smoked and danced and gave me the wildest show that I had seen in months. Unaware that I was standing close to her as she danced with her eyes closed, I smacked Stacey on that fat booty and watched as she made her butt cheek's clap repeatedly. Turned-on, we rolled onto the bed and went at each-other with heated passion. This time, I was pretending to be Stacey and she was the dude, as she flipped me into her favorite positions. Telling me how she wanted to be served, and taking it the way she wanted it.

Despite the various positions, she was unable to keep up with a long and strong brother like me. I had her so wound up that she was practically pulling her hair out as she screamed for more and more. Eager too oblige, I fed so much meat into her that the condom broke. I felt it break and before I ejaculated into her womb, I pulled out and came on her stomach and breast. Excited, Stacey pulled me close and began sucking me until I was dry.

I sat on the side of the bed, trembling, as I tried to gain control of the situation. Stacey lay on the bed and allowed her fingers to play between her legs as she was overcome with lust. "I could stay here and do this with you all day. Are you sure that you don't want to hit this? Your cousin got this for me and it is the bomb. If you try this and we both get high, we can "freak" all afternoon," she said. I shook my head as I turned around and leaped on her. First, I sucked her gum drop nipples, and then I sucked on her earlobe.

While lying on top of her, Stacey smacked my butt and locked her legs around my waist. Moments later, I was pipe-deep inside of her. As we bucked and rolled across the bed, Eric burst into the room and yelled, "My mom's home!" Stacey didn't seem to care that Eric had come in on us as she kept forcing my penis deep into her womb. I stopped my strokes and climbed off of Stacey. "Didn't you hear what 'E' said? Get up and move this stuff before we get caught," Adam said frantically.

Stacey moved at a snail's pace as she put her clothes back on. I hurried to get dressed as fast as possible, as I was nervous about my aunt coming downstairs and catching us in the "raw." As I slipped my shoes on, I heard Aunt Joyce walking around upstairs. She walked heavy and that gave me the opportunity to guess where she was in the house. Aunt Joyce talked loudly, and I followed her voice along with her footsteps. Thumps were all I heard as she went through the house calling for Eric to come downstairs and get the kitchen cleaned. "Tell your company to come by later, because I'm expecting company and I need some privacy," she said.

Stacey went into the bathroom to wash-up before she fastened her shorts. I followed her into the bathroom and fondled her body as she writhed from my touch. "Damn, you feel good," I said while licking her neck. Stacey took my hand and placed it inside of her panties and I ran my fingers through her pubic hairs. Tilting her head back, she gave me a kiss and grind her butt on my crotch. As I heard Aunt Joyce coming down the stairs, Stacey and I moved away from each other as Aunt Joyce crept into the bedroom.

"Hey baby, how long have you been here? I talked with your mom last night for a few hours. She was telling me how proud of you she was for being the big man on campus. How are things going for you? Are you making good grades," she asked while attempting to tidy-up the basement? "Things are great, Aunt Joyce. This is Stacey, a friend of Eric. We were on our way upstairs," I said. Aunt Joyce spoke to Stacey as she continued cleaning. "You guys know what this basement smells like, right? Although, if you're a friend of Eric, what more should I expect," she replied.

Stacey walked ahead of me as I followed her upstairs. Her curvaceous behind moved gracefully as she looked behind to see if I was paying attention to it. Once we were upstairs, Stacey made her way into the family room as I remained in the kitchen. As I closed the refrigerator door, Eric shocked me as he was standing behind the door with a grin on his face. "Did you hit it the right way, Adam," he asked as I opened a can of soda-pop? "I hit it for a few minutes, but I couldn't go nuts on it like I intended too. However, I think Stacey is attractive, with her big thighs."

"What are you guys getting ready to do," I asked? "I'm going to drop these girls off at home and then I'm going to the east side to get with my real girl," he said with a devilish grin. "Well, I guess I'll go back to the campus and hang around for a while. Someone should have told me that this wasn't a good time to come by," I said with a hint of disappointment in my voice. Eric placed his hand on my shoulder and shook his head as Stacey yelled for him to hurry.

I followed Eric outside where I found Stacey standing at the backdoor of the car. "If I give you my number, will you call me Adam," she asked coyly. I approached Stacy and planted a kiss on her lips as I palmed her butt cheeks. "I'll call you," I said. Stacey gave me her number and got into the car. Eric shouted, "Do you know your way back, Adam?" I nodded my head and climbed into my truck. Once I pulled away from the house, my cell phone began ringing. To my surprise, it was Lisa calling to find out if I had any plans and would it be possible for us to see each other. I made the conversation as short as possible, regretting that I had to return to Ann Arbor so early.

CHAPTER

FOUR

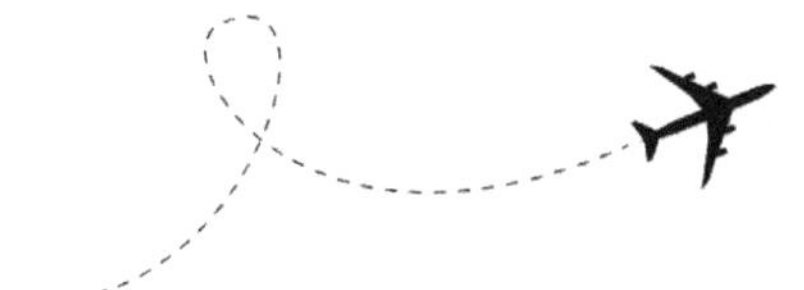

When I hung up the phone, I waddled over to the couch and collapsed. Smiling as I rubbed my round belly, I felt overjoyed to be carrying this man's baby. Although I had refused to tell anyone whom the father was, I was proud to finally be pregnant. Many of the girls I had gone to college and grad school with had already had one or more children. It felt as if my dream to become a mother had finally come true. Each time I rubbed my stomach I felt a thump. 'Ooh, I wish Adam was here to share this moment with me,' I thought. I hoped for a girl and he hoped for a healthy child.

Months into the pregnancy, I was beginning to feel as if it was time to reveal to my parents whom the father actually was. Telling them is better than having them believe that their daughter was a tramp who was sleeping with anyone who came along. The advantage for them is that I'm independent and responsible, with sense enough to take care of a child. If I didn't have anything going for myself, they would probably disagree to the idea. However, if I tell them before the baby is born, they will be satisfied with that. Although, I know that my dad is racking his brain trying to figure out who the father is, and what does he do for a living.

After an hour-and-a-half of waiting, Adam finally arrived. I met him at the door with a big kiss. He hesitated to grab me because he didn't want to hurt the baby. "It's okay, I won't break," I said with a grin. Adam came inside and my emotions began to go haywire. "There's something that I want us to do, but before we do it, can we do it," I asked nervously.

Adam didn't bother keeping me waiting as he began to remove his clothes. Horny, I slid my shirt over my head and he approached me and began kissing my stomach. Pleased, I placed my hand on Adam' head as he ran his tongue along every inch of my swollen belly. I moaned as he gently licked around my navel. Down on his knee's, Adam slid my shorts down and they fell to the floor. "Baby, please make love to me," I whispered. Once he removed the shorts, he slid my panties down around my ankles. The crotch of my panties was soaking wet. Gently, he ran his fingers along my swollen clitoris and labia. Leading me to the bedroom, Adam helped me onto the bed, as I watched him undress. As he climbed into bed, I said, "Come and get some, daddy!" Adam grinned as he slowly entered my womb. Applying long strokes to me, I wanted to come immediately, but I held back.

Trying not to hurt the baby, he gave me all that I wanted and more. Adam sucked my fat breast as if he was the baby that I was carrying. My nipples felt so good in his mouth that I wanted to scream. He sucked them slowly, licking the areola. Suddenly, we came together and it was "beau-ti-ful." I managed to writhe on his rigid penis as his body shook profusely.

Eager for us to leave, we showered together and I broke the news to him. "I want you to meet my parents, today. They've been asking me to tell them who the father of my baby is and I think its time for me to tell them," I said boldly. As he washed my back, Adam agreed to go along with me. I was so surprised that I turned around and gave him a wet kiss. The feeling of him palming my bottom overwhelmed me as I gripped his manhood. 'The times that we spent together was like a dream come true,' I thought. Adam did such a good job pampering me that it was almost frightening. The sex, back rubs and long walks in the park were decadent.

Once we were out of the shower, I sat on the edge of the bed and gave Adam a good "head" job. The more I sucked, the more it turned me on. Just watching him standing there with his eyes closed and his hand resting on my head was more than I could stand. I took so much of Adam into my mouth that my lips actually touched the base of his penis. Unlike most guys who would be trying to knock a girl's tonsils down her throat, he took his time as I applied slow strokes to his member. As I felt his sperm rising, I took the towel from the bed and jerked on Adam' penis enough for him to reach his climax. Within seconds, Adam gripped my head tightly and released his sperm onto the towel. Watching him come made me so excited that I couldn't sit still. "Get dressed so we can go," I demanded as I shook my head in anticipation of more.

CHAPTER
FIVE

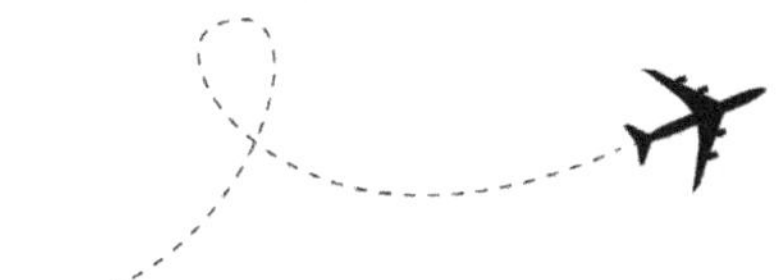

It felt as if I was asleep behind the wheel as we drove to Lisa's parents home in Plymouth Township. Between the sex and the "head" job, I was drained. Oh, and I can't forget the round I had with Stacey. Thank God, I wasn't too worn out to take part in another performance. Stacey felt good, but Lisa's sopping wet hole was much better. There's no better person to monitor than the mother of my first born. The funny part about this whole pregnancy thing is that I'm going to school to become a gynecologist, so what's better then studying you own child.

I had been nervous, but through prayer and preparation, I had become excited about the gift of life that was growing inside of her. Although, I wasn't excited about meeting her parents, because I know how fathers can be. Lisa told me that her parents were kind, but I assumed that was her impression of them. Despite their disposition, I wanted to show them that Lisa was being cared for, by her baby's father.

Lisa and I arrived at her parents home and were greeted by her mom and the family German Shepard, Lazy. Their home was large to say the least. It gave me visions of my parents home in Illinois. The home was made of red brick with white shudders to add accents to the aged home. If I were to guess, I would say that the home was built in the early seventies or late eighties. Lisa told me that her dad was in construction and her mom was a retired school teacher. Her dad was not only in construction, but he was one of the owners of the company that he was employed with.

"Hi, baby! How is my little girl...looking as pregnant as I did before I gave birth to you? Please come inside and have a seat. After all, a pregnant mother needs all of the rest that she can get, and who is this," she asked? Lisa cleared her throat and introduced me. "Mom, this is Adam. He's the father of my baby," she said proudly. Mrs. Daly looked stunned as she looked me over, staring above the rim of her glasses. Mrs. Daly was a petite lady with wide hips, and long black hair. It was apparent that Lisa had gotten her good looks from her mother. "Hello, young man," she said softly. "Are you a sports athlete, maybe a basketball player," she asked? Shaking her soft hand, I grinned and said, "No, Mrs. Daly, I'm not an athlete." Smiling nervously, she replied, "Oh, I was expecting someone much shorter."

We then followed Mrs. Daly inside where we found her dad putting a fan together. Mrs. Daly approached Mr. Daly and said, "Your little girl is here and she has her babies' father with her." Mr. Daly turned around and looked at me with the same look on his face that Mrs. Daly had on hers. Spontaneously, I said, "You have the same expression on your face that Mrs. Daly had on hers. Hi, my name is Adam and it is a pleasure to meet you." He wiped his hands on his pants and gave me a firm handshake.

Both of her parents made me feel welcomed as they were both very outgoing. While Mrs. Daly discussed parenting issues with Lisa, her dad and I sat in the den and watched a sports program. "If we had known that you and Lisa were coming, we would have prepared something to eat. As you can see, this is a large home and my wife and I aren't big when it comes to cooking. Maybe we would be better cooks if there were someone else here in the house besides the two of us," he said jokingly. As he spoke, I looked at the pictures that adorned the walls of the den. "How long have you two been living in this home, if you don't mind my asking?" Mr. Daly stood up and walked to the bar that accented a corner of the room. "We've been here for five years and we love it. The home was built in the early seventies and when I came across it, the homes hope was fading. We purchased it at an auction for less than what the original owners wanted for it and it became a project. Lisa may have told you that I've been working in construction for most of my life and after we finished remodeling this home, things went flat. When Trump's term was over, my partner and I had to downsize and just last week the company folded. Therefore, we've decided to remain here for another year or two and we're going to put the house on the market," he said in a discouraging voice. Mr. Daly asked me not to tell Lisa as he poured a large glass of scotch whiskey and downed it in two sips.

I continued admiring the home as Lisa and her parents discussed life after the baby arrived. Eventually, we all sat down and had a wholesome talk. Mrs. Daly asked, "So Adam, what are you planning to do after college?" I cleared my throat and replied, "I'm studying to become a gynecologist. It's my way of following the family tradition." "What do your parents for a living," Mr. Daly asked curiously? "My mom heads her own law firm and my dad is one of the chief physicians at one of Chicago's finest hospitals," I replied. Glancing at each other, Mr./ Mrs. Daly raised their eyebrows with a surprised expression on their faces.

As the visit came to a close, Mrs. Daly decided to ask my age and what was my plan for taking care of her grand baby. I told her my age and assured her that her grand baby would be well-taken care of. With a look of joy on their faces, both her parents hugged me and wished us the best. This moment made me uncomfortable because I knew exactly what Lisa would want to discuss on the way back to Ann Arbor. Once we said our final goodbyes, she and I headed back to the places that we called home.

For the first twenty minutes we sat in complete silence. In an instant, Lisa began her discussion about she and I moving to Chicago. I didn't want to discuss it so I said as little as possible. However, without adding any pressure, she said her peace and changed the subject. The trip to Ann Arbor wasn't all bad as we found things to laugh and joke about. Lisa and I tossed out possible names for the child and that made her day more than anything else. It was the first time that we had gone over possible names for the child and it felt different. However, we kept searching and exploring our possibilities.

Lisa and I picked up a pizza and returned to her home. As I was preparing to get out of the car, she handed me a set of keys to her house. "I want you to have these, so please make yourself at home. You can come here whenever you choose to and you can stay as long as you want," she said with a smile. Before

I could say a word, Lisa had gotten out of the car. While I sat behind the wheel of the car in shock, she made her way into the house. Slowly, I followed her inside and took a seat in the first chair that I came to. Something in my mind was telling me to accept the keys and not to make a fuss about it. Accepting the keys did make sense, because God forbid that something was to happen to her or the baby.

Yelling from down the hall, Lisa asked if I had brought the pizza into the house. Pushing my chair underneath the table, I went back to the car for the pizza. As I walked to the car, I couldn't take my eyes off of the keys in my hand. If this is a question of trust, then I'm surely being put to the test. Obviously, this key idea was something that she had thought about before, because I didn't see it coming. Maybe I should have prayed for more insight, because I'm at a loss for words, right now.

I came back into the house and took the pizza to the bedroom where I found Lisa completely nude with her protruding frame lying across the bed. "I would like for us to finish what we started before the baby and I fall asleep," Lisa said as she pinched her nipples. It was at that point that I began undressing, and moments later I was back where I started. As the sun began to set, Lisa let her hair down and screamed like she did during our earlier performance. With her legs slightly raised, I gave her long, slow strokes that eventually pushed her over the edge.

Lisa came repeatedly while I kept digging into her. The more I gave, the more she wanted. "I bet you didn't know that a pregnant woman could be so horny," she said between moans. I got Lisa on her knee's and increased the pace of my strokes. "What's my name," I asked repeatedly? Lisa then began to call my name over and over as I held her cheeks apart, plunging directly into her. The sound of her cries and moans put me on the brink of ejaculation and it wasn't long before I released a wad of sperm into her womb. Lisa fell forward as I slowed my strokes. Surprisingly, that's where she remained as she and the baby fell asleep.

CHAPTER

SIX

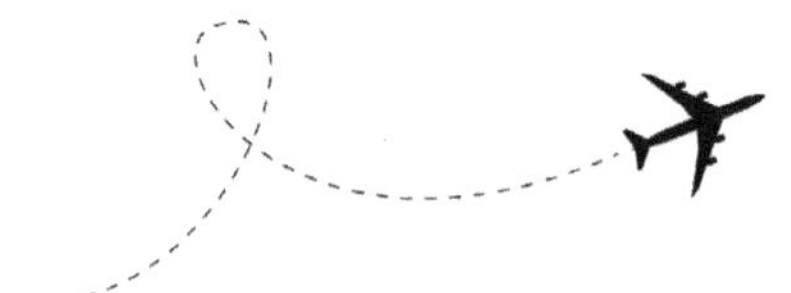

As the months went by, Lisa kept me busy as she began having false labor pangs. This particular night was a long one as I sat by her side in the emergency room. Puzzled and unsure about what was about to happen, I managed to call my mom while I sat by her side. When my mom answered the phone, she was surprised to hear my voice this late in the evening. "Is everything okay," she asked nervously? I told her that I was at the hospital and she immediately began to panic. "No mom, everything is okay, but I got my girlfriend pregnant and we're in the emergency room waiting to be seen," I replied.

Mom was full of questions as she tried to explain to my dad that I had gotten someone pregnant and that we were in the emergency room. What didn't surprise me was that my mom was getting dressed to fly to Michigan to find out exactly what was going on. Flying wasn't a problem for her during the late hours, because she had total access to the company plane. Before I could talk her out of flying, an intern came into the cubicle to assist us, and the call ended. Having sat at the hospital for hours, I received a call at 5am from my mom saying that her plane had landed and that she should be in Ann Arbor within the next hour or so. While traveling home, Lisa sat nervously in the passenger seat, worrying about how my mom would respond about her being pregnant, and my telling her about it one month before the baby was due. I held her hand as I tried to assure Lisa that my mom was open minded and that everything would be okay. "Have you thought more about coming with me since the last time we discussed my moving to Chicago," Lisa asked as she held my hand? I replied,

"Can we talk about this some other time." Angrily she said, "We need to talk about it now, because once the baby is born, I need to start planning to leave. I'm still taking this job offer, Adam." I gave a long sigh as I tried not to think about it.

Once we were home, my mom called to get directions to Lisa's home while I sat nervously at the kitchen table patting my foot on the floor. I had no idea how close my mom was to Lisa's home and it was too late to call her and find out how long it would be before she arrived. Standing at the bedroom door, I watched Lisa sleeping when suddenly the doorbell rang. I knew it was my mom, so I put a smile on my face and answered the door. Dressed in relaxed fit pants, tee-shirt and sandals, my mom came into the house as the chauffeur got her bags from the car.

Excitedly she yelled, "Hi, son. Where is the mother of my grand child? Is she sleeping? Should I go and wake her?" Mom talked a mile a minute as I stood speechless. Once the bags were brought into the house, I took her to the bedroom and she stood in the doorway and looked at Lisa's sleeping body. "Oh, the poor girl," mom said as she walked over to the bed and took a seat. "What is her name, Adam," she asked while placing her hand on Lisa's shoulder? "Her names Lisa, mom," I replied as I walked toward the restroom.

My mom shook Lisa until she awakened, and with a smile, she took Lisa into her arms. "My name is Gayle and I'm Adam's mother. Are you feeling okay? Is there anything that I can do for you," she asked in a compassionate tone? Lisa returned the embrace and immediately they began to make a bond with each other. I left them alone to talk while I laid across the Futon sofa in the basement. It was a real pleasure having my mom in town, but I hoped that she wouldn't allow Lisa to get her involved in my decision making process. Knowing my mom as well as I do, I can remember how well she does when it comes to influencing others.

Through the air vents, I heard distinct conversations and laughter. "Adam," my mother yelled as I was beginning to drift off to sleep. Unaware of why she was calling for me, I got up from the sofa and ran upstairs to the bedroom. "This girl is pregnant and she's hungry, so find something for me to prepare for her and the baby to eat. If you want me to fix breakfast for you, then thaw out enough food, because I'm starving," mom demanded as she continued consoling Lisa. Without saying anything, I went to the kitchen and removed an unopened pack of bacon from the freezer. Exhausted, I poured a glass of orange juice and sat at the kitchen table.

"I like her Adam," mom said as she entered the room. "Why didn't you call and let your dad and I know that you were about to become a father," mom asked as she placed strips of bacon in the skillet? Not knowing exactly how to answer the question, I said, "You and dad may not have liked the fact that I had gotten someone pregnant after only being in Michigan for a few months. That's not what I'd consider being responsible, and besides I was in shock up until I heard the babies heart beat. No-matter how hard I tried, I couldn't deny the fact that the baby is mine because we were together for days at a time."

As my mom scrambled seven eggs, she replied, "That's no excuse not to tell me and your father. After all, we're not upset, because you're a grown man and things happen when you're not careful." My response to her last statement was, "I took precautions and the condom broke." Mom stopped beating the eggs for a moment as she stood speechless. "Well, Adam, if the condom broke then her pregnancy must have been meant to be, so thank God. You do remember who Jesus is, right? Don't beat yourself up, because what's done is done, and who knew that it would turn out like this, except the Lord," mom said as she prepared a pan of   hash browns.

As we ate breakfast, mom and Lisa talked as I read the morning paper. I then heard her tell Lisa that she would be around until after the baby is born. The statement didn't bother me. because with mom around I could get some other things accomplished. "Baby, when you get some time, I would like to go and visit your aunt Joyce. Have you seen her since you've been here," she asked as Lisa sat at her side? Careful not to give the wrong answer, I replied, "We saw each other for a few moments at the beginning of summer." It was at that point that I was saved by a 'kick' as Lisa buckled over with pangs. "Is the baby okay, Lisa," my mom asked with a hint of concern in her voice? Lisa managed to nod her head in response to the question. "I'm okay," she whispered.

After spending the day with my mom and Lisa,

it was time for a little R & R. Once Lisa fell asleep, my mom came into the basement where she found me enjoying 'Three Stooges' reruns. "I remember how much you like the 'Stooges' when you were growing up. Some things never change," she said jokingly. Mom took a seat in the recliner as I sat near by on the Futon sofa. We sat there watching the 'Stooges' for twenty minutes before she hit me with the interrogation. "Lisa told me about the job offer in Chicago; the one that you don't approve of. Lisa said she asked you to come along with her and that you refused. What I want to know is why are you refusing to go along with her," she asked in a very sarcastic tone of voice?

My mom did not realize that I wanted to avoid this discussion, but I managed to give her an answer. "My life is here in Michigan and I'm not willing to relocate to a university back home. If there were any schools back home that interest me then I would have remained there. I'm not doing this to be stubborn and I don't believe that Lisa got pregnant to keep me in her life, but this is not the right time," I replied. My mother is easy to talk to and after listening to me she only nodded her head and said, "Okay, baby. It's your life and you can live it as you choose. Now, Lisa is giving me my first grand child and I'm probably more excited than both of you, so here's my suggestion. You remain here in Michigan and once you're done, you can come home and take care of your child. Lisa told me that she's planning for this to be a permanent move, so you know what responsibility you're going to be faced with. You are going to be a long distant parent and your job will be the same as a 24-hour parent. My daughter- in-law needs you and I want you to be there for her," she said in the most caring manner.

When I heard the word 'daughter-in-law', my mouth practically dropped to the floor. "Did you say the daughter-in-law? Did she tell you that we were going to get married? Is this some kind of conspiracy against me," I asked with a curious tone? Mom sat on the edge of her chair and said, "Whether you marry Lisa or not is unimportant to me, but as long as she's carrying that baby, she will be looked upon as a daughter-in-law." Once I heard my mom explain herself in that manner, I didn't have any more questions. Mom seemed to have agreed with what I was saying, so she dropped the subject.

CHAPTER
SEVEN

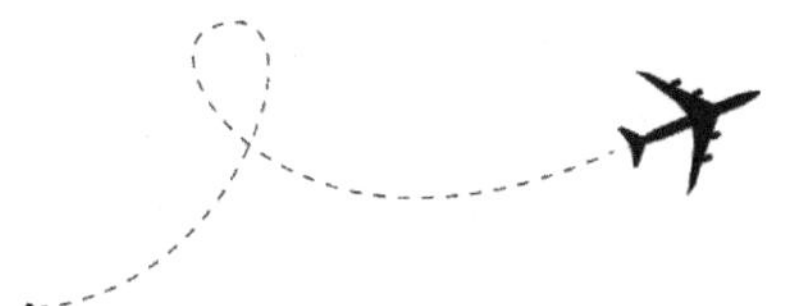

The three of us woke up early and drove to Southfield, MI to visit my aunt Joyce and her family. Mom cooked breakfast before we left and with her sense of humor, she kept us laughing. Lisa wasn't having as many labor pangs as she was before my mom arrived, and that was a good thing. As far as I was concerned, it didn't matter to me if she didn't have any more pangs until the actual time to deliver. She and my mom discussed plans for a baby shower, and where it should be held. Before I crossed the county line, Lisa began having multiple labor pangs and I had to come off of the expressway.

We arrived at the hospital and it was the same thing as usual. The baby wasn't on the way and because we had spent so many hours there, we postponed the trip. When we pulled up to the front door of the home, she had several more sharp pangs but we didn't get alarmed. Holding her hand, I lead Lisa into the home where she took a seat on the living room sofa. The sofa was made of very soft material that didn't bother her back, and there she remained for the majority of the evening. My mom and I waited on Lisa hand and foot. Both of jumping at her every request.

Lisa wasn't much for talking on the phone, but this was one conversation that she did not want to miss. The cousin from Flint, MI whom I had heard about, but not met, called to say that she was having a surprise baby shower for Lisa. The news shocked her so much that it brought tears to her eyes. 'At last, I'll be able to have a moment of silence to my self' I thought as I wiped away her tears. My mom was so excited about the shower that she immediately left the home in my truck to visit a nearby shopping mall.

As soon as Lisa heard the truck pull out of the driveway, she ran to the bathroom. It didn't dawn on me to ask if everything was all right, but seconds later she came out of the bathroom wearing her bra and panties. "I think your mother is a jewel, but I need some sex, right now," Lisa said as she fell onto the bed. Lisa removed her bra as I removed her panties. Once she was nude, I slid out of my track pants and tee-shirt and climbed into bed. We went at it like two wild animals, as she begged for long, hard strokes. The wetness of her crotch drenched my member in her succulent juices. With her legs spread, Lisa gripped my butt and forced me further into her womb as she kept crying for more.

I discovered that I couldn't hold out any longer and I shot a large wad of sperm into her. Lisa felt the warmness of the sperm and she shouted and bucked like someone having a fit. Using slow strokes, I kept working my member inside of her. She and I held each other for five minutes or more as I kept gliding within her soft flesh. Overwhelmed with lust, Lisa held me close as she began pulling me closer, forcing my penis further into her.

Stroke after stroke she yelled louder until I heard a squishy sound and I realized that she had come extremely hard. My entire pelvis was wet with cream as beads of sperm rested in the crack of her anus, which now resembled a glazed doughnut. Pushing me out of the way, Lisa crawled out of bed and went to take a shower. While she showered, I fought to catch my breath as I was ready for more. I knew that she wouldn't mind my getting into the shower with her, so I joined Lisa for a bath before we fell asleep in each others arms.

When the sleep was beginning to get good, someone began ringing the doorbell. I leaped from the bed as Lisa continued snoring. The closer I got to the door, the more the bell rang. "I'm sorry for ringing the doorbell so much, but I have to use the bathroom," my mom said as she ran down the hall. I closed the front door and returned to the bedroom. Mom came out of the bathroom and knocked on the bedroom door and asked, "Is everything okay, because I didn't hear any voices so I wondered if you guys were cuddling? I cut her off in the middle of her question and replied, "We just wanted to take a nap. You know where everything is so help yourself. " As mom closed the door she said, "I'm going into the office and e-mail your father and from there I'll be in the basement."

I got out of bed around 9p.m. and went downstairs, where I found my mom lying on the sofa reading a magazine article. "Hi, Adam. Your father wants you to call him when you have the time. Is Lisa asleep? I purchased some terrific things for the baby shower. I had everything gift wrapped so that she won't have a clue as to what it is. Have a seat. You know, I really like Lisa. She's the kind of person that you need in your corner. She's bright, and educated, and..." I stopped her sentence and said, "Pregnant!"

My mom sat the magazine down and looked into my eyes. "Are you okay, baby? I mean, are you having any doubts about anything," she asked in her motherly tone? "Well, I care about Lisa, but I'm not in-love with her, if that makes any sense. I've been out of high school for exactly one year and I'm a father to-be. She has every right to accept that job in Chicago, and I don't want to lead her on. Just the other day she gave me a key to the house, and that's cool, but I need some more time to continue growing and to discover what I want. Lisa's older than me and she appear to have lived a sheltered lifestyle, and I don't want to lead her astray," I said with my head in my hands.

Mom cleared her throat and said, "Your father and I raised you to do what's right and there's nothing wrong with you feeling this way. Becoming a parent can be frightening, but the Lord will see you through, and never visualize this baby as a mistake. The Lord gave this baby to you guys because he knew what he was doing. All he wants you to do is love the child he has given you and try to provide for it as best that you can. You're going to be a good father and Lisa is going to be a good mother. Just stay strong and you'll see."

As mom finished her lecture, Lisa made her way downstairs. "Am I disturbing you two," Lisa asked as she waddled over to the recliner? I got up from the sofa and approached Lisa to aide in helping her to sit down comfortably. "You know, Ms. Gayle, I have gotten so much attention from Adam these past months that I'm starting to feel like a spoiled brat. The two of you together are remarkable! I get breakfast in bed, back rubs and a lot of TLC," she said with a sparkle in her eyes.

Mom reclined on the sofa and said, "Baby, this is only the beginning. By the time we're finished with you, you're going to be bouncing around this house like a ball. Believe me, I've had three children and his dad has always been there for me. Most men have hang-ups after seeing a woman give birth. They wonder if the vagina snaps back into place and when? However, once I snapped back into place, James and I were going at it like rabbits. A woman tends to be exceptionally horny after being told that she can't have sex for six weeks." Embarrassed, I held my head in my hands as I could not believe what I was hearing. "Mom, can we change the subject," I suggested. "Hey, daddy, this is girl talk!"

CHAPTER
EIGHT

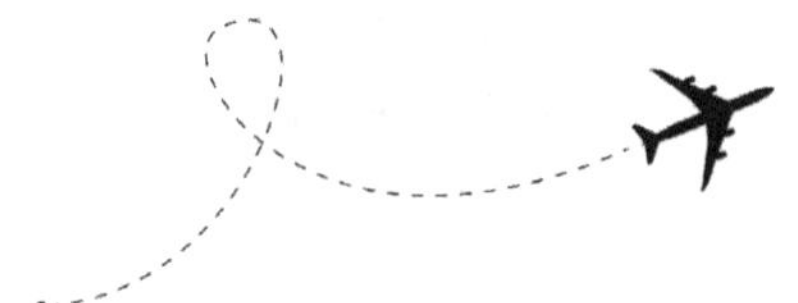

This is the day before the baby shower and we're all excited. When we awakened, we made a second attempt to drive to Southfield, MI to visit my aunt Joyce and her family. My mom and I left with the clothes on our back and Lisa packed a bag for just in case of an emergency. The highway isn't as congested as it is in the early hours of the morning, so we got on the highway around 11:30a.m. and traveled to our destination. My mom had never traveled Michigan roads, so she sat in the back seat and enjoyed the sights. She noticed how things changed as we drove through Livonia, MI and surrounding areas as opposed to the sights she saw once she entered into Detroit. The sights weren't bad, but there was a difference in billboard ads. There were more teenagers and young adults on the road than she expected. "This area is no different from the streets in Chicago," mom said as she peered out of the window.

We pulled into aunt Joyce's driveway, and she greeted us with her dog, 'Cuddles.' Aunt Joyce gave my mom a big hug as I opened the door for Lisa. "Come here. I want to show you something," mom said as she brought aunt Joyce around to the passenger side of the car. Aunt Joyce looked at Lisa's stomach and laughed hysterically. "Oh, I don't believe this. I'm going to be a great–aunt and no one told me. How many months are you," she asked with joy in her eyes? Aunt Joyce and my mom acted as if I wasn't there as they gave all of their attention to Lisa.

As they made their way into the house, my cousin Eric came out onto the front porch with a soda pop in his hand and a smile on his face. Damn, "A, where did you meet her? I have to admit that she is attractive, and she's pregnant. Is the baby yours or are you keeping her warm for someone else," he asked with a devilish grin? I laughed and shook my head as I knew that he would be surprised to find out how we met each other. "She's one of my instructors from school. We started messing around and she became pregnant. The baby is due next month," I said.

Eric poured the remainder of his soda pop onto the grass and said, "Damn, Adam, you didn't waste any time. I've been in Michigan all of my life and I don't have any kids." Eric pulled me close and asked, "Would you like to go for a ride with me? Stacey and Angela just moved into their own crib and I'm on my way there to help break the place in. Are you game?" Before giving him an answer, I went in and mentioned to Lisa that I was leaving with my cousin and that I'd be back shortly. Lisa gave me a kiss and told me to have a good time. My mom and aunt Joyce were so busy talking that they didn't notice that I was in the house.

When I got into Eric's car, it smelled of marijuana as he took short drags from a cocktail. "If you want some I can roll one up," he said between coughs. I shook my head and he proceeded to drive away. There were so many girls out that I got dizzy trying to look at all of them. Eric was a fast driver and before I knew it we were pulling into the driveway of the apartment which wasn't far from aunt Joyce's home. He took a few minutes to roll up a blunt and we went up to the apartment. Eric and I flirted with some older ladies who were waiting in the lobby while we waited for the elevator. Once the elevator came, we rode up to the 8th floor and when we stepped off, all we could hear was loud music coming from the apartment.

Eric knocked on the door and Stacey answered it. "Please, come in gentlemen," she said with a smile. When we entered the apartment, Angela came out of the back room wearing a tight bikini. "I didn't know what time you'd be here so I was going out for a swim," she said before giving Eric a kiss. Without saying a word, Eric pulled out the blunt as Stacey approached him with a lighter. "Are you smoking, Adam," she asked inquisitively?

After seeing everyone gathered together to hit the blunt, I said, 'I'll try it." Eric took two puffs. Angela and Stacey took two puffs and I took one as I damn near choked off of the smoked. I sat down on the sofa to gain my focus as they continued smoking. "Was that your first time hitting a blunt," Eric asked with laughter in his voice? I managed to nod my head between coughs. He and Angela took their last hits off of the blunt and went into the bedroom. Slams were all I heard as they closed the doors, leaving Stacey and I alone. I felt so high that it appeared as if I was going to pass out. Stacey took several drags from the blunt before putting it out.

Standing in front of me with her hair braided and her shorts unbuckled, Stacey joined me on the sofa. "I've been thinking about you since the last time I saw you. Eric told me that he was going to hook us up the next time you came by and I've been waiting patiently," Stacey said as she placed her hand on my crotch. Running her fingers along my erection, she asked, "Can we finish what we started or are you too high?" I laughed and said, "If you've got the time, then I've got the time." Stacey took me by the hand and led me to her bedroom. Before closing the door, she went into the living room and turned the volume down on the radio. When she came back into the room, Stacy found me sitting on the bed in my 'drawers' and she began to undress.

I laid on my back with my penis pointed toward the sky. My eyes widened as she stood over me wearing a thong. Before I could say a word, Stacey climbed onto the bed and began giving me some damn good "head." My toes curled as she sucked like a wild woman. Her mouth was wet and her nipples were as hard as quarters. I managed to pinch them as she took all of me in her mouth. This girl's mouth went down to the base of my erection and I damn near screamed because it felt so good. The more she sucked, he more my body writhed with pleasure.

Once the sucking stopped, I began fondling her breast. They were as soft as a baby's butt. I placed my mouth on her nipple and she began to moan uncontrollably. "Suck this titty, baby," she cried. With her nipple in my mouth and my finger stuck deep inside of her womb, she begged me not to stop. Our foreplay lasted for twenty minutes before I whipped out a condom and let her put it on me. Stacey laid on her back and I pushed her knee's toward her chest. She played with her tits as I shoved all of myself into her. Eyes closed, she began to moan and cry out for more. As I stroked her sopping hole, Stacey spread her lips and asked me to come inside. I gave her everything I had as she bucked like a horse. "Ride this hole college boy," she said as I began to grind my penis deeper into her flesh. This girl was on fire and it appeared as if she didn't want to stop.

Stacey pushed me off of her and got onto her knee's. I shoved so much of this pole into her that she began to cough. "You can stop coughing, because by the time I'm finished, your gonna want to clean your colon, I said as I pushed into her. She met every stroke with precision timing. "Spank it, Adam," she begged. I spanked her rear and she began coming. "Every time you spank my fat butt, it makes my "flower" hot and I just want to keep coming." 'Why did she tell a guy like me a thing like that,' I thought. The more I spanked, the more she came. "I want to come all over your rod so I can lick our juices off your balls," she said with her head buried in the pillow.

One smack, and then another, and she came. Stacey's body shook as I kept digging into her. "Oh, baby, you're the best," she screamed. Suddenly I came as waves shot through my body. Stacey unwrapped my penis and sucked all of my juice. High-as-hell, my eyes rolled into my head as she would not stop sucking. "Damn, this has a good taste," she said. Filled with more lust than I could contain, I pushed her away and fell onto the bed. "That was g-o-o-d," I said as I struggled to catch my breath.

I thought the show was over when I heard a knock at the door. "Come in," Stacey whispered softly. Angela came into the room with a drink in her hand and her nipples staring at me. "Your cousin wants me to take care of you," Angela said as she placed her drink on the dresser. Stacey moved away as Angela began sucking my limp penis.

While she played with my rod, Eric came into the room and asked Stacey to follow him. Once my penis was ready for round two, I got behind Angel and began drilling into her hole. It was obvious that Eric had already taken her for a few laps, because her hole was extremely wet. I gave her all of me like a pro as she bounced her butt up against me. The blunt made me light headed and I felt like a super brother. We gave all that we had until we finally came together. Angela was much prettier than Stacey, but her hole wasn't as wet. However, it was worth a second try.

Taking her head into my hand, I held Angela close as I rode her in the missionary position. With her slender legs stretched wide, she took all that I had to give. She wasn't much for talking dirty, but her moans and sighs managed to get her point across. I laid my body on top of her and she held me close as I grind deeper into her gaping hole. Her womb made all sorts of sounds as I kept drilling. Moments later, we came together, once again. As we laid there drenched in sweat and our own juices, her hands caressed my back. At this point I was unable to speak as she rolled me off of her. While we caught our breath, we could hear Stacey screaming for more as Eric spanked her. Glancing at each other, we laughed.

Angela and I went into the bathroom and showered while Eric and Stacey continued their performance. When we came out of the shower wearing towels, Eric and Stacey, both dressed in their underwear, were sitting on the bed smoking a blunt. Angela joined them on the bed as I searched for my clothes. "Do you want to hit the blunt cousin," Eric asked? Without saying a word, I took one hit and passed it to Stacey. Everyone continued smoking while I got dressed. I wasn't trying to be rude, but we had been there for three-and-a-half hours and I was becoming concerned about Lisa.

As that thought passed, my cell phone rang and it was my mom asking how long was I going to be, because Lisa wanted to get something to eat. Eric and I went into the living room and I told him my situation and he left to go and get dressed. Angela immediately stopped smoking and followed him into the bedroom.   I could hear Eric and Angela arguing through the door. Apparently, he made her feel cheap, because he passed her to me. However, the argument didn't last long, as I heard Angela agree to wanting to do it again.

After he had showered and dressed, we made plans to get with Angela and Stacey again before we kissed them goodbye. Stacey tried to shove her tongue so far down my throat that it turned me off. "We'll finish this kiss later," I said as I followed Eric down the hall. I could not believe what had just happened. The sex part I understood, but the freak swapping blew my mind. It's obvious that we were all game for it, but I personally didn't expect it to happen. Smoking the marijuana took the cake, because I had never smoked that stuff in my life. Judging from the way that I was feeling, I don't want to try it again.'

CHAPTER
NINE

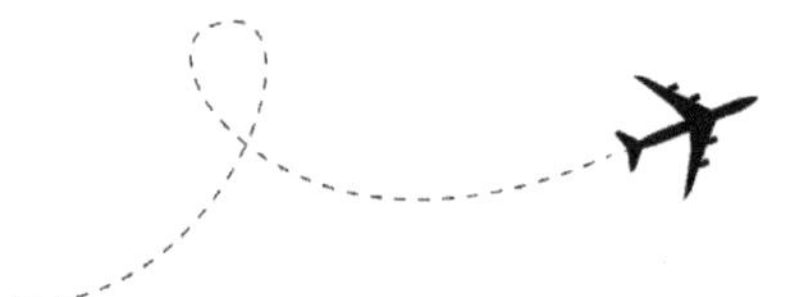

As we sat in the driveway of aunt Joyce's home, Eric laughed as he took short glances at me. He shook his head and said, "I hope you enjoyed yourself, Mr. College man. I didn't plan anything, but things worked out for the best." I laughed and said, "Your girl Angela is a freak. Was it your idea to get her to come across the hall," I asked? "Man, Angela will do anything that I tell her to do. She's proud to be a freak. However, Stacey is the freak, with her big legs. That was our first time, and it was nice; body as soft as cotton," Eric said as he opened the door to get out of the car.

Eric and I walked through the front door and headed for the basement. Mom, Lisa and Aunt Joyce were sitting in the basement watching a 'Lifetime' movie. "Is everyone ready to go to dinner?" Mom laughed and said, "You and Lisa go back to Ann Arbor and after Joyce and I finish shopping tomorrow we'll drive there to attend the shower." I helped Lisa out of the recliner and she said, "I'm ready to go, because the baby is getting hungry. We can stop at a restaurant on the way home. We have a taste for some seafood." I then formally introduced her to Eric before he left to go upstairs to answer the phone, and we followed him. Lisa walked slowly as I stood behind her for support. With my weak legs, it took a lot to help Lisa maintain he balance; I felt like falling.

My mom came outside and helped her into the car as I hugged Aunt Joyce. "Take care of that girl, Adam. Also, get as much sleep as you can, because you're going to need it," she said jokingly. We pulled out of the driveway and traveled south to the expressway. As we drove through the city, Lisa said, "I spoke with your mom and she told me about your plans to remain in school here in Michigan, but I have a serious concern." Lisa cleared her throat and asked, "Are we to remain a couple, while I'm away or are you going to move on to someone else?" I replied, "I'm going to date other girls while you're away, but that doesn't have anything to do with us." Angrily, she said, "If we're going to raise this child together then you should focus on doing that. If you decide to get another girl pregnant then I'll be crushed. Your mom said that she will give me all of the support that the baby and I need, but I still want you to be apart of our lives. I can't believe that you would actually date someone else while I'm away. Do I mean anything to you or do you consider me to be a ship passing through the night," Lisa asked?

I explained to Lisa that I had needs and although it's not about sex, she wasn't going to be able to help me if she's hundreds of miles away. "I'll come and visit you and the baby every chance that I get, but that will only be on certain occasions. What's more, you and I need to take some time to figure out what we want and what we expect out of each other." Crying, Lisa said, "I care about you Adam and I'm willing to fight for you. You can be with any girl that you want, but she needs to know that I've already put my bid in for you. I don't like the fact that you will be dating someone else, but I guess you're entitled to that. After all, you are a man and I'm aware of your needs. Now, that doesn't mean that I'm going to seek out another mate, because I know whom I want to be with." She then took hand and squeezed it. "I love you, Adam. No one has made me feel as special as you make me feel, and that's special to me. However long that it takes, I'm gonna be waiting for you." I felt like such a heel. "I'm going to be here for you and the baby, I said.

We held each others hand as we traveled to our destination without saying a word. 'I was amazed at what I had I said to Lisa. It was freaking me out to believe that I was actually having feelings for the woman. 'My mom told me this day would be coming, but I never imagined that it would be coming so suddenly. Hell, I had a good woman by my side, a baby growing inside of her and a lot of responsibility to face up too. There was no need of me to be upset with Lisa, because she was only expressing to me how she felt. The amazing part was that I really wanted to be with her, but the timing was all wrong. It would be naive of me to say that these months together didn't make me feel anything for her,' I thought while staring at the road.

With my hand in hers, Lisa placed our hands together on her stomach. The feeling of my child kicking made me feel a joy that I couldn't describe. Lisa moaned softly as I rubbed her stomach. "Yes, this is your daddy. I can't wait to see your face and count your fingers and toes," I said as we drove through Livonia. "Pull up at the next exit so that we can find a restaurant because I'm hungry. I mean we're starving," Lisa said with a smile. I came up at the next exit and there were several restaurants in the area. She and I pulled into the parking lot of an Italian restaurant and we proceeded to go inside. The line in the restaurant was stretched outside of the entrance door. We had our names placed on a waiting list and we took a seat that had become vacant. Within minutes we were led to a table for two. Lisa and I sat down and prepared to have dinner together. Ironically, there was a pregnant, Caucasian woman setting across from us and her and Lisa immediately began sharing pregnancy stories.

Once our food arrived, we ate and talked more about our future plans. When we were done, we felt more comfortable about my dating, while trying to maintain a close relationship together. "I'm not a jealous person, Adam, but I'm serious about what we talked about," Lisa said as we waited for our waitress to return. I removed the credit card from my wallet and replied, "As long as you're aware that I'm not looking for anything serious, we shouldn't have any problems. After all, I'm going to be here for a long time by myself. Sure, you can expect me to visit you and I expect you to visit me, and that's only fair. However, despite what I do or whom I do it with, I promise not to bring you anything that a doctor can't cure."

I felt so much better after that conversation that I was anxious for more sex. As I helped Lisa into the car, she said, "We need to get home as fast as possible, because I'm horny and I need to take a rest. I closed her door and walked around to the driver side of the car. Once I got in, I leaned toward her and we gave each other a long, passionate kiss. "Let's go, baby, because we have some unfinished business to take care of," I said as I put the car in reverse. Like

children, we laughed with mischievous expressions
on our faces, as we seductively looked at each other.

CHAPTER
TEN

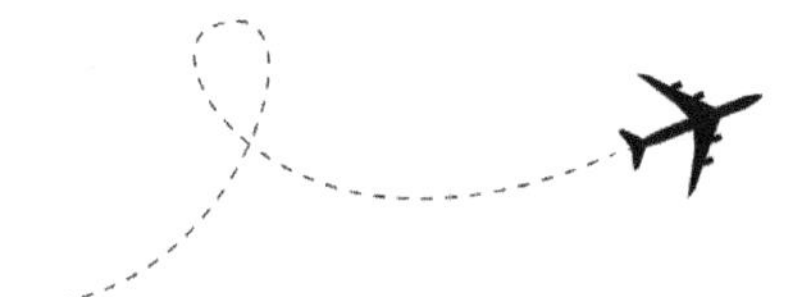

Lisa slept the entire trip as I struggled to remain awake. I wasn't sleepy, but the effects of the marijuana had my eyes feeling heavy. The ride home was smooth, although I did get mixed up in rush hour traffic. What surprised me was how well I was finding my way around town. I exited the expressway and realized that we were practically at home. 'I'm actually calling her home my home,' I thought to myself. When Lisa awakened, we were pulling into the driveway of the complex. We pulled into the garage and once the car stopped, she took my hand and placed it inside of her shorts. "See how wet I've gotten," she said, as she moved my hand across her rigid clitoris.

I got out of the car, and then I helped Lisa out. We held hands as we entered the house. "Damn, I can't wait to get you out of your clothes," Lisa said in an aggressive tone. She began to undress, leaving her clothes behind as a trail for me to follow. Once the doors were locked and the blinds were shut, I joined her in the bedroom. Lisa laid on the bed and with both hands she spread her legs. "Don't keep me waiting, Adam," she said as I removed my shirt. The desire to get into Lisa was overwhelming as I watched her play with herself. "You really know how to torture a guy," I said while removing my underwear.

I laid in the bed next to her and began rubbing her clitoris and sucking her nipples. For the first time in my adult life, I actually tasted fresh breast milk. It didn't have the best taste, but I proceeded to suck more of it. Lisa placed her hand on my head as I did not want to stop sucking her full breast. "You've got to save some for the baby," she whispered. Lisa turned onto her side and I slowly entered her. I grind my penis into Lisa as she moaned and dug her nails into the mattress. Eventually I increased my pace as she began to buck against me. With my hand resting on her butt, I parted her cheeks and put more manhood into her womb. "Go slow, baby," she said. Lisa began bucking slowly and I decreased my pace as well. We stayed in this position for what seemed like forever. I didn't mind because the feeling of her warm butt cheeks against me was mind blowing and soothing. Lisa was wetter than ever before, and I savored each moment inside of her juices. As I picked up my pace, she spread her legs and I went in a little further. The sound of her moans and whimpers made my penis harder with each stroke.

Lisa and I faced each other as I continued stroking her hole. Changing positions, Lisa's tongue flickered in my ear until her moans became deeper and her juices flowed over my member. While her heaving body writhed underneath mine, I released my load. As my sperm splattered inside of her, Lisa pulled me closer into her womb. Sucking on her finger, Lisa moaned deeply as she dug her nails into my arm. The pain of her nails was more pleasurable than excruciating, as my penis became limp.

Lisa panted uncontrollably as I laid there with my eyes closed, waiting for more. "Let me give you something that you need," Lisa said as she reached for my penis. On my knee's, I hovered over her as Lisa licked our juices from my cock-head. I once thought this was a disgusting act, but I had grown to like it more and more. Lisa liked it when I made love to her mouth, so I thrust deeply into her throat. She always managed to take all of me into her mouth and this is what heightened my excitement and interest. As she licked my shaft, I fingered her to a hot climax. She wanted to scream, but it was difficult to do with nine and-a-half inches of beef in her mouth.

I watched as sperm ran down her thighs and dripped from her mouth. Because I had taken part in a wild sex act earlier this evening, I was almost certain that I would not climax again. Lisa paused for a second and I withdrew my aching penis head. 'What a day,' I thought to myself as I collapsed onto the bed. Lisa crawled out of bed and went into the bathroom and turned on the shower. I listened as she brushed her teeth and gargled with mouthwash before closing the shower door.

While she showered, I toyed with the television remote and savored the cool breeze that came from the fan. When she was done, I went into the bathroom, brushed my teeth, and showered. Once I was done, she called me into the bedroom to put lotion on her body. I approached her with my penis hanging and a towel thrown over my shoulder. As she watched the evening news, Lisa poured 'baby oil' and lotion into my hands and poised herself on the bed. Gently, I rubbed Lisa down as she sighed with pleasure. "Your hands feel so good," Lisa said as she laid there with one leg spread and the other one resting on my forearm.

Lisa turned on her side and I squirted 'baby oil' onto her back and her butt cheeks and began to slowly massage the oil into her skin. "I can't wait to lose this weight and regain my figure. After the baby is born, I'm going to join a gym and get myself back into shape while you're in class. I'm sure that my mom won't have a problem coming down to assist me. When I get to Chicago, your mom said that I can use the gym at her home," she said. The more Lisa told me things, the more I tried to imagine some of it. Deep down inside, much of what we're experiencing feels like a dream. Sometimes I wished that someone would come along and pinch me, just to be sure that I wasn't sleeping.

While Lisa watched television, I applied lotion and 'baby oil' to my own skin. She tried not to be obvious, but each time I rubbed different areas of my body, Lisa would turn her eyes away from the television and watch me. After sneaking a few peaks at my muscular build, I decided to give her a show, as I began rubbing my body slowly. Every few seconds, I would hear Lisa let out gentle moans as I was turning her on. All of a sudden, I kept rubbing myself and she became quiet. I looked over my shoulder and noticed that Lisa had fallen asleep. Hunching my shoulders, I tossed the lotion and 'baby oil' bottles onto the chair and laid down beside her. With her butt acing me, I curled up behind Lisa and placed my arm over her shoulder and pulled her close. "Thank you," Adam, she whispered before drifting off into a deep sleep. Before I knew it, the television was watching us as I could not stay awake.

CHAPTER
ELEVEN

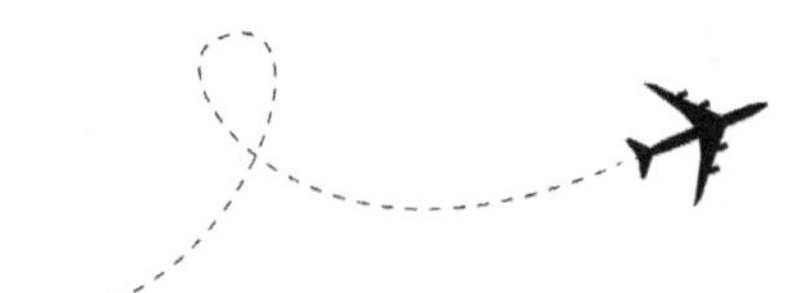

The next morning Lisa and I were awakened by the ringing of the phone. She rushed to the bathroom and I answered the phone. My mom was on the other end asking about Lisa and telling me her plans for the day. Sleepily, I told her that she would have to talk to Lisa about the baby shower and where it was going to be held. When Lisa came out of the bathroom, I handed her the phone and she and my mother talked for 10 maybe 15 minutes. I felt sorry for giving her the receiver, because my mom knows how to keep someone on the phone. However, Lisa didn't seem to mind as she wiped the sleep from her eyes.

Lisa hung up the receiver and called her cousin Tracy to confirm where the shower would be held. She and Tracy stayed on the phone for one hour, while I prepared breakfast. "Adam," Lisa called as she made her way to the kitchen. When she entered the room, Lisa was surprised to see that breakfast had been laid out for her. "Oh, this is so sweet of you," she said while giving me a hug and a kiss. "Guess what today is?" I looked confused as I pretended not to know. "Today is our baby shower. I can't wait to see what we'll receive for the baby. We need everything, and that's exactly what I'm hoping for. The shower is going to be held at my parents home and it begins at 6pm. Before I sit down for breakfast, I need to call your mom and tell her the time and place," Lisa said as she hurried out of the room. I ran behind Lisa and turned her around and said, "First, I want you to feed the baby and then you can call my mom.

Once Lisa was done with breakfast, she called my mom, talked for a few minutes and fell asleep.

While she slept, I watched the sports highlights and bits and pieces of several movies. As I stared at Lisa, I thought she looked as beautiful as the day we met. Her skin had a glow about it that I couldn't describe. The more I stared, the more I could see the baby moving in her stomach. Gently, I put my hand on her stomach and felt the vibrations as the baby kicked. Just as I rubbed her stomach, Lisa 'passed gas' and the smell had me devastated. I then remembered her telling me that a pregnant woman passes gas for two. It was difficult to believe that an attractive behind was capable of putting out such a foul odor. I thanked God that the A/C was blowing, so I caught my breath and continued watching my programs.

Lisa slept for hours before she was awakened by the sound of the doorbell. Dressed in a pair of panties, she ran to the bathroom while I answered the door. When I opened the door, there were three gorgeous black females standing on the porch. "Yes, may I help you," I asked as I hoped that they were there to see me. They looked me up and down and one of them said, "Hi, I'm Tracy, Lisa's cousin. I told her that we were coming by. Is she here?" I invited them inside as I went to inform Lisa that her guest were here. When I walked into the room, Lisa had put on a maternity short set and was styling her hair. "Were those my cousins at the door," she asked? I replied, "Yes, their waiting for you in the living room." As I searched for her sandals, Lisa asked, "Did you introduce yourself?" I walked out of the closet and said, "No, I wanted you to formally introduce me to your cousins."

Lisa put her purse on her arm and walked toward the bedroom exit. She called for me to come out and meet her cousins, and I rushed at the opportunity. "This is Adam, and Adam this is Tracy, Brenda and Brittany. These were my road dogs back in the days," she said jokingly. I said "Hi" and Lisa and her cousins opened the front door and walked outside. I followed Lisa outside and she gave me a kiss and said, "I'll be back tonight, so keep it warm for me." She placed her hand on my crotch to signify what she was talking about. Her cousins noticed the gesture and they began laughing and whispering. My pride wouldn't let me feel embarrassed because they knew what time it was. Besides, they knew that she didn't become pregnant through some fertilization technique. I followed Lisa over to her cousins' truck and helped her inside as they continued laughing. Once they pulled out of the driveway, I ran into the house and locked the doors, closed the blinds and leaped onto the bed. "Now, it's time for me to relax," I said to myself.

CHAPTER

TWELVE

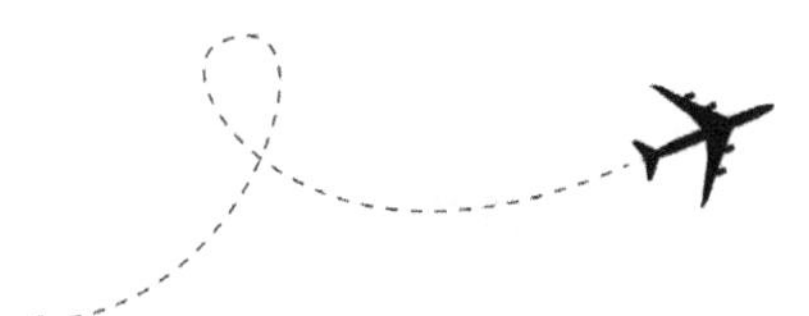

The foursome was on their way to celebrate this joyous occasion, as everyone was excited to be together. "Girl, how in the world did you get pregnant by this man you just met? He's a nice, young, strong looking black brother. Does he live around here, because if he does, then ask him to hook me up with his brother. I know there's got to be another one around here," Brittany said in a joking manner. Everyone in the truck laughed as they took turns making cracks at one another. "Girl, Adam is a student. This guy challenged my intelligence. One thing lead to another and I got pregnant," Lisa said as she pointed to her stomach. "Although he's younger...Brenda cut her sentence and asked, "How much younger?" "He's nineteen. No...and he's mature for nineteen is a better expression. I have to give the man some respect. Hell, I'm only four years older than he is if you really want to know what's up, and it's all good," Lisa remarked in a sassy tone.

"Leave her alone," Tracy said as she took a glance into the rear view mirror. Turning her attention back to the highway, Tracy remarked, "I'm happy for Lisa having a real brother who's trying to get somewhere in life. He looks intelligent, in a sexy chocolate kind of way. He's tall, and athletic. Most brothers don't have anything to offer but some limp "dick." When he's giving it to you he has the nerve to ask "is it good to you," and you be like, "yeah, sure!" Lisa then asked Tracy what she meant by her "sexy chocolate brother" statement? "Hey, I'm just kicking it like it is. My whole point is that I'm happy for you and your man. Have that baby and raise it together," Tracy responded.

Almost as if she was in another world, Lisa looked at everyone individually before closing her eyes and saying, "I know you all are going to be upset with me, but I've accepted a position as a 'director' with a company in Chicago. Due to the pregnancy, I won't be leaving until late September/early October." Everyone looked at Lisa with 'Surprise' written all over their faces. "When were you going to tell us," Brenda asked? Laughing, Lisa replied, "I forgot to tell you guys. But seriously, I've accepted a position in Chicago. I'll come back to visit, especially on holidays. Besides, it's on four-and-a-half hours away."
"Girl, you're full of surprises. Got a good job and leaving for a better job. Got a 'fine' brother living up in your crib. Damn, Can you tell me what I'm doing wrong," Brittany asked in her usual playful manner? "So, what are you going to do about your boy? Is he leaving also," Tracy asked inquisitively? Lisa replied, "Adam going to remain here until he finishes his education, and we'll meet up after that. Besides, he doesn't want to go with me because he's from Chicago. There weren't any universities there that appealed to him, so he decided to take a chance in Michigan." Brenda lit her cigarette and asked, "What is he studying to become, if don't mind my asking?" "He's studying to become a doctor. Adam Harris, the black gynecologist," Lisa said as she rubbed her stomach.

Just as Lisa was taking Tracy's hand to put it on her stomach, she parked the car in the shopping mall parking structure. Quickly, Tracy came to a stop, her tires screeching to a halt. "Ooh, I'm sorry," Tracy said as she leaned toward Lisa to feel the baby move. "Yeah, you've got a 'big fella' in there. He's going to kick his way out," Tracy remarked jokingly. Lisa playfully pushed her away and said, "Get out of the car, fool." Everyone climbed out of the vehicle and proceeded toward the entrance. Mocking Lisa's walk, everyone made fun of each other. Lisa tried to run after them and found it difficult to do. "You can't keep up with 'us' slim girls. Maybe, after you have this baby you can get back into your 'track star figure.' I remember when Lisa would be out whooping everybody's behind out on the track. I even remember you getting your 'track and field' trophies," Brenda said playfully.

Everyone ceased from playing and entered the entrance way. Inside the mall, they went their own way, but they managed to stick together. Lisa was enjoying herself so much that she had forgotten about the shower. At this point the shower didn't really matter because she was beginning to feel insecure. Lisa had never had anyone to make those sort of remarks about Adam. For Tracy, Brittany, and Brenda, any one of them could want a piece of him. 'The very thought of him sticking one of my cousins is too much to bear. Hell, anything is possible because after all, they are slim and more attractive. They could give it to him in ways that would be uncomfortable to me. But, I'm having his baby,' she thought with a smile.

Brenda and Brittany then ran up along the side of Lisa and carried her off to another store. "Do we have to walk this entire department store," Lisa asked in a whining voice? "Girl, we've got to walk that baby down. Hell, I'm anxious to see whom it resembles," Brittany said. Lisa laughed along with Tracy, whom had just joined the group. Together they strolled from one store to the next. They went to jewelry stores to tease each other about their taste in wedding rings. The more they walked, the more Lisa's appetite grew. Eventually, they all took time to have lunch together.

"Seriously, what's going to become of you and Adam. Are you guys committed or is he negotiable," Tracy asked as she wound spaghetti on her fork? Lisa drank some water and said, "Adam is going to stay here and finish his education. We'll keep in touch… long distance." With a whimsical look on her face, Tracy said, "That's what I'm talking about. If you leave him here, then you know that he's going to do someone else. Are you willing to trust this long distance thing? Remember the old saying, When the cat's away, the mice will play." As she noticed the expression on Lisa's face, Tracy thought, 'I would love to keep your young friend company, cousin. Hell, it would be better than knowing that he's sleeping with a stranger. If you're going to leave him behind, then it's better if we just keep it in the family,' she thought.

Brittany noticed that Lisa was looking uncomfortable regarding this topic and said, "Can we change the subject? Why don't you tell us about this guy who was up in your face, Tracy?" As Tracy began telling her story, Lisa practically ignored every thing she was saying and got an instant attitude. Although she didn't want her attitude to be obvious,

Lisa pretended to pay attention to Tracy. Inside, Lisa was a raging fury. She was in such a rush to leave the restaurant that she began making several trips to the restroom. Everyone noticed that Lisa was uncomfortable, so they ate their lunch and left the restaurant, and then the department store.

CHAPTER
THIRTEEN

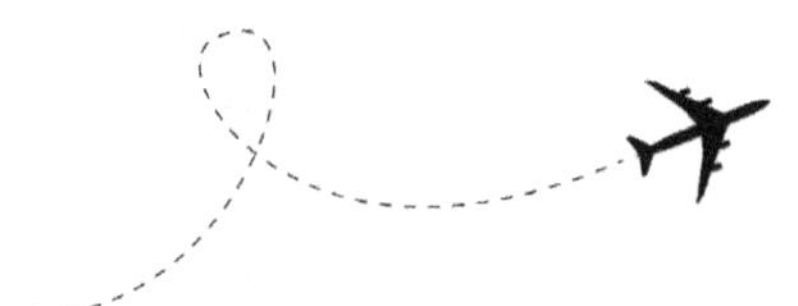

While Lisa was away from the house, Adam, dressed in 'boxer underwear,' spread his tall frame across the bed and watched television. He had become so use to being around Lisa that it felt like something was missing. The thought shocked him, because he has never felt this way about anyone. It was that thought of them being old, and the scene where she's about to give birth that played in his mind. Desperately, he tried to not think about anything, but nothing seemed to work. As the thoughts continued playing, Adam stared at the picture of them, taken at a carnival.

Adam was beginning to wake up to what he was actually getting into. There was some sort of feeling about commitment but it wasn't well thought out with details. Suddenly, he felt out of place because he was actually 'chilling' at her crib. Although Lisa told Adam to 'make himself-at-home,' he just felt as if something was missing. Having given it a lot of thought, Adam realized that 'his' girl was still away. "Hell, I must be tripping," he whispered to himself.

Once he snapped out of his daze, Adam leaped from the bed and went into the kitchen. "Let me see, what does the baby have a taste for," he asked himself. Much like his father would have done, he decided to order out. Taking the receiver into his hand, Adam glanced at the different coupons from 'pizza-to-you-name-it'. He settled for pizza and hot wings over the seafood meal. Dialing the 'Pizza Hut' phone number, someone answered the phone and Adam was quickly put on hold; Adam began to place his order. They told him that it would be 30minutes and he hung up the receiver. Running from the kitchen, Adam ran into the bedroom and leaped onto the bed. Horny, he grabbed his penis and said, "Bring your body home, Lisa." He then fell onto the bed and regained his composure. As he went through the cable channels, he waited patiently for his food to arrive.

After the food was delivered, Adam slammed the door and went back into the bedroom. Slowly, he folded the cover back on the 'meat special,' while savoring the smell. "That smells delicious," he remarked. Taking a slice from the box, Adam lowered his head to say grace before diving into the pizza and hot wings. Adam sat up in bed and like a black prince, he ate pizza, and drank soda-pop from the bottle.

Slice after slice, he devoured the pizza. Once he was at the last three slices, Adam closed the box top and opened the hot wings. Piece-after-hot-piece, he continued eating. Minutes later, Adam put the food away and drank soda-pop to wash it down. "Burp!" "Excuse me," he said before curling up on the bed. 'If I keep this up, I'm gonna need to go on a diet,' Adam thought to himself. No one has ever told me that the man eats as much as the pregnant mother-to-be.

As he scanned the channels, Adam came across a special report and he couldn't take his eyes off of the women on the screen. Considering how he was feeling sexually, Adam would have taken his pick from any one of them. 'Every one of those 'dime pieces' could do me right about now' he thought. The more he looked at the ladies gyrating on stage, the more Adam wished Lisa would say, "Forget this social time," and just come home.

Adam's desire was surging through his body as he began to reflect on past episodes with Lisa. He thought about what she did, and what she does now. Neither one of them saw a problem in the bedroom. Lisa liked the way he worked it and he liked the way she worked it. He had always admitted to himself that Lisa was addicted to the sex and she loved it. 'Hell, I'm glad we hooked up, because I like her sex just as much as she likes mine,' he thought, laughing to himself.

CHAPTER
FOURTEEN

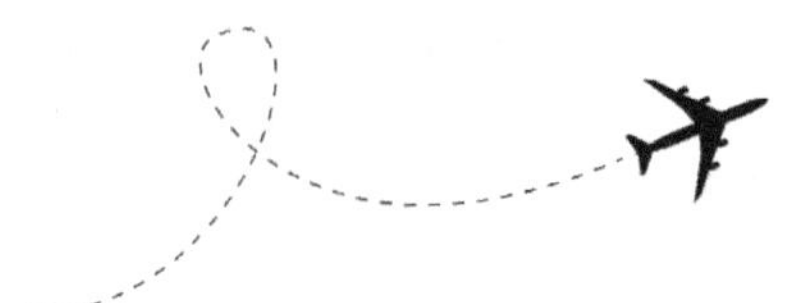

Everyone was gathering for the shower, as Lisa took a nap. She and her cousins stopped and had their nails done for the evening, and the 'sleep' had crept in. Lisa struggled to keep her eyes open while the technician did her fingernails and toenails. For heat purposes, Lisa wore sandals that helped to accent the color of the polish. Riding home from the 'nail salon,' Lisa 'got her sleep on' and once she arrived to her old bedroom, it-was-lights-out for her and the baby. After a long day, Lisa felt she deserved it.

Although enjoying her sleep, she was awakened by the sound of people gathering together. Slightly dazed, Lisa looked around the room to remember where she was. Noticing the room, with a huge smile on her face, Lisa rolled across the bed. Running her fingers across her crotch as she thought about Adam. Seconds into her thoughts of Adam, an old friend came into the room and whispered, "It's time to wake that baby up," as she crept to the bed. Shocked, Lisa got out of bed to greet her. "What's up, Denise? I haven't seen you in some months, girl." Helping Lisa off of the bed, they embraced one another. 'I don't believe she burst into 'my room,' like she's already heard about my man from Tracy,' Lisa thought to herself during the embrace.

Having spent a few minutes talking, Denise stood in the restroom doorway while Lisa brushed her hair. "Hey, Tracy told me about your man. Is it true that he's younger than you," Denise asked as if to pry? Lisa looked at her through the mirror and asked if they could discuss him later? "Tell me what's going on with you," Lisa remarked. Denise began telling her life story as Lisa was not paying attention to her. The more Denise talked, the more time Lisa spent brushing her ponytail. Placing the brush onto the counter, Lisa replied, "I don't mean to cut you off, but I need to pee." Denise stepped out of the doorway as more friends piled into the bedroom. Setting on the toilet, Lisa shut the door and shook her head as she couldn't believe it was time.

When Lisa came out of the bathroom, there were five additional well-wishers standing around the room. They were all eager to celebrate the moment and get into 'girl issues.' For the next three hours, Lisa was going to be pushed from one person-to-the-next. It was a moment that was ready to go down as it did. The food had been catered and everyone was ready to get nosy. Cautious about leaving Adam behind, Lisa looked at everyone suspiciously as they kept coming into her bedroom.

Once she got out of the bedroom, the shower began. Sensitive, Lisa cried as she was reunited with so many familiar faces. The women all gathered around and played games while they awaited the big moment. Eager to find out what gifts she was going to receive, everyone chanted for Lisa to open her gifts. Happily, Lisa decided to go with that idea. For the next 45 minutes, she tore through a mound of gifts. Once she was done, the floor looked liked 'Christmas in the summer time.' Everyone, including Lisa, was surprised at all of the gifts she received. Friends and family members gave her a car seat, a stroller, and plenty of other nice things.

Once the party was over, Lisa had her gifts taken out to the car she'd be riding in. Glancing at her watch, the time read 10:14pm and everyone were eager to leave. There were more hugs and kisses taking place than Lisa expected. Always pleasant, she didn't mind the attention. "Girl, I've got your things in my car. Just say the word when you're ready to leave," Tracy said cheerfully. Lisa said her last goodbyes and she and Tracy left the house.

On the way to Lisa's home, she and Tracy talked and laughed over particular events. They hadn't laughed together like this in a long time. Tracy coughed after laughing and managed to ask, "Who were those two ladies that resembled each other?" "That was Adam's mother and his aunt Joyce. The mom had on the denim shorts and his aunt wore a sun dress. His mom heads her own law firm and his father sits on the hospital board," Lisa replied. Tracy's eyes widened as she could not believe what Lisa was telling her. 'She's got good connections,' is what Tracy thought to herself. Tracy then pulled into Lisa's driveway and turned the engine off.

Adam saw the headlights pull into the driveway and he knew that Lisa was home. He opened the garage door to greet her as she climbed out of the truck. "Hi, baby! I've got some great things to show you," Lisa said as she gave Adam a kiss. "Tracy's going to need some help with those gifts," Lisa said as she tried to keep her eyes on Tracy and Adam. He and Tracy grabbed the gifts and followed Lisa into the house. Lisa was in front and Adam brought up the rear as he enjoyed looking at Tracy's rear.

Innocently, he noticed that both Lisa and Tracy have similar body structures. 'These girls got a 'tight' looking family,' he thought to himself and grinned. "Just stack the stuff anyplace, and I'll go through it tomorrow. I want to thank you, Tracy, for a wonderful day and now I would like to enjoy my man," Lisa said in her 'sexy' voice. Unnoticeably, Tracy rolled her eyes and replied, "Yeah, you and Adam have a good night, and have some fun. If it were my choice, I'd be having some fun also." Lisa had turned her attention away from Tracy and had begun flirting with Adam.

After Tracy had gone and the house was quiet, Lisa yelled for Adam to come into the bedroom. He was shocked at the way she called him, so Adam stopped in his tracks. 'I know she didn't just call me like there's a problem.' He then rushed to the bedroom to find out what was wrong. When Adam entered the bedroom, he noticed Lisa had began to undress. Wearing a playful smile, she asked, "Do you think my cousins are attractive and would you try to get with them?" This question shocked Adam, whom didn't see it coming. He thought for a minute and said, "I think your cousins are attractive, but that doesn't mean I want to get with them. Do you know something that I need to know," he asked? "If you've got a problem, let it out."

Lisa reached for Adam, and taking his hand, said, "I just got jealous for a minute because they're in shape and I'm bloated. Sometimes I wonder if you're tired of looking at me; I can't even see my toes. Adam said softly, "Baby, I'm here! Get rid of those crazy thoughts. Besides, I think you look sexy. You look sexy enough to 'ride,' if you know what I mean." Adam then removed his shorts and drew closer to Lisa. "I've been waiting all day for you to come home. Are you ready for a little taste," Adam asked playfully? Lisa gently squeezed her breast together and fell backwards onto the bed. Adam hovered over Lisa to remove her panties. "Oops, I'd better use the bathroom before we start. This might go on all night...change that to a few minutes," Lisa said jokingly as she got out of bed.

Lisa came out of the bathroom and fell onto the bed. Lying on her side, Adam began working his penis into her mouth. Lisa's mouth was hot and wet, and it shot chills down Adam's spine. He knew that Lisa enjoyed giving head, and the moment seemed 'just right.' She engulfed as much as possible without spilling one drop of semen. Adam, who was fingering Lisa, increased the speed of his strokes. Lisa grind on his hand as-if-for-dear-life. Moaning, Lisa rolled over onto her back and motioned for Adam to lie on top of her. Adam climbed on top of Lisa and began to slow the grind into her womb. Lisa's eyes rolled into her head as Adam increased his thrust. "Oh, Adam... let me have it. Give it to me, baby. I've been waiting all day for you to satisfy me. Slow down, because I don't want you to upset the baby," Lisa whispered. Adam began applying long, slower strokes to Lisa. 'Pregnant hole feels really good,' Adam thought to himself.

With her hands on his butt, Lisa took control of the strokes she wanted. Lisa would have Adam to speed up, slow down, and do a combination of both. Adam's torso glistened with her juices as the moon light shined on him. He gave Lisa a few more strokes and they came together. Both their bodies shook uncontrollably as they held each other. This climax left both of them feeling drained. Although he remained inside of her, Adam noticed that she wanted more.

Adam's penis was still rigid, so he held Lisa close and gave her a combination of strokes. He started out with the 'piston' stroke, where he took straight aim, and then playing inside of her. She enjoyed every minute of the love making as Adam feasted on her breast. Lisa's nipples were extremely sensitive, but 'the doctor' knew exactly how to treat them. The feeling of his tongue flickering across her nipples was more than enough to make Lisa scream. Between the strokes, the tit sucking and the closeness, Adam and Lisa felt as if they were on fire. Hot sweat covered their naked bodies as they groped at one another. Wet, and unable to hold out, Lisa came a second time. She shook her head so many times that it looked as if it was going to come off. Waves of ecstasy took control of her body as the strokes continued. With her stomach between them, Adam applied even longer strokes. He kept each stroke at a slow pace as he held onto Lisa's calves. "Take this thing, girl. You can have all of it," Adam whispered. Still writhing in front of him, Lisa was unable to say anything. All she did was scream, moan and make circular motions with her torso.

As Adam was withdrawing the glistening penis, his sperm rushed forward, leaving him on the brink of coming. Adam increased his strokes while Lisa rubbed her clit. Just as her moans increased, he unloaded into her. The sensation felt so good that it brought Lisa to another climax. This time she screamed louder than ever as Adam kept applying slower strokes.

Lisa began giving Adam kiss–after–wet–kiss. "You make me feel so good that I could scream louder and louder. I like the way you take your time and make sure that it's right. The lovemaking feels special," Lisa whispered as she tried to lie comfortably. "Good night, daddy," she said. Adam was too drained to respond. With her back turned to him, he placed his hand on her rear, as a non–verbal cue of responding. Sighing repeatedly, Adam smiled when he considered how good the lovemaking felt. 'Oh, I'm starting to feel like a fiend for this woman's hot body. Hell, I can't wait to see what the lovemaking will be like after she has this baby,' he thought.

CHAPTER
FIFTEEN

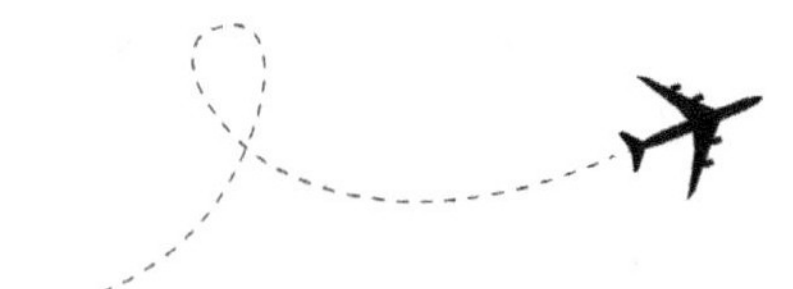

the weirdest faces. He humped really fast, like he was in a rush. It was obvious that Jason was only out to get his 'nut.' This actually worked for Tracy, because it was better than having him stab her repeatedly with his nub. Noticing that Jason was about to come, after two minutes, she faked an orgasm to help get him off.

Tracy would laugh to herself, because Jason looked like he was having a 'fit' when he came. She knew he was about to go to sleep, so Tracy asked him for a loan. This was her sucker move because she knew Jason's answer. "Go in my wallet, baby, and get what you need, just leave me some," Jason said as he worked to catch his breath. Seconds later, Jason fell asleep and Tracy went into his wallet and removed four–hundred dollars. She placed it into her purse, and went into the bathroom to wash–up. By the time she was done in the bathroom, Jason was asleep.

The next morning, Jason rose early and tried to get Tracy stimulated. She had gotten what she wanted, so Tracy brushed him off. Like the wimp she thought he was, Jason laid down beside her and gave up trying. Tracy didn't want to be a complete 'arrogant woman, so she got up and made him breakfast. She served Jason breakfast in bed and the look on his face proved that the breakfast was as good as sex. He didn't show any manners as he gulped down his food. "Aren't you going to have some," Jason asked with his mouth full? Tracy shook her head and left the room.

As she left the bedroom, Tracy wished that it was Adam that she had prepared breakfast for. Naked, she looked at a picture of her and Lisa and wondered why Lisa was always so fortunate. Although looking at a picture, she ran her fingers between her legs as she envisioned Adam feasting on her juices. Just as she slipped a finger in her hole, Jason came out of the bedroom carrying a cup of coffee. "Are you okay? Did you leave me some money," he asked while chewing the remainder of his food? Tracy replied, "I'm just tired from a long week. There's been a lot on my mind. After I shower, I think I'll just sit around the house and take it easy. Jason placed his cup down and said, "I have to spend the day with my daughter, but I'll give you a call later. Maybe we can get together and have a late dinner." Tracy smiled at the offer, but she wasn't the least bit interested in seeing him. Throwing him a hint, Tracy said, "If you can't make it back, then I'll understand. Your daughter may want all of your time...daddy's girl." Jason kissed Tracy and went to then began to get dressed.

CHAPTER

SIXTEEN

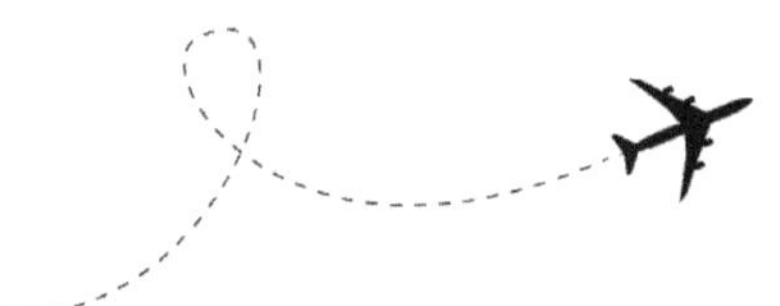

Lisa made it to her ninth month and she was miserable. Between the heat making her uncomfortable and the baby kicking, she was ready to give birth. Adam's mom had flown home to take care of some things, but she had returned. A week into the month of August and her and Adam was on 'pregnancy' patrol. They continued to wait on Lisa hand-and-foot and when she wasn't cranky; she managed to enjoy the attention. Gail helped Lisa through a lot of her discomfort by saying things to console her. While Adam was away at the college selecting classes and so forth, Lisa and Gail spent a lot of 'girl time' together.

The date was August fourteenth, which was Adams' father's birthday, and the day of extreme importance. Just as Adam pulled into the complex, his cell phone began ringing. He ignored the phone and pulled into the garage. As the garage door opened, his mom was standing in the garage panicking. Adam got out of the car and asked, "What's wrong?" "Lisa's going into labor, his mom shouted as she ran toward Lisa's bedroom!

Leaving the back door open and the garage door raised, Adam ran behind his mom. When he got to the bedroom, Adam found Lisa dressed as she lay on the bed and held her stomach. "It's time, Adam," Lisa said as he took her by the hand. Gail handed Adam the suitcase as she walked along the side of Lisa. The three of them went out to the car and left for the hospital. Adam's mom had spoken with Lisa's doctor and she mentioned that she'd be waiting for Lisa.

At the hospital, Adam pulled into the emergency entrance' and an officer wheeled her into the hospital. Adam had the car parked by the valet attendant as he rushed to be by Lisa's side. She was quickly taken to the delivery room as Adam nervously rode the elevator. Adam got off of the elevator and ran to the room where all of the nurses were standing. Once in the room, Lisa's doctor assured him that everything would be okay. "What time did the water break," the doctor asked as she washed her hands? "I'm not sure," Adam replied. Lying on her back, Lisa squirmed as the labor pains grew closer. Quickly, the doctor began working to deliver the baby. "Adam, I love you," Lisa screamed as she pushed!

Inquisitively, Adam watched as the doctor delivered the baby. As Lisa squeezed his hand, the sound of the baby crying took Adam's mind away from the discomfort he was feeling. "It's a boy," the doctor shouted. Once the baby was out, Adam pried his hand away from Lisa's as he went to get a full view of the baby. Gail stood in the corner crying as it was too much commotion in the room to move around freely. While they stitched up Lisa, Gail stood by her side with tears in her eyes.

The nurses took the baby to be washed up while Adam sat by Lisa's side. "You did well, baby. I can't believe that he's finally here. We've got to come up with a name for him. Although I was hoping for a girl, a boy will do," Adam said while reclining in the chair. Minutes later, the nurse brought the baby into the room. "Here's your bundle of joy," she said with a smile. Holding him close, Lisa kissed him as Adam did a recount of his fingers and toes. "This is your son, Adam," Lisa whispered. "I hope you're happy," she said with tears in her eyes.

Adam kissed her forehead and said, "I'm very happy, Lisa. Nothing that I've experienced in Michigan has made me happier." "Do you want to hold him," Lisa asked as she handed the baby to Adam? Just when he had taken the baby, his mom entered the room. Smiling, she asked, "Where is my grandson," as she approached the blushing father? Gail hovered over Adam as he cuddled the baby. "This is the new generation of doctors," Adam said jokingly. He handed the baby to his mom, as he offered her his chair. "I called your mom, Lisa, and I tried to contact the other people whom you wanted to see," Gail said as she held the baby close to her chest. "Adam, your dad wants you to call him. It's still his birthday, she said.

Adam left the room to go outside and call his dad. The phone rang three times and his dad answered. His dad congratulated him and they proceeded to have a father and son conversation. They remained on the phone for twenty minutes before ending the call. Adam stood outside and called some of his friends to inform them that he was a 'dad.' The calls didn't last long as he was anxious to get back to Lisa. When he arrived to the room, he saw his mom giving the baby it's first meal. Adam smiled as he sat on the bed next to Lisa. Happy, she looked at the baby who sat with his eyes closed as his grandmother fed him a bottle. Placing his arm around her shoulder, Adam pulled Lisa close to him and kissed her. Grinning, she laid down with the look of a proud mother on her face.

Hours later, Brenda and Tracy arrived at the hospital. They made their way to Lisa's room, where they found five of the women from the shower standing around. "Hi, Aunt Marie," Tracy said as she hugged Lisa's mom. "Let me see the baby," Brenda said. The women were so concerned about the baby that they didn't notice Adam sleeping in the corner. Lisa had washed up, and was in good-spirits as the sun had gone down. There was only an hour left for visitation, so everyone did their best to hold the baby once. Tracy took the baby in her arms and looked at Adam to see any resemblance.

Smiling, she kicked Adam's foot to wake him up. Lisa noticed her action, and became annoyed by her waking Adam. She didn't want Tracy to have anything to do with him. "Wake up, daddy," Tracy said in a friendly voice. Adam opened his eyes and was surprised to see all of the unfamiliar faces. He stood up as Tracy held the baby close to him. "You guys did a great job. When will there be a second one," Tracy asked playfully? Handing the baby to Adam, he took it in his arms and remarked, "This is it for now. Catch up with us in a few years." Tracy wasn't happy with that statement as she smiled and looked at the baby's curly hair. "He has your eyes, her nose and both parents' hair, " Tracy said. Making his way through the crowd of women, Adam gave the baby to Lisa and exited the room.

With her cell phone in hand, Tracy exited the room after Adam. Lisa noticed Tracy as she began to fell helpless. She knew that Tracy was up to no-good and it's been obvious since the day of the baby shower. As Lisa watched her leave the room, she heard Tracy call out to Adam. Standing in the corridor, Adam waited for Tracy to catch up to him. "Where are you going," Tracy asked? "I'm going downstairs to get a soda pop," Adam said as he stood in front of the elevator doors. "How did you feel watching Lisa giving birth to your son? Was it scary," Tracy asked in an effort to make conversation? Adam stepped onto the elevator and said, "I enjoyed the experience. It's not every day that a man watches his child being born." "If you're going to be a doctor then you might as well get used to it," she said, trying to be humorous. Adam ignored Tracy's last statement as they exited the elevator. Tracy followed Adam to the vending machine and he purchased a soda pop for himself and a bottle of water for Tracy. "Let's go upstairs before the visitation is over," Adam said as he rushed to catch the elevator. Once inside, he held the door for Tracy as she got on after him.

On the elevator alone, Tracy turned and placed her lips against Adams' and began kissing him. Stunned, Adam asked, "What was that for?" Tracy said, "I just wanted to congratulate you on a healthy baby." "Why don't you try shaking my hand next time? I don't think your cousin would have liked that," he said. As Tracy switched in front of him, she said, "My cousin doesn't have to know." Adam couldn't take his eyes off of her as she walked in front of him...teasing. The skirt Tracy wore highlighted her figure and she looked sexier than the last time they had seen each other.

Adam followed Tracy into the room where he found everyone preparing to leave. Women kissed Adam, Lisa and the baby as they said their goodbyes. The room was filled with so much love that Lisa remained in bed as her eyes filled with tears. Because everyone was passing out kisses, it was the perfect chance for Tracy to kiss Adam. She approached Adam and kissed him on his cheek. "Congratulations, Adam. I hope you have fun being a daddy." Tracy then gave Lisa and the baby a kiss before leaving with everyone else.

"Call me if you need anything," Lisa's mother said as she left the room. Standing with her purse on her shoulder, Gail said, "I've had a long day, so I'm going home to shower." She kissed Lisa and the baby while Adam stood nearby. "I'll see you in the morning, Lee," Adam said as he kissed Lisa. "Good night little man," Adam said as he kissed his son's forehead. As he was leaving the room,

Lisa said, "Adam, I want to name him 'Andre,' after my grandfather. Andre Harris will be his name." Adam agreed to the name before making his way down the hall.

Adam and his mom walked to the car with smiles on their faces. "My son's a father, and I'm so excited that I don't want to leave. The Lord has finally given me a grandchild and it feels wonderful. Now, when I go shopping, I can buy a 'few' extra's," Gail said as Adam shook his head between yawns. "Who is Tracy, Adam?" As they got into the car, he said, "She's Lisa's cousin...they grew up together." Gail closed her door and said, "Don't trust that girl. She's up to no-good. Her attitude makes people think she's happy for you and Lisa, but her eyes say something else." "What are you getting at, Mom," Adam asked? Taking her cell phone from her purse, Gail said, "Just watch your back, baby. I'll bet my money that she makes a pass at you. It may not happen now, but it is going to happen."

After a good night sleep, Adam and his mom, rushed to the hospital to pick-up Lisa and Andre. Adam drove the car around to the entrance door, and Gail helped Lisa into the truck. As Gail helped Lisa, Adam safely secured the baby in the 'baby seat.' Hungrily, Lisa had Adam to stop at the nearest restaurant. They each ordered a value meal and left for home. Jokingly, they all laughed as Andre slept. Unable to wait, Lisa began eating. Gail snacked on her 'french fries' as Adam drank a milk shake. "Well, I have to say that I've got to leave the day-after-tomorrow. I have a lot of things to tend too and I've already called to have the plane ready. However, I can do anything you guys need me to do before then," Gail said as she kept eating. Adam glanced at his mom through the rear-view mirror and nodded his head in agreement to her last statement.

"Do you know when you'll be moving to Chicago, Lisa," Gail asked? After swallowing her food, Lisa said, "It should be around the end of September or the first week in October." Gail then explained that if she needed help finding a place to stay, she'd be more than happy to help. Lisa asked her to check into a condominium for her and to call and let her know the asking price. Gail saved Lisa's information as they were minutes from the house.

CHAPTER
SEVENTEEN

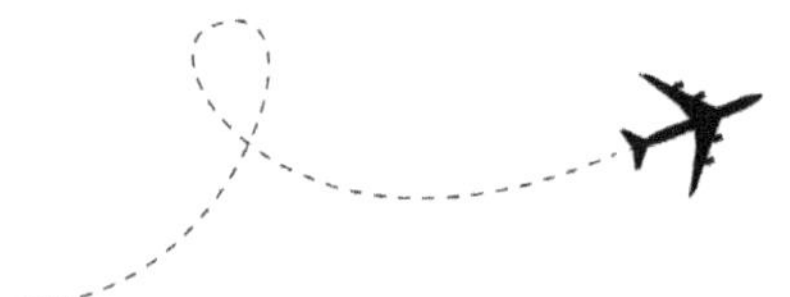

On the morning of her departure, Adam drove his mom to the airport. The private company jet waited for her as she and Adam said their goodbyes. Adam watched as his mom boarded the plane and took off to her destination. Continuously, Lisa called Adam every 15 or 20 minutes. She called regarding something to eat, the baby, and when was he coming home. Her actions had made Adam furious as he didn't want to play husband and wife. Angrily, Adam drove to Lisa's as she kept calling his cell number. The more the phone rang, the louder he turned the volume on the radio. Adam was rushing to get home, but after the disturbing calls, he slowed his pace. Getting there in a rush wasn't much of an issue as he thought it was.

When he arrived at Lisa's, Adam entered the house and it was obvious to her that he was upset about something. "What's wrong," Lisa asked as she laid the baby down? Anxiously, Adam replied, "You're making me upset! The phone has been ringing constantly and it's been driving me crazy. I can't recall you calling me this much when you were pregnant. Now, my phone rings all day. Maybe you can say something to explain your actions." With her hands on her hips, Lisa remarked, "If this is too much for you, then maybe you need to reevaluate your responsibilities. I never thought that calling you would be a problem. There are certain things that I want to share with you. Is that a problem?" "Understand that I'm going to be a man and take care of my responsibilities, but I don't need any drama from you about how to do it. I've been here since the semester ended, and now it's time for me to return to the dorm. We're not married, so don't put me through the non sense that married people go through. You're a woman and I'm a man, and we had a baby together. Please don't make me begin to dislike our situation, Lisa?"

With tears in her eyes, Lisa cried for a few minutes before speaking. As she cried, an angry Adam stared out of the living room window. His emotions kept telling him to get up and leave, but he wouldn't because it was important for him to spend some time with Andre. Lisa sat across from Adam and worked to regain her composure. Softly, she said, "Adam, I don't like it when you're angry with me. You are the first guy to treat me this way and I'm still adjusting to it. When I look at Andre, I see your face. I picture the times we spent before I got pregnant. The first, real orgasm, that I had was with you. It's not all sexual between you and I, but the sex did play a major role. I apologize for the way I've acted today, because it was selfish of me to act that way. It seems like the smallest things are making me jealous, and I don't like it."

Lisa stopped talking and placed her head in her hand. Adam turned to face her and said, "Don't let that happen again, okay? Jealous or not, you've got to trust me at some point. Having said that, let's raise this baby together." Adam walked up to Lisa and took her in his arms, and they began kissing. "I love you Adam and I'm sorry for what I did," Lisa said as she held him tightly.

After the embrace, Lisa laid in Adam's arms as she let a breast pump extract the milk from her breast. "Do you think my tits are ever going to be the size that they were," Lisa asked as she removed the suction device? Adam grinned and said, "If you keep using that thing, they're going to be smaller than they were." "I hope this thing works because I don't care for huge tits." After placing the device on the bathroom shelf, Lisa came back into the living room and began giving Adam some 'head.' He stood with his eyes closed as Lisa sat on the edge of the sofa.

Stopping for a moment to undress, Lisa kept giving him 'head' as she placed his hand on her breast. Gently, he rubbed her nipples as her head bobbed-back-and-forth. Pushing her away, Adam began sucking her breast. They were so sensitive that she could have screamed, although, his tongue did feel good. He made circles around her areola and Lisa began to squirm and moan. "Suck my titty, Adam," Lisa said as she ran her fingers along his back. This behavior lasted for about thirty minutes, until Lisa started coming. Her body shook as the orgasm overwhelmed her. 'I didn't know that a woman could have an orgasm so soon after giving birth,' she thought to herself. Laying on his back, Lisa jerked on Adam's penis until he came. With his eyes closed, Lisa licked the sperm drops from the head of his 'manhood.'

CHAPTER
EIGHTEEN

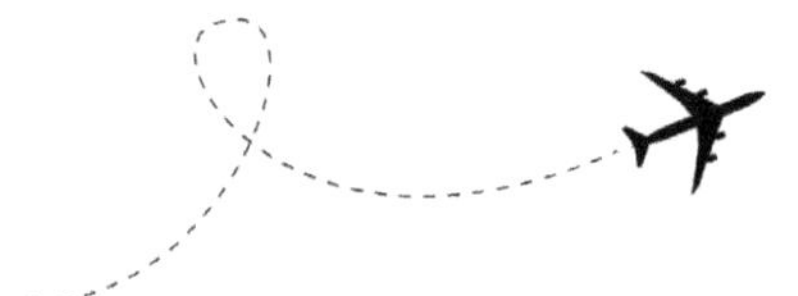

As the weeks went by, Adam's classes began. He was anxious to attend, and with Lisa's support, he was able to stay focused. Adam spoke to the proper officials who made it possible for him to offer his tutoring services. One-by-one, students began coming to him in large numbers. It worked out for him because Adam was able to tutor students on different types of sciences. Adam continued making 'A's while managing his other responsibilities. When he wasn't busy tending to Andre, he managed to spend time with 2-to-three students a day. The majority of the students were females, and he tutored two males. Adam believes that the ratio of males would pick up because more guys were having trouble in science classes this semester.

While Adam was busy at with his classes, Lisa became more familiar with the duties of being a full-time mom. Although she enjoyed it, there was still a lot that she had to learn. Sure, most of her day was consumed of thoughts regarding Adam and another girl, but Lisa didn't let it stand in her way. As she neared her sixth week, she lost weight and felt more comfortable about winning Adam's complete attention. When they were together, he made her feel special, but Adam' charm was his natural quality. He resided at the dormitory, but on the weekends Adam spent his time at Lisa's condo.

Adam always enjoyed being there because he was allowed to relax. Lisa gained an understanding about her young lover, and she ceased with the pressure that she had put on him. Instead of behaving like husband and wife, they behaved like a couple who were dedicated to raising their child. As the outdoor temperature drew colder, they managed to do a lot of things together. There were dinners that they enjoyed together, and moments when they would play, and bathe their son together. It was a new experience for both of them, and one they liked participating in.

However, things weren't great for Adam. Due to his charming nature, girls were practically standing in line for a chance to sleep with him. Each one of them was attractive in they're own way, and he struggled to resist the temptation. Eventually, he met a girl named Kelly and he lost control. Kelly's descendants were from Germany and she had a thing for black guys. Adam did his best to ignore her over-friendly gestures, but she wouldn't let up.

Near the middle of October, things really got bad when he had to tutor Kelly in his dorm room. Kelly had a sensational body and she wanted him to see it. Arriving at Adam's room around 1pm, dressed in tight jeans, and a matching denim top, Kelly looked extremely hot. She wore a perfume that was captivating, and her smile only helped to entice him. Kelly noticed from Adam's facial expression that he was interested in her. Therefore, she proceeded to bend and stretch her body in different positions, so that he could get a good look at her. Adam looked, but he didn't say anything as he watched her bend for this, and reach for that.

Things were going well at the beginning of the session, but Kelly became a little too comfortable. "Can we stop for a moment? My brain feels like it wants to explode," Kelly said as she laid across his bed. Running her fingers through her hair and looking around the room, she said, "I think you have a nice room, Adam. I didn't know that students were allowed to decorate their rooms like this. Do you have any pictures of your girlfriend?" Adam turned the radio on and replied, "No, I don't have any pictures." "Well, do you have a girlfriend," Kelly asked as she kicked her shoes off. Adam took a basketball in his hands and sat in a chair across from the bed. "Everyone has someone," he said. Flirtatiously, Kelly remarked, "I must be the only freshman without someone. Can you introduce me to some of your friends, Adam?" Adam shook his head and laughed. "What's so funny," Kelly asked with a smile? Before Adam could answer, Kelly walked over and sat on his lap. Her skin was soft and she smelled good. "Do I make you nervous, Adam," Kelly asked as she twisted, and grind her butt onto his crotch? Adam pushed her off of him and said, "You should be careful, because you might get more tutoring than you need."

Smiling, Kelly dropped to her knee's and said, "I'm here to learn." She then put her hand on his erect penis and proceeded to pull down his track pants. Adam slid his shirt up as Kelly put her mouth on his penis head. She sucked his 'head' like a lollipop as he thrust deep into her mouth. Unaccustomed to a man his size, Kelly tried to engulf as much of him as she could. Adam placed his hand on her head and increased the strokes. Kelly removed her mouth and walked over to the radio and turned up the volume. Removing her jeans and top, she laid on the bed. Adam undressed and hovered over Kelly as he began shoving more manhood down her throat.

Turned on, he rubbed her clit as she sucked and moaned. "You're supposed to suck and jerk," Adam said as she writhed before him. Adam withdrew his penis from her mouth and got between her legs. As Kelly parted her legs, she said, "Be gentle, because I've never been with a black man your size." Adam grinned as he put on a condom and closed the blinds. Kelly took Adam's prick and placed it against her hole opening. Gently, he thrust forward until she accepted him. With slow strokes, he went as deep as possible inside of her womb. Overwhelmed by the size of his penis, Kelly parted her legs further apart and began to moan softly. "Oh, your dick feels so good. Go ahead and teach me something 'daddy.'

Adam picked up his pace once her juices started to flow, as Kelly worked to keep up with his strokes. Kelly placed her hands on Adam's broad shoulders and begged him for more. Graciously, Adam gave her more and more. He didn't want to stop and Kelly felt as though she couldn't stop. "I like this wet hole," Adam whispered as Kelly got on her knee's. Adam entered her from the back and she began yelling like a wild woman. Wet, he plunged deeply into her. To enhance the moment, Kelly began rubbing her clit until she came. Screaming over the music, Kelly shouted, "Yes!" As the sperm flowed, Adam increased the pace of his hard thrust. "Take this rod," Adam whispered as he continued pumping.

Two hours had gone by and they were totally unaware of the time. Kelly and Adam laid in their juices as they caught their breath. "Damn, Kelly, I didn't know that you could go like that. Judging from your small stature, you can put up quite a fight in the bedroom. Oh, my legs feel weaker than ever," Adam said as she ran her hand along his shaft. "German women love a big cock and sex," Kelly said as she leaned over and sucked the head of Adam's penis. With her mouth open wide, she allowed Adam to push himself in so far, that he nearly touched the back of her throat.

Moments later, Kelly whispered to Adam, "I have two classes on Friday and one of them is about to start shortly. When can we get together for some more tutoring?" With his forearm resting on his forehead, Adam told her to check his calendar in the tutoring office to see when he'll be available. "What's my usual day," Kelly asked? Adam said, Monday and Wednesday. Kelly hunched her shoulders, got out of bed and walked over to the sink and began washing her crotch. 'I'll leave my scent on the towel so that he can smell it and remember me' she thought to herself. "Throw your towel in the basket when you're done," Adam remarked. Surprised by his response, Kelly frowned and thought, 'Damn, I thought I was going to be able to leave my scent behind.' Kelly had a long distance to walk to her first class, so she dressed and left in a hurry.

Slipping into his robe, Adam left the room to go and take a shower. Just as he was leaving, his cell phone rang. Adam noticed that Lisa was calling him and he said to himself, "I'll call you back in a little while," as he tossed the phone onto the bed. Removing his robe, Adam noticed all of the dried up juices that Kelly left on him. Adam grinned and proceeded to shower as he tried to remember the last time he had sex. 'I should have waited to get with Kelly, but the temptation was too strong. Waiting six weeks to get some sex after you've become accustomed to getting it on the regular is difficult. Lisa's got one more week to go before she can have sex, and I can't wait,' Adam thought as he lathered his body.

Adam returned to the dorm room and immediately returned Lisa's phone call. He told her that he would be there shortly and that he would watch the baby if she needed to go somewhere. They ended their conversation and Lisa laughed as she could not wait to see him. She had one more week left before she could have sex, but tonight was going to be their night. With the baby asleep, Lisa took a hot shower as she began getting prepared for a long afternoon. Filled with lust, she fingered her clit as she thought about the good time she was going to have. The shower was exhilarating, that is until she heard the baby crying. Just as she got out of the shower to quiet the baby, her mother rang the doorbell. Lisa picked the baby up from the crib and ran to answer the door, hoping it was Adam. "Hi baby," her mother shouted as she entered the house.

Dripping wet underneath her robe, Lisa hurried to get away from the cool breeze coming through the door. "Mom, I wasn't expecting you. What made you come by," Lisa asked as she handed Andre to her mom? "Well, I was out and I thought I'd come by to see how you and my grandson were doing. Did I catch you at a bad time," she asked inquisitively? Lisa shook her head and replied, "No, and as a matter of fact, I was hoping that you could watch your grandson while Adam and I go out for dinner." Anxiously, her mom gathered the baby's things and left the house.

Lisa phoned Adam and said that he would need to get a box of condoms. Adam was excited to finally hear those words, but was reluctant to reply. After two hours with Kelly, he was about to put in overtime. Adam stopped a few blocks from the house and purchased a 24-count box of condoms. The sales lady grinned as he handed her his credit card. With a smirk on his face, Adam hurried out to the car. Minutes later, he parked his truck in front of Lisa's garage and entered through the front door.

Lisa practically tackled Adam when he came into the house. She ran and jumped into his arms, placing her warm thighs around his waist. With her robe open, Adam held Lisa in his arms as he stared at her erect nipple's and shaved vaginal area. "You remembered how much I like surprises," Adam said as he walked Lisa over to the sofa. Flinging her robe open and parting her legs, Lisa said, "I've got a real surprise for you, daddy My mom has the baby for the night, so we can get it on until the sun comes up. After all these weeks, you know I'm horny." Adam tossed his jacket onto the sofa as Lisa followed him into the bedroom. "I don't want any foreplay, I just want to get down to some hard-core S-E-X.," Lisa said as she ran her hands along her thighs."

Adam put on a condom and they went at it for

two hours. Hungry for each other, they gave all that they had to give…for now. Lisa's hole was so wet that after sex, she had Adam to finger her until she came again and again. The bed drenched in their juices, they held each other like first time lovers. "I wish you didn't have to wear a condom, baby. However, it's a good idea that you did, because I don't want to take a chance at getting pregnant again. The doctor said that it's best to wait six weeks to heal and lessen the chances of getting pregnant. I hope you're not upset," Lisa said as she placed her head on his chest. Adam was overjoyed by the idea, because he wasn't ready for another baby. He then replied, "Hey, the doctor knows best." They laughed and after several more hours of sex and soaked condoms, they fell asleep.

Lisa slept 'spread eagle' and the next morning, she woke up with a hard rod inside of her. Slowly, Adam grind his penis into her tight hole. Once her hole had opened up to receive him, they began having sex like rabbits. Throughout all of the humping, they managed to come together. Adams' wad filled the condom while her juices soaked the bed. That was just the beginning as they continued having sex throughout the remainder of the morning. Surprised, Lisa was shocked at how much her womb could take after five weeks of having delivered a baby.

They were so hungry for each other that they ignored the phone ringing or the rough winds blowing outside. "I'm leaving next week, Adam," Lisa said softly. Adam listened attentively as she went on about what she expected to take place between them. Lisa explained that she would be in his corner and that she didn't want to be disappointed. Adam reiterated his terms. They came to a mutual conclusion and then proceeded to screw each other for another hour.

CHAPTER
NINETEEN

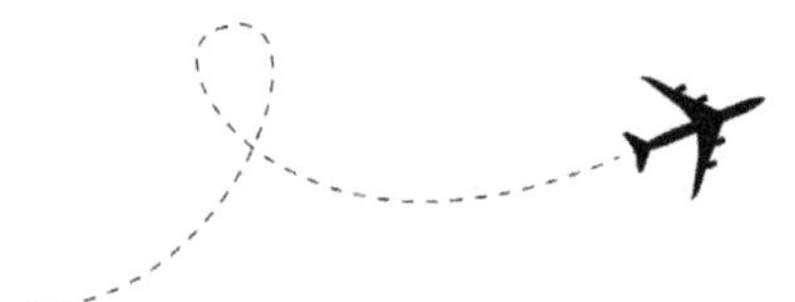

The day before Lisa was scheduled to leave for Chicago, she and I spent the entire evening having sex. When Andre was awake, I tried to spend as much time with him as possible. Lisa and I knew that it would probably be another month or so before we saw one another again, and each moment spent together was important. It amazed me that I actually had a child that I was going to miss. Lisa had mentioned that she would miss the hot sex, but I hoped that we would have something more to 'miss' than that. She and Andre's belongings had been packed for weeks and as a special favor, my mom took time from her busy schedule to fly to Michigan to get her new grandson.

My sister, Krystal, accompanied my mom to Michigan, which was a real treat for me. Instead of staying at Lisa's condo, they resided at a nearby hotel. They arrived the day before which gave us a chance to spend some quality time together. Krystal teased me about being a father, but it only heightened her interest in wanting to become a mother. However, she didn't have the time to focus on such a thing, because she was being groomed to take over the law firm. I believed that Krystal should be placed over the day-to-day operations, because my brother was living in his own world.

Lisa and Krystal got along well, but Krystal managed to keep her distance. She wanted to be close to Lisa, but not so close that it interfered with my relationship with Lisa. My sister has a mothering quality about herself that tends to cross certain boundary's. Although close to my brother James, he and Krystal had to keep a certain amount of space between them because James believed that she sabotaged some of his relationships. James had been engaged twice and after going out with my sister, his fiancee's came to an understanding about their engagement. They realized that they really wanted to be single, because James could be a control freak when he wanted to. He's very intelligent, but he uses his intellect to control others.

Being the oldest grandson, James received a financial inheritance from my grandfather, years before he passed, which helped to make him an asshole. He and I got along like best friends, but if it were left up to me, I'd like to be the one to introduce him to Lisa. I trusted Lisa with him, but I didn't trust him with Lisa. Given the opportunity, I knew that he'd try to sleep with her because she was his type. Not much older than Lisa, he'd probably see her as a possible mate.

After we had sex for the last time that evening, Lisa continued packing some small items. My mom had purchased a place for her and Andre to live, and it was for that purpose that she was more than obliged to transport them to the 'windy city.' Because my mom had to be at work that next morning, Lisa was to be ready to leave at 4am. Krystal had rented a small car to drive around, but they were being taken to the airport via limousine service. If I wanted to see them off, I was to follow them to the airport.

"How would you like to take over this condo, Adam," Lisa asked? "I'll have the deed transferred into your name and you could take it from there," Lisa said as she packed the remainder of Andre's belongings. Startled, I accepted the offer and said, "Give me a call at your convenience and we can work out the details. It's a good idea, because we had never discussed your plans for the house or the furnishings. The good thing about it is that it's close to campus." As she zipped up the bag, Lisa replied, "Please don't bring any of your 'friends' in here to spend the night." I didn't agree with the statement, but I shook my head as if I did.

Lisa and I managed to sneak in a quickie before the limousine arrived. We rushed as if things were out of place. I envied Andre, because he was able to sleep while we ran through the house, bumping into each other. As soon as we got him dressed, the car pulled into the parking structure. When I saw the headlights, I yelled, "Let's go, Lisa." Lisa tossed me a bag as she took one and ordered me to put Andre into the car.

Once everyone was in place, I got into my truck and followed them to a nearby airport. Actually, it was more like a landing strip with several private planes on the property. When the car stopped, the driver got out and immediately began unloading the luggage. Because my mom had already furnished the house with the necessities, Lisa didn't have to worry about carrying a lot of things. I kissed Lisa, my mom and my sister Krystal goodbye as I held Andre close. "Hey, take care of my son. Don't call me with any bad news, like he accidentally got stuck in the toilet like my man in Soul Plane," Adam said jokingly.

Adam then got off of the plane and stood outside as he watched it taxi onto the runway, and then lift off into the sky.

Adam didn't have class on Friday, but he did move all of his tutoring schedules up one hour. He had planned to spend the day studying, but to be well rested, he rushed to the condo to get more sleep. When he arrived, Adam felt a touch of sadness because the house was empty. There was no Lisa walking around in her panties, nor was Andre lying in his crib waiting to be picked-up.

Adam never had a problem falling asleep unless something was on his mind, so he leaped onto the bed and began to drift off. As soon as he drifted off, the phone rang. Sleepily, he answered it and Lisa told him that they had arrived and that she was going to be at his mom's until Saturday or Sunday. Dazed, Adam mumbled a few words, asked about the baby and got off of the phone. He then struggled to fall asleep, as he had been awakened so suddenly.

That morning, having already showered, Adam quickly got dressed and left for the university. Once he arrived at the tutoring center, he waited for the first student to arrive. While going over course material, Adam glanced toward the door and in walked a short pudgy looking girl with braces. He didn't think she was unattractive, but she wasn't his style. It turned out that she was from Iowa and she knew of the schools reputation. "Hi, my name is Sara, are you Adam," she asked coyly? Adam didn't bother standing up, so he put out his hand to her. Sara took his and said, "I hope I'm not late." They both looked at the clock and it read 9:07am. She quickly sat down and removed her text books from the book bag that she wore on her back.

Sara and Adam met for an hour, and to his surprise, his other three students arrived on time. 'This day is going perfect. After I'm done with this guy, I'll be free for the day. I can pick up some boxes from the maintenance room and pack a few things' he thought. The time flew by and within minutes, the session was over. Adam took a sigh of relief and before he could exhale, Kelly walked into the room. They hadn't seen each other in weeks and this was a pleasant surprise for both. "Hey, what's going on, Adam. I see you're still tutoring," she said cheerfully. With a smile, Adam replied, "Yeah, I lucked up and got another crazy schedule. I've got a Friday night class." "What time does your class start," Kelly asked? Adam took a second and noticed that Kelly was wearing spandex pants. "Damn, you look good in those, but don't you think it's a little chilly outside." Turning up her nose, Kelly asked, "Can we talk out in the hall?" He then took his bag and followed Kelly into the corridor. With her back facing him, Adam marveled at her appearance, as he could not see any pantie lines.

"It's good to see you, Adam. Do you still live in the dorms," Kelly asked? With a devilish grin, Adam replied, "As a matter of fact, I do. If you don't mind the walk, you can come and help me break the room in again." Kelly saw the look in his eye and playfully pushed Adam away. "Seriously, You can come over and we can watch one of my new DVD'S. Maybe just kick it about classes or something. Oh, come on," Adam said jokingly. Kelly believed his hint of innocence, because if something happens, then something happens. "So, will I be seeing you on the tutoring schedule this semester," he asked. "I'm not sure Adam. I mean classes started practically four weeks ago, so it's difficult to tell. Although, I hope, my professors have better attitudes this semester. How are your classes going? Do you like any of your instructors," Kelly asked as she waved at someone she knew?

Adam and Kelly had so much to talk about that the walk to the dorms didn't take long. "I want to check my mailbox," Adam said as he held the door for Kelly. After checking his mail box and finding nothing, they went to his dorm room. Once inside, Kelly immediately noticed the change. I see that you've got a flat screen television. Put in a movie so I can see the type of picture it shows," Kelly said excitedly. Adam closed the door behind them and handed her a case of movies. He kicked his shoes off, popped pop corn, and got comfortable. Kelly removed her shoes and joined Adam on the bed. "Do you mind if I watch Cradle to the Grave," Kelly asked? "I love this rapper's movies, and his music," Kelly said. "We'll watch whatever you put in," Adam remarked.

Leaning against the throw pillows, Adam crossed his right leg over Kelly's left and they relaxed. Twenty minutes into the movie, Kelly asked, "Would you explain the conditions of your scholarship to me?" Talking with pop corn in his mouth, Adam mumbled 'yes.' Taking a handful of pop corn, Kelly said, "I'm here because of the scholarship committee, also. The scholarship was offered to me in high school and I accepted it. My parents could have sent me to school, but why bother if you see where you can be accepted by the scholarship committee." What area did you receive your scholarship? Sports or something," Adam asked as he increased the television volume? "I received the sport scholarship in soccer. That's why my legs are so toned. Do you like my leg's Adam," Kelly asked as she flexed her calf muscle? Adam grinned and said, "Of-course I like your thighs. I like all of you. You're cute and freaky."

Kelly continued talking while Adam paid more attention to the movie. He didn't mind the conversation, but Kelly talked constantly. "You know, my mom is German and my father is African American." Surprised, Adam looked at Kelly and replied, "I guess that explains why you look so damn cut...in a sexy way." "You're talking like you want to start something. Are you trying to start something, Adam," Kelly asked playfully? Adam removed the empty pop corn bag and tossed it across the room, making a basket. "Whatever happens is meant to be," he said in his charming tone.

Without hesitation, Kelly began removing her shirt. Adam removed his shirt as he tried to keep his eyes on Kelly. Watching Kelly undress had Adam filled with lust. He couldn't wait to taste her, and feel her body up against his. Kelly slowly removed her spandex pants, revealing a dark-blue thong. As she tossed her clothes onto the floor next to her side of the bed, Kelly held her rear end high, just to give Adam a close view. He tossed his underwear across the room and Kelly turned and placed her mouth on the head of his penis. She took him in deep as he slowly worked his fingers into her 'wet' hole.

Kelly grind on Adam' fingers as he moved them back and forth. Adam wasn't sure if her moaning was coming from the vaginal attention or from the way he stroked her mouth. As he lay on his back, Kelly turned her torso toward Adam's face and placed her crotch in his face. "Just try this one time; it really gets me hot," she whispered. Adam wasn't much for 'eating out,' but as he looked at Kelly's swollen lips, he took a chance. Her round-behind twist and turned as he began satisfying her soft spot. Kelly continued sucking as Adam brought her close to a climax. After a few minutes of oral sex, Adam turned Kelly onto her back. "It wasn't what I expected, but it was okay," Adam replied about the oral sex. "Well, you're going to love this," Kelly said as she help put on his condom. "Just work out the kinks, Adam," Kelly said as she drew his body closer to her.

With one push, Kelly was so wet that Adam slid inside on the first try. This was one time when he didn't have to work it in. Bucking like a horse, Kelly grabbed his behind and took control of the strokes. Kelly would speed up the strokes, slow them down, and do a combination. Adam was familiar with the way she liked sex, so he let Kelly do her thing. Stroke-after-stroke, Kelly dug her nails into his forearm as she moaned and begged for more. 'This girl can never get enough,' Adam thought to himself as he gave more of himself. Kelly's eyes rolled into her head, letting Adam know that she had reached her point. Her moans grew louder as Kelly kept her calves wrapped around his thighs. "Don't stop, Adam," she said repeatedly.

Adam kept stroking as he neared ejaculation. As Kelly took his hard strokes, her mind remained relaxed as she enjoyed each moment. It was a pleasure for her to beg for more, because Adam's performance was excellent. With each thrust, Kelly pulled him closer. "You feel so good," she said. Suddenly, Adam's sperm filled the condom. His body shook as she thrust her pelvis into his. "Let it out, baby," Kelly whispered as she worked to drain him. "Oh, you're too much," Adam remarked as he caught his breath.

He climbed off of Kelly and fell onto the bed. Her legs raised, Kelly noticed that her thighs were trembling. "You know the sex is good when your legs tremble," Kelly said as she stared at Adam's limp penis. The sight of something that large lying next to her made Kelly's juices flow faster. "I'm ready when you are," Kelly said cheerfully as she laid next to him. After a few minutes, Kelly put another condom on Adam and climbed on top of him and took a seat on his now erect penis. Adam saw the struggle Kelly was having trying to put his penis inside and said, "Now, don't hurt yourself." "It's just so large, Kelly responded as she began riding him.

Up-and-down, Kelly rode Adam, bucking her hips against him. To help her maintain control, Adam lye still as she worked at her own pace. "I love this Adam," Kelly whispered as she closed her eyes. Eventually, he began thrusting into her and she said, "I can take it like that. Give it all to me. All of it! Make me come all over you. Let your condom explode." After a few more strokes, Adam noticed that sex with Kelly felt different. It felt good, but different.

Adam and Kelly came together, unleashing their juices into and onto one-another. Still erect, Kelly bounced on Adam's penis as he kept thrusting. Judging from the way she felt inside, Adam realized that the condom had burst. 'I'm actually putting a straight rod up in her,' he thought. It was too late to stop because Kelly had begun writhing above him. Out-of-control, she came as Adam spanked her butt. "Oh, this feels so good." Unable to hold out, he came inside of her, one-more-time. Kelly leaped off of Adam and began sucking his wet penis head. She was so hot that she didn't notice that the rubber had burst. When she stopped sucking, Adam removed the condom ring from the base and tossed it aside. Kelly slowly rubbed her crotch to soothe the burning sensation.

"You really know how to make a girl sweat. Have you thought about becoming a fitness instructor," Kelly asked playfully? Adam rolled over and started sucking her perky tits and replied, "No, I've never had a desire to be a fitness instructor." Turning to her side, Adam curled up behind Kelly as he nuzzled his face into the pillow. "Are you tired, or do you want some more?" "I'll let you know in a few minutes," he said. Kelly grind her butt into him, and turned off the television and both of them fell asleep.

Hours had gone by and Adam was awakened by the sound of other students going into their rooms. They were talking, playing music, slamming doors and doing a host of other things. Adam glanced at Kelly who was lying with her legs spread. 'This would be the perfect time to get her,' he thought. At that moment, he glanced at the clock and the time read, 6:23pm. "It's time to wake up Kelly." I'm about to be late for class," Adam said in a hurried voice. Kelly turned her butt to him and Adam spanked it before standing up. "You'd better not do that again or you won't make it to your class," Kelly said invitingly. Adam was in such a hurry that he overlooked her remark as he washed his penis. "You can take a towel from the closet if you want to wash-up."

Kelly got out of bed and began washing up as she watched Adam getting dressed. "I hope that I don't get pregnant," Kelly said. Eyes wide, Adam told Kelly not to think like that. "I noticed that the rubber was gone when I was sucking you. So, there is only one thing that could have happened to it. I felt it, although I hoped that I wasn't feeling it. It was hard to stop because it felt so good. It was hot and it was inside all of me," Kelly said as she washed the soap from her pubic hairs. Adam saw that she wasn't going to change the subject, so he ignored it. 'She looks good enough to make a baby with, but that's not about to happen,' he thought.

Once his class was over, Adam listened to his cell phone messages, and read his text messages. As he walked to the dorms, Adam returned Lisa's call. When they spoke, she mentioned that she was going-out dancing with James and Krystal. Adam wasn't too happy to hear that she was going out with James, because he knew what time it was. James would get her alone and before you know it, he'd be trying to get in or would be in her panties. Adam hoped for the best and told Lisa to have a good time.

Suddenly, there was a knock at the door, as Adam wondered why someone would be knocking on his door at 10:30pm. He opened it and found Kelly standing there with a huge grin on her face. "What's up Kelly," he asked inquisitively? "I just came by to finish the movie," she said innocently. Adam invited her inside and asked, "Does your parents know that you're out, or is it just because it's Friday that you decided to stop by?" Kelly tossed her jacket onto the chair and replied, "I called my parents and told them that I'd be staying at the dorms tonight. My folks aren't strict. I know how to take care of myself."

Adam, who had removed his jacket and sweater, turned and faced Kelly. She stared at his broad chest and became speechless as he asked, "So what are you really going to do?" "I'm staying at the dorm with you," Kelly said playfully as she removed her sneakers. "Welcome," Adam said as he pointed to the bed. As Kelly removed her sweater, Adam stared at her gorgeous body, as he read her non verbal statements.

Kelly and Adam managed to watch two movies without intercourse taking place. Toward the end of the 2nd movie, Kelly started teasing him. During the slow scenes, she would give him 'head' and maybe suck his nipples. Just before the credits began, Adam began doing some playing of his own. He turned Kelly onto her knees' and rode her from the back. She made very little noise as she bounced her butt against him. The dirtier she talked, the more he would spank her for being a 'bad girl.' When the credits stopped, Kelly came repeatedly as Adam kept stroking. Their performance went on for hours as they had no place to be.

CHAPTER
TWENTY

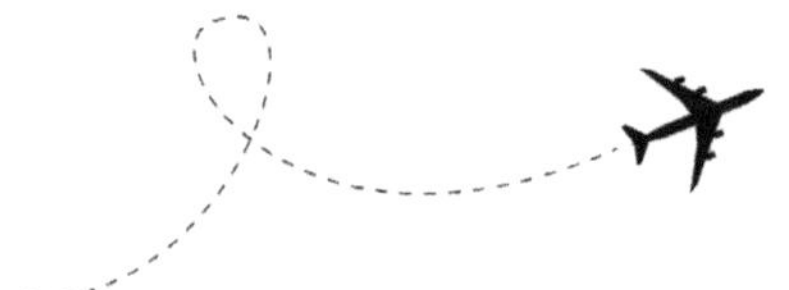

Back in Chicago, James and Krystal took Lisa out dancing and 'club hopping.' Krystal's friend arrived at the club, leaving Lisa alone with James, on the dance floor. James has always been a good dancer, but tonight there was something different about it. He danced close to Lisa, enticing her with his every move. Once the music changed the mood, James held Lisa close as the lights were lowered. "So, tell me, who are you doing in Chicago," he asked seductively?

Lisa grinned as she could not believe the question. "Are you implying that I should be doing someone? I don't think it's that simple," she replied in a sassy tone. James then whispered, "I know that you may be waiting on my brother, but I know he's out doing someone. What I'm trying to say is that it can get lonely sometimes. One day you're going to get tired of playing with yourself, and once you do, feel free to call me." They didn't say another word as he graciously moved her across the dance floor.

Lisa was mesmerized as she thought about his option. She couldn't deny that Adam may be with someone at this very moment. 'James bring up a good point because I know that Adam won't be around when I'm on fire. It would be wrong to do this behind his back with anyone. However, this isn't anyone, but it is his brother. Yeah, they look identical, but it doesn't seem right. What if I get with James and he blows my mind? I need to sleep on this,' she thought. She and James continued dancing as the morning hour crept in.

James returned Lisa to his parents home and

said, "Think about what I told you. Here, take my card, because it has all of my numbers on it. Give me a call when you get tired." Lisa opened the door to get out and James whispered, "I know that your panties are wet." Lisa thought that she heard him say something, so she asked James to repeat what he said. "I said that I know that your panties are wet." Lisa rolled her eyes and said with a smile, "Have a good night James."

Lisa went into the house and immediately called Adam. As his cell phone rang quietly, Adam and Kelly continued building up a sweat. Lisa began to call every 15 minutes as her conscience was telling her that he was with someone. The thought that he could be doing someone who's more attractive or does a better job, was driving Lisa insane. "Why doesn't he answer the phone? I know that he keeps the volume up. He wouldn't go to bed this early," Lisa worriedly said to herself. Lisa remembered what Adam said about dating and she became afraid. Her thoughts raced toward a future that may not happen.

However, Adam awakened early and called Lisa at the break of day. Expecting her to answer not to answer her cell phone, he dialed the home phone number. Unaware that Lisa was asleep, his mom answered the phone and explained that she was gone. She assured Adam that she was going to give Lisa the message and have her to call him. Adam started having imaginary visions of what may have happened between her and James. "Did he get it, or didn't he," Adam asked himself? Within a second, Kelly opened her eyes as Adam laid beside her. "I like sex in the morning," Kelly whispered as she moved her butt closer to him. Adam took another condom from the box, parted her cheeks and began applying long strokes.

Once the sex got hot, Kelly turned from her side and got onto her knee's. Arched behind her glistening globes, Adam gave her longer strokes. With her head faced upward, he licked her neck as he leaned forward. Placing his tongue in her ear, Kelly started bucking faster. Screaming for him to take her body and do as he pleased. With her face buried in the pillow, Kelly screamed as she came. Her juices forcefully splashed against Adam's penis. Applying faster strokes to her gaping hole, Adam released his wad into the condom. 'This is how a hole is suppose to feel with a condom,' he thought after his orgasm.

Kelly left to go spend her day with her grandmother, while Adam remained in bed. They went four rounds and he was exhausted. He was surprised at how much rod Kelly could take, and she still walked straight. She promised Adam that she would be back, but not before calling. After a few hours of rest, Adam drove a few small items over to the condo. Having belonged to a woman for so long, he wanted to change the atmosphere of the condo.

Taking some food from the freezer, Adam remained at the house for the entire day. Just as he finished preparing the food, Lisa called to give him the third degree about his whereabouts. They argued over the issue and she hanged the phone up on him. Adam didn't bother calling back as he turned off his phone. Knowing that he was at the house, Lisa began calling the house phone. After several rings, Adam answered the phone, told Lisa some of what she wanted to hear, and concluded the conversation.

Three weeks had passed and Lisa was becoming weary as she hadn't had sex since that night before she left for Chicago. She wasn't talking to Adam often, and nor had she had sex in what seemed like longer than three weeks. Lisa would make so many calls to Adam and he seldom answered any of them. She was becoming angry at this point because she feared the competition. However, Lisa had a long day, Adam hadn't returned her calls, and she wanted to be risky. Lisa phoned James and they agreed to meet at her new home. She had planned to keep it innocent but this was undoubtedly a 'booty call.' 'This has been a long time coming, kind of booty call,' she thought with a smile.

James pulled into the driveway, just as Lisa was getting out of the car. Together, they walked into the house. She told him to make himself-at-home, as she went to take a shower. "Where's my nephew," James shouted? "He's at your mom's," Lisa replied. James' mind raced into sex mode and he couldn't wait to taste Lisa. Once she got into the shower, James went to her bedroom and took a seat on the bed. Within a few minutes, Lisa came out dressed in a towel. Surprised to see James sitting on the bed, Lisa thought, 'Oh, I can't wait to feel this hot sensation. If we click, James can keep me warm while Adam and I are apart. I know that he's sitting here because he wants to see my body. This feels strange, but here goes nothing.' Lisa then removed her robe.

"I'm not going to play with you, James. I've thought about your offer and I'm ready to take a chance. However, your brother must never find out about this. So, get undress because I'm about to explode," she said with anticipation. Lisa couldn't believe what she had just said, as she hoped that Adam wouldn't find out about this. 'I'm afraid of what he might do or whom he might do,' Lisa thought nervously.

Unlike his brother, James gave Lisa what she wanted. He placed his head between Lisa's thighs and brought her to repeated climaxes. "Adam won't do it like this," Lisa whispered as her legs shivered and shook. James' tongue was almost as long as his penis, as he licked her juices. Kneeling between her legs, James stroked her with skill. She didn't want to make comparisons, but the sex was different with James than it was with Adam. They were both good, but different in other ways. James turned Lisa every way but loose as he kept putting more of himself into her. Lisa found herself doing things that she hadn't done in months. Although she'd rather be with Adam, Lisa made do with what she had. "Adam never has to know," she whispered to James as he gave deeper thrust.

The next morning, Lisa gave James some more hot sex before he left. Returning to bed, she wondered what Adam was doing. 'I should feel bad about last night, but I don't. Hell, something had to give. Between adjusting and taking care of Andre,

I'm exhausted.' Thinking back to last night, Lisa said, "Well, I was exhausted, but now I've exhaled." She didn't plan on getting with James again, but Lisa wasn't certain about that idea.

Rationalizing her options, Lisa agreed to get with him as much as possible. 'I could really use his help until Adam comes to visit,' she thought. It was too early to plan the future, but her thoughts now drifted to the possibility of Adam finding out. "I'll be able to have something worked out by then. If it comes down to it," she said.

Back in Michigan, Kelly was giving Adam a morning ride. As he laid with his eyes shut, she rocked back and forth. 'I can't believe this girl is so horny,' Adam thought as he thrust into her womb. No-matter the position, they moved in-time. Rolling Kelly onto her back, with his eyes closed, Adam kept stroking her. With her hands around his neck, Kelly held on for dear life. His hands underneath Kelly's buttocks and holding her body off of the bed, Adam gave Kelly deep, slow thrust. "Good morning sunshine," Kelly whispered as Adam brought her to climax. She bucked wildly as he stroked her repeatedly. Within seconds, Adam released his load and they shook together.

Both moaning, their sounds were like music to Kelly. "You've got me addicted, Adam. I'm addicted to your 'dick.' Can I be your girl," she asked? Adam asked, "Why are you giving it any thought? I'm about my books and I don't have the time to be your man. We can get together on occasions and 'get-our-freak-on,' but nothing more. Why don't we take things one day at a time, because that's the kind of relationship we have? After all, I don't want to break your focus. Our tutoring sessions are great, but grip on things.

Kelly didn't argue as she laid her head on Adam's chest. "You're right Adam, because I need to be thinking about my classes. It's amazing how I'm a sophomore who's being tutored by a sophomore," she whispered. Neither could sleep, so they decided to go for another round of sex. What Adam told Kelly about staying focused went out of the window. She rode him with passion as Kelly was taken away by the way he made love to her body. Kelly thought she was in a sexual oasis, as Adam placed her in different positions. "Oh, I like Michigan," Adam said. They both came together and fell asleep, awakening at noon.

As the sun beat its way through the blinds, Kelly said, "I've got some running around to do, so we'll definitely get together some other time." She kissed him, dressed and left. Kelly left like someone who had seen a ghost. After she had gone, Adam laid still as he pondered what Kelly had said to him. The more he thought about it, the more distressed he became. Although, Kelly was a sweet person, Adam didn't share the same desire that she shared. Adam saw her interest as merely infatuation, and he believed that with some time, it would pass.

Adam left for the shower minutes after Kelly had left his dorm room. Dressed in a robe, he sauntered down the hall. Once in the shower, Adam let the water thrash against his body, as he enjoyed the exhilarating feeling. When Adam was done, he returned to his room, he dressed in a cotton track suit, and left for the university. Joining some friends who were on their way to the university, he walked and chatted with them about their classes. When they split up, Adam went in the opposite direction of everyone else, except two freshmen whom he didn't know.

'I've had enough sex to last me for a while, and now its time for me to hit the books. Kelly would come around every day if I let her. She's not fooling me by saying that she needs to get focused. She's not a bad catch, but her life appears to be missing something. However, she's freaky, just the way I like them. Here I go, thinking about sex when I should be focusing on my thing. I've got a dream to fulfill, and a son to raise and put through college. Maybe, just maybe, I'll consider marrying Lisa, someday. Ah, I can't believe I'm thinking like this,' Adam thought as he walked to the library.

After hours of studying, Adam arrived at the dorm hall and found Kelly sitting in the lobby. 'Damn, what's up with this girl,' Adam thought as he approached her. "What's up Kelly," he asked in a stern voice? Nervously she replied, "I was hoping that we could get together and do something. Is that okay with you? Oh, then again, I forgot to call first." Adam nodded with a grin and said, "That's right, so why don't you call my phone number and maybe we can do something at another time. It's been a long day and I'm ready to get some sleep. I've got some exams to prepare for, and you should have some coming up, also." "Well, yeah, but I enjoy being with you. Don't make me beg," Adam, she asked in a whining voice? Standing 8inches taller than Kelly, he looked down at her and said as he walked away, "We'll get together some other time, Kelly. Go home and get into those assignments, and if you need something, call my cell."

The doors closed and Kelly stared at Adam until he was out of sight. She wanted so badly to believe things wouldn't change once sex was put into the picture. In an instance, her mind had all sorts of thoughts roaming around. 'Should I go and buy him something. Maybe I should try to get him from another angle. I know he likes me and this good stuff. However, he is a smart brother and I should not stand in his way. He's going to be 'somebody' in the field of medicine,' Kelly thought as she left for her car.

As she drove away, Kelly kept playing the events that she and Adam shared over in her mind. It was obvious that the sex had put their relationship in a spin, but it was something that she liked. Kelly only hoped that Adam would see things her way, and give in to the opportunity to be with someone who made him feel good. However, the more she thought about it, the more lame the idea appeared to her. Kelly believed that he wasn't giving himself to anyone else and she wanted to prove it by taking up Adam's free time. With all of the competition walking through the university, she wanted to be the first to seize the Chi-town man with the chocolate body.

CHAPTER
TWENTY-ONE

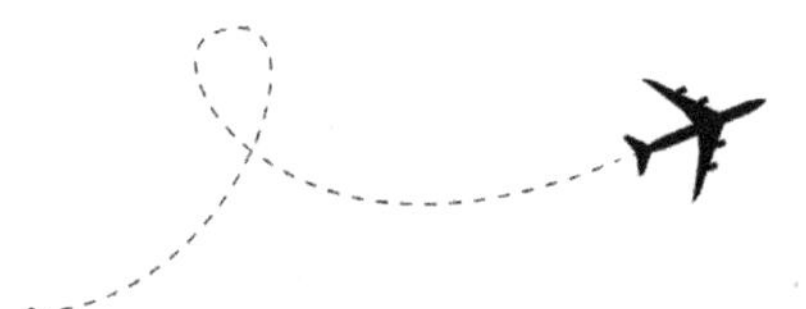

Lisa maintained her on-again-off again relationship with James, to a point that she thought less about Adam. They moved to having sex twice a week and it only got better. James' rod had gotten so good that she would call Adam while James slept next to her. Lisa was beginning to see it as something more than a fling. James was the heir to a law firm and only God knows what else. He appealed to her, from head to toe. James gave her positive vibrations. She knew that he thought with his penis, because he gave her money each time they got together. Lisa wasn't interested in the money, but she did want the sex. However, James played the 'field' and his demeanor spoke for itself. Busy working, Lisa was with James for convenience.

Thanksgiving will be on a Thursday, and to surprise everyone, Adam arrived on Monday. He knew exactly where Lisa lived, and because she was home from work, the time was right. When Adam rang the doorbell, Lisa ran to the door, and was shocked to see his face. She fumbled her words as she greeted him. Stepping inside, Adam gave her a hug and headed for the bathroom. Standing there with a look of worry on her face, Lisa had planned to be with James that night. 'Think fast, think fast, Lisa. Damn, I can't call him now, because Adam might get suspicious, although James isn't returning my calls,' she thought. "Where's Andre, Adam asked?" "His daddy is here. Is he asleep? Am I talking to loud, he asked with a whisper?" "Everything is okay, because he's awake," Lisa remarked.

Taking Andre into his arms, he and Lisa lay on

the bed, looking like the happy family. Adam wasn't sure if Lisa had been with James and he sure didn't want to find out. He envisioned he and Lisa having a family and this was the start. With Andre in his arms, Adam got out of bed. "Let's go to the kitchen and get something to drink," he playfully said to the laughing baby. 'Good, maybe I can use the bathroom before James calls. After all, he probably wouldn't answer my text' Lisa thought.

Just as she sat down, the phone rang and she thought it was from the television. Standing next to the house phone, Adam picked it up on the first ring. Before he could say a word, the person on the calling end said, "What's up, baby? Is that hot thing ready for daddy's loving touch?" Shocked, Adam noticed the voice and said, "James? What's up man? This is Adam and I'll be here for a while." James spoke nervously as he was surprised to hear Adam's voice. He knew that from the sound of his voice, Adam had put two and two together to come up with sex. "James, why are you calling Lisa to say something like that? Be real, and tell me if you're hitting it?" James didn't say a word as he held the phone to his ear. "Your not saying anything proves to me that you've been tapping it. That's okay, big brother. Oh, and I'll tell her that you called."

Adam hang up the phone and grinned. "This woman is out here giving it to my brother when I'm thinking that she's doing something else. She was celibate when we met, so why not be celibate now? Why did she give it to him of all people," Adam asked himself? Thoughts raced through his mind as he sauntered down the hall to Andre's bedroom. Meanwhile, Lisa turned off the phones ringer moments before Andre and Adam returned to the bedroom. Leaping from the bed, Lisa ran to the kitchen and turned off the phones ringer. Followed by Adam, Lisa turned and paused. "Do you want something," Lisa asked Adam as she searched for something to snack on? Adam didn't bother replying as he rocked Andre to sleep.

Once Andre was asleep, Adam forcefully gave himself to Lisa. He held her wrist so tightly that they were bruised. With her legs raised, Adam gave every inch of himself to her. Lisa squealed as she took everything he had to give. They had always enjoyed sex, but this time it was different. Adam was having sex like someone who had been locked up in a prison cell. Every stroke was controlled by him as he only wanted her to be submissive. Lisa liked this because it was his control in the bedroom that added to her attraction to him. However, this time the sex was different because it was rougher than before.

He shifted Lisa around so much that she felt like a rag doll. Lisa huffed-and-puffed as her vagina tingled from the penetration. As she laid with her legs spread, her hole remained open as it gasped for air. The fat vaginal lips looked sweaty, as it craved for a moment of rest. "Something is wrong, Adam. I can feel your vibes and they're strong and angry," Lisa said. Hoping that he wasn't going to say that her womb felt differently, Lisa closed her eyes as she waited for a response. "How long have you been sleeping with my brother," Adam asked in a strong voice? Lisa was shocked, as her mouth dropped and her eyes widened.

Pretending to be angry over the question, she asked, "Do you think that I would sleep with your brother? Do you think I'm that kind of woman? We have a child together and that should stand for something." Adam sat with his eyes closed as he waited for Lisa to confess. He actually enjoyed her show, because she put so much energy into it. "If you think I would sleep with your brother, then why would you consider inviting me to Thanksgiving dinner with your family," Lisa asked as she held back her tears? Lisa knew that she was wrong for fooling him, but she was more shocked about how he found out. Afraid of what Adam might say or do, she continued the charade. Besides, what makes you think that I'm sleeping with James, she rudely asked?

Adam was about to enjoy his confession to Lisa, but first he teased her by going into the bathroom. Lisa waited, although afraid of the results. 'He just got here, so how does he know? Adam couldn't have spoken to anyone, because we've kept it on the down-low. Maybe he's psychic. He knows that I hate it when I have to wait for an answer,' she thought with a surprised expression on her face. Adam came out of the bathroom and laid next to her.

Your house phone rang and I answered it, and heard a familiar voice say, "Baby, are you waiting for daddy to come over and hit that thing for you." "I recognized the voice, Lisa, and I couldn't believe he was calling you. What I did was put 2-and-2 together and came up with, James screwing Lisa, and Lisa is screwing him. Tell me that it's not true," Adam asked as he laid his head on her thigh? Lisa was speechless, but she went ahead and took a chance. "I'm not sleeping with your brother, Adam. I promise you that I'm not," she said nervously. Laughing, he replied, "You're telling a lie Miss Daly.

I've known my brother for a long time and I know how he works. It's okay that he slept with you, because you've played yourself. James is a pussy-go-getter, and you are another victim. The way I see it, he can have you, because you can't have both of us. Now, what's this about your making a promise that you're not freaking him? Listen, this is one time that I'm glad that I bothered answering the phone. Hell, I couldn't rely on you telling me the truth," Adam said sarcastically.

"Okay, Adam, you've got me, because we did get together. It was late and I couldn't talk to you, so I invited James to come by. One thing lead to another, and that's it," Lisa said with tears in her eyes. Before she could say another word, Adam said, "It doesn't matter when it happened, because it shouldn't have happened. I could understand someone else giving it to you, but this is different.

You've crossed a thin-line and you've got to make some decisions."

Pausing for a moment, Adam further stated, "Here's what we'll do. You can keep James, because I'm out," Adam said in a rude tone. As he raised his head, Lisa reached for him, saying, "It was a mistake. I don't feel the same thing for James that I feel for you. Okay, we did it more than once, because if I've got to confess then I might as well be honest. What we had was a fling. I just needed someone and your brother was there. Remember that I invited you to come with us and start a new life. Please understand, because behaving this way doesn't solve anything." "I don't believe this is happening," Adam remarked as he turned away from Lisa. Thoughts raced through their heads as they sat in silence. "Can we start this over," Lisa asked softly? Adam did not give a reply as he stared at the wall. Hours later, the discussion was put to rest and they both fell asleep.

This was Lisa's day off so she spent it with Adam and Andre. Having gotten some sleep, they were cordial with each other. They laughed and played all evening, acting as though yesterday was a bad dream. Adam didn't feel compelled to bring the issue up, so he didn't. After all, he does know his brother. Lisa wanted to bring it up, although she didn't. Mental pressures fueled with guilt feelings were getting the best of her. Lisa had to force herself to smile, knowing that there was something 'important' between her and Adam. 'Maybe it was a dream, or a bad nightmare,' Lisa thought as she strutted around in her panties.

The day was going great, but Adam wasn't making a play for the sex. He acted as if it wasn't an issue. Adam knew that he was going to hit it again, but now she needs to make a choice. 'For now, she'll just think I'm upset. This woman slept with my brother and lied to me. I think she needs to be with him for a while,' he thought with a grin. After all, it may be overwhelming to satisfy two brothers in the same city.

Adam and Lisa put the baby to sleep and she asked, "Why haven't you bothered to touch me today? Do you think I'm dirty or do you have someone else in mind?" Taking a drink of water, Adam sat the glass down, looked into her eyes and said, You're sleeping with James and you can't have both of us. You made a choice, so now just live with it. The best brother won. You know, the family name sake." "Are you telling me that you don't want to hit this because I slept with your brother," Lisa asked with her arms folded? "That's crazy, because I love you. Why are you doing this, Adam? You sleep around and I don't say anything," Lisa said. "Maybe so, but I haven't slept with anyone in your family. If I did, then it's because I didn't know," he replied.

Immediately, Lisa began thinking about her cousin's interest in Adam. 'Damn, I hope Tracy doesn't try to get with him,' Lisa thought as she picked at her fingernails. "We can still do it, Adam. I'm not going to call you James," Lisa said with a smile. "Let me think about it. A nut is a nut, okay, and I'm finished thinking," Adam said. He then slipped on a condom, and taking Lisa into his arms, Adam began grinding inside her womb. Dripping wet, her lips clasped onto his penis as Adam drilled her. The intensity of the whole event made Lisa feel wetter than before. Screwing as if everything was okay between them, she and Adam put on their best performance.

At Thanksgiving dinner, they acted like the perfect couple. Posing for pictures and introducing Lisa and Andre to people they may never see again, was the highlight of Adam's schedule. Lisa met all of his aunts on his fathers' side of the family, and three of his moms' brothers. Everyone took turns holding Andre as he was as playful as ever. Wearing a big toothless grin, he captured everyone's heart. "This is little Adam. Look at his features and the curly hair. His mom and dad have good hair, also. It's a perfect combination. This little boy is going to be a heart breaker. Go ahead and put your name on something," Uncle John said playfully. Uncle John is Gail's older brother, who knows everything and everyone, or so he thinks. His intelligence could be compared to a rock. Although he held 2 degrees, he refused to follow his majors. Uncle John was really unstable and everyone tolerated it.

Things were going great for Adam, until James came through the door. They embraced each other as usual, but this time they shared a secret. James teased Adam about his success in school and congratulated him on becoming a dad. "Hey, man, you know how I get sometime. I've got a problem, but I'm sorry for getting with your girl. I mean that from the bottom of my heart," James said apologetically. Adam replied, "This is Thanksgiving, so let's not even discuss it."

James, Sr., lead the prayer and everyone sat down to eat. Lisa felt uncomfortable having both brothers in the same room, as she kept her attention focused on Adam. However, after dinner, James followed Lisa to the bathroom. 'It's a large house, and there's no one around, so why not take a chance,' James thought. Before Lisa could sit down on the toilet, James burst into the bathroom. "Wait, I just wanted to talk for a minute," James said as he closed the door and took Lisa into his arms.

Running his tongue along her neck, Lisa could not stand the pressure. They kissed wildly as she sighed loudly. "What are you doing? Don't you know that Adam will kill us," she asked? James kept licking her neck and earlobe. "I've got to see you again. Call me when he leaves. I'll take care of you. It's a secret, so don't mention it to anyone. This is our thing," James said as he placed three hundred dollars in Lisa's hand? James scurried away from the bathroom and joined everyone else. Startled, Lisa sat speechless, as she could not believe James' nerves. Eager to leave, she was only being polite because of the occasion.

After a large dinner and plenty of laughs, Adam made sure that Lisa and the baby got home safely. "Are you coming in for a few minutes or do you have some place to go," Lisa asked inquisitively? Turning off the engine, Adam replied, "I had plans, but the other party never called back." "You're welcome to stay here," Lisa said as she got out of the truck. In the backseat trying to untie the baby, their eyes met and both Adam and Lisa rushed into the house.
Asleep, they put Andre in his crib, turned out the lights and got freaky. Lisa placed her legs over Adams' shoulders and bucked against him as he breathed heavily. The sensation made Lisa's toes curl as Adam gave it to her just the way she likes

it. Holding her legs high and wide, Lisa let Adam go deeper into her womb. His thrust grew stronger and she came. Before he could withdraw himself, Lisa came again, screaming like someone being chased. In the missionary position, they're sweaty bodies remained joined together.

Later that night, Lisa left for work after awaking from her nap. Adam got out of bed and walked her to the door, to assure her safety. As she drove away, Lisa thought about the mess that she was in. 'I can't believe that I got busted by Adam! Days before, I said that I would have things worked out by the time he arrived. Adams's here, but soon he'll be leaving for Ann Arbor. James doesn't need to do any more than he's doing. However, since I've been sleeping with him, the sex has been so good that I've ignored other guys. There are plenty of them at the hospital, but if it's good at home, then why should I go out to get it. What I should try to do is wean myself away from James. Soon, Christmas will be here and I don't want this to happen again. Now, I've got to worry about Tracy trying to get with Adam. She could hang out on campus and make a pass at him. Knowing Tracy the way that I do, she'll probably wait until she runs into him.'

Lisa drove at a slower speed as thoughts raced through her head. I'll just have to wait and see how things work out. Adam's no fool, and he could easily find out something else, Lisa whispered as she pulled into the hospital parking structure. As her thoughts continued racing, she desperately searched for a parking space. Once she found space for her car, Lisa sat for a few moments, as she tried to devise a plan.

At the condo, Adam laid awake thinking about what was going on between James and Lisa. He wrestled with the thought, because it wasn't easy to accept. 'Maybe I'll feel different in a few weeks. I can't believe this happened! But, it takes two. This woman was so gullible that she gave it to my brother and lied about it. She left herself wide open for that mess to take place. I can't stay upset with my brother, because he was only doing what he does. The man has no morals about sex. Just give it to me is all he knows,' Adam thought.'This is going to be a tough one to work our way out of, because I can't forget about Tracy flirting behind. She wants a piece of 'this.' Lisa probably told her some stories and now she's wired-up. It would be nice to run into her. I'd go nuts on that girl. Tracy even looks like the freaky type, and those soft bedroom eyes really set-it-off.' Rolling onto his side, Adam thought about Tracy until he fell asleep.

Lying close to Andre, Adam smiled and said, "Your mom has me feeling uncomfortable, son. Yeah, she's been sleeping with your uncle to stay warm. However, now she's got me thinking some wild thoughts; thinking bedroom thoughts...with someone else. Do you think dad should do what he feels like doing?" Grinning, Adam sighed loudly and whispered, "Yeah, let's go day by day and see what happens."

CHAPTER

TWENTY-TWO

Adam returned to Michigan on one of the worst snow days ever. From the county line to Ann Arbor, Adam took his time driving to his destination. Due to the weather and the fact that he had to be in school, he chose to stay at his dorm room. When he arrived, everyone was sitting around the lounge talking about their holiday and sharing stories. Adam put his things away, went back into the lounge, turned on the radio and got a card game started. Everyone was eager to play, as the snow kept all of the students inside. As the card game continued, Adam was interrupted when Kelly came into the room. Dressed in a dark sweat suit and gym shoes, Kelly sat nearby as she waited for Adam to finish his game.

"How was your holiday," he asked with a smile on his face? Taking Adam by the hand, they left the table and slowly walked to his room. "Adam, I think I'm pregnant. I haven't had my period and I'm afraid. My parents would kill me if I had a baby before finishing school," Kelly said as she walked with her head down. Adam walked quietly as he thought that this was the worst state to be in, because Michigan girls appear to get pregnant so easily. "Are you suggesting having an abortion?" Kelly nodded her head as she looked at Adam.

"An abortion or not, I've got to have you... tonight. Please, I don't want you to tell me anything negative," Kelly said as she pleaded with Adam. "Should we still be doing it, I mean, am I going to hurt something," he asked nervously? "It's okay, Adam, just do it the way you always do," Kelly said invitingly.

Adam squeezed her hand as he looked at her and sighed. "So, have you given this abortion some serious thought," he asked as they walked slowly down the corridor? Kelly looked up at Adam and replied, "I've given it a lot of thought, and I believe that it's the best thing to do. Even if I were to put the baby up for adoption, it doesn't change the fact that I'm pregnant and I've got to carry it for nine months. Both Kelly and Adam chuckled in agreement.

They entered his dorm room and Adam undressed and let Lisa give him 'head' as he thought about her current condition. Filled with lust, Kelly took all of Adam into her mouth. "Oh, you taste so good," she whispered. 'Every time I get with someone, they get pregnant. Maybe, I should just settle for getting head,' Adam thought as he pushed deeper into her mouth. Moving away from her as he reached a climax, Adam told Kelly to undress. Once she did, Adam turned Kelly onto her back and inserted his penis into her tunnel. Push, after push, he drove deeper into Kelly's hole. 'She must be pregnant, or her hole must have been on lock down over the holiday,' Adam thought as he considered how tight her hole was.

With each thrust, Kelly moaned louder. Unable to hold back, Kelly came as she dug her nails into Adam' back. He screamed as the feeling of her nails brought about intense pain. After a few moments, Kelly wasn't sure if he was screaming from pain or from the thrill of ejaculating. Kelly wrapped her legs around his waist as she tried to drain Adam of all the sperm he had inside. As droplets of semen dripped from his penis, Adam's body shook as Kelly held onto him.

Once they were done for the evening, Adam sat and talked with Kelly for hours. Afraid to tell her that he had a child with someone who has been affiliated with the university, Adam sat in silence. "I could be with you every day. The more I see you, the more I want to see you. No one has ever made me feel the way you do. It's like magic. I think that you would make a wonderful father, but we can't take this step now. What we need to do is decide how we're going to pay for this abortion," Kelly said as she played with Adam's limp penis. With his back against the head board, Adam looked at Kelly and said, "I'll pay for it. It shouldn't be any more than two, or maybe three hundred dollars." Putting her fears aside, Kelly kissed Adams chest as a show of affection. "Can you go along with me," she asked? Adam nodded his head.

The next day, Kelly called and set up an appointment with the abortion clinic. Afterwards, she explained to Adam how much it would cost, and where it would be done. That Tuesday morning, she and Adam agreed to meet at the university so they could travel together. Once they arrived at the clinic, the doctor performed a quick procedure, and they dismissed her. Kelly stood nearby as Adam waited for his payment receipt. Surprised, Adam couldn't believe how long the procedure lasted. He expected to be there for an hour or so. But, to his surprise, the procedure only lasted a few minutes.

Adam left to go and get the truck, while Kelly was wheeled to the lobby. As they drove away, Kelly asked, "Can I spend the day in your room, because I don't want anyone to get curious?" Adam had been excused from his classes, so he found nothing wrong with Kelly staying with him. Although feeling uncomfortable after the procedure, she managed to hold Adam's hand as he drove through the blizzard. "Are you comfortable with the decision we made," Kelly asked? Squeezing her hand, Adam glanced at Kelly and nodded his head. Feeling relaxed, Kelly took a sigh of relief. "We can't let this happen again," she said as Adam drove slowly through the storm.

Once Kelly was in the dorm room, she laid across the bed and fell asleep. Puzzled by what had happened, Adam collapsed beside her, placing his arm over Kelly's shoulder. He then pulled her close to him. They rested like this for hours as they were both tired. Adam slept best with the television on, but because he wanted Kelly to be well rested, he sacrificed his own interest. As they laid quietly, Adam felt Kelly's hands grab her butt cheek and spread it. Adam grinned as he thought that Kelly didn't realize that she was nude.

Parting her cheeks wider, Kelly asked, "Do you want to get some, or are you straight?" Unaware of what she was talking about, Adam asked, "What are you talking about?" Kelly remarked, "I thought you were horny, and if you are then I'm into anal sex." Adam's eyes widened, as he could not believe what he was hearing. "Nah, I'll wait until you're well," he said with his face buried in the pillow. "Thank you for being so patient with me," Kelly said as she drew closer to him.

It was now two weeks before Christmas, Kelly is all better, and it was time to party. Adam' friends from the fraternity invited him to a dress-to-sweat party in celebration of Christmas, and he was ready to leave. Once they got into the truck, Adam and the fraternity brothers traveled to their destination. "When you arrive, Adam, all of the drinks are on the house," someone shouted as the truck pulled up at the club's back entrance. Inside, the DJ played 'techno' and 'house' music, as swarms of gorgeous women came through the front door. Adam recognized some of the faces, and for others, he noticed the bodies. One-by-one, he took girls to the dance floor. Working up a sweat, half the girls in the club wanted to dance with Adam. His graceful movements captivated everyone, as they shouted for him to keep dancing.

After hours of dancing, Adam felt someone tapping him on his shoulder. "What does a girl have to do to get a dance," the soft voice whispered? Turning with a drink in his hand, Adam was surprised to see Tracy. He stared at her as he could not believe how good she looked. "What are you doing at this party," Adam cheerfully asked? Staring at his sweaty chest, Tracy said, "I just wanted to let my hair down for the holiday. Are you staying here for the Christmas break, or are you making other plans?" Adam licked his lips as he ignored the question.

Adam then grinned and asked, "What are you drinking?" Tracy ordered a 'Scotch' and soda. They talked over their drinks and when they were done, Tracy took Adam onto the dance floor. Together, they made the perfect dance couple. No girl was able to get close to Adam as Tracy became his private dance partner. As they danced, other girls noticed how Tracy would grind onto Adam and grab his butt. This gave others the impression that he was taken for the night.

Adam and Tracy stood at the bar, as patrons began to leave. "Did you have a nice time," Tracy asked flirtatiously? Grinning, Adam replied, "This party was great. I can't wait to attend another one." Stepping close to Adam, Tracy asked, "What's your plan for the night? Are you hanging out with your friends or someone special?" Adam knew what she was trying to get at, so he asked, "Is there a place that you want to take me?" Tracy laughed and said, "Why don't you say goodbye to your friends and come with me." Tipsy, Adam waved goodbye to his friends and left with Tracy. "Do every thing that I would do, Adam," a voice shouted. Grinning, Tracy replied, "You're going to do everything that he wished that he'd be doing." Staggering, Adam asked, "Oh, is that right?" Smiling, Tracy walked faster as she held Adam's hand.

Inside of her truck, Tracy tore away at Adam's crotch, trying to pull down his sweat pants. Once his penis was staring her in the face, she engulfed all of it. Mouth wet, Tracy sucked his equipment with intense fury. 'This girl is acting like she's never given 'head' before,' Adam thought as he reclined his seat. Tracy was so eager to suck his manhood that she didn't mind if someone had seen them. Breathing heavily, the windows remained fogged until Tracy stopped sucking.

Tracy started the car and pulled away, as Adam held his still erect penis in his hand. "I know that you want this," he said playfully. Tracy took short glances at Adam as she tried to stay focused on the road. "You need to put that away before I crash," Tracy remarked. Holding his penis firmly, Adam replied, "You're not going to crash, because you can't get this if you're in the hospital." Tracy laughed and drove faster through the 5 inches of snow. "Besides, you've got to drive me back to my truck tomorrow, so keep it together."

They went to her apartment in Plymouth, Michigan, and before they could get out of the car, Tracy leaned forward and began kissing him. With one hand behind Adam's neck, Tracy rubbed his crotch with the other. "Let's get out of here," she whispered. Running across the parking lot, Adam followed Tracy through the back door of the apartment complex. As she struggled to unlock the door, Adam envisioned her body next to his. 'I'm going to wear-her-out,' Adam thought as he walked behind her. Anxiously, Tracy ran to her apartment. Squatting, Adam looked at Tracy's butt as she ran in front of him. Shaking his head, he said, "Damn, she is fine!" As he glanced between her legs, all he could see was the space between her inner thighs.

Adam then went into the apartment and got attacked. Tracy pushed him against the wall and began groping Adam's body and kissing him. Unable to say a word, Adam took Tracy into his arms as she guided him to her bedroom. Placing her on the bed, they started to undress. Tracy tore away her clothes like a wild woman. Believing that Adam was taking too long to undress, she proceeded to help him. "Baby, you've got to move faster than that," she remarked.

Taking Tracy by the ankles, Adam held her legs high and wide as he plunged into her. Stroke-after-stroke, he didn't even notice that he wasn't wearing a condom. Tracy didn't bother to tell him that he wasn't, because she had hopes of becoming his next 'baby momma.' However, by the time they began having sex, she was too overwhelmed to say anything. This is the moment that she was waiting for, and she didn't want to ruin it with meaningless conversation.

Placing Tracy on her knee's, Adam rode her doggy-style as she bucked against him. She bucked so hard that he thought she'd break her back. Tracy begged for more as she tore the sheets from the bed. Adam wanted her to feel the results of 'Gin' and juice as he played inside of her womb. She didn't seem to mind, because he was better than anyone whom she had been with in the past. As he stroked her, Tracy closed her eyes and bit her finger like someone who was insane.

With her legs held high, Adam gave her a few more strokes and Tracy exploded. Writhing beneath him, she screamed and bit into the pillow as the orgasm rushed through her body. At that moment,

Adam picked her up off of the bed, and standing, applied more strokes until he came. Tracy wrapped her arms around Adams' neck and whispered, "I've never had anyone do me like that before. I like it, she said while humping against him.

The sex didn't stop, as they were hungry for more. For the first time, Tracy really understood why her cousin is so protective of Adam. Angry that Adam had only ejaculated once, Tracy hoped that he wouldn't remember to wear the condoms that he had. Although, once he realized that he wasn't wearing one, Adam pulled them out faster than a deck of cards. The more they screwed, the more condom wrappers he tossed onto the side of the bed. He and Tracy screwed until day break and she surprised him with breakfast in bed. It began to snow again, so after breakfast, Adam hung around and satisfied Tracy's sexual needs.

As he came, she begged him to stop. "Wait, because my hole is drying up," Tracy said as she laid with her legs spread. "Damn, you believe in giving a girl all that she can stand. Why don't you become a porno star," she asked? Adam ignored Tracy as he caught his breath. Tracy rubbed her vagina to cool the burning sensation, as she ran her fingers through his pubic hairs. "Are you going to spend the evening with me, Adam?" Shaking his head, Adam replied, "I've got to return to the dormitory, Tracy." Saddened, Tracy turned her back to Adam and said, "I hope you think about my proposal before you decide to leave." Clearing his throat, Adam said, "I've already thought about your proposal, and you have my answer. Sex, or no sex, my books come first."

Managing to make it to the dorm on Sunday night, everyone one was setting around wondering if there would be any school for students. The snow storm had gotten worse and the streets weren't clear. As he entered his room, Tracy called him to say that she was thinking about him. "Are you home," he asked in a concerned voice? Unlocking her door, she said, "I'm home and everything looks okay. I really enjoyed having you with me, Adam. You could have stayed longer if you had driven your car last night. I hope Lisa doesn't find out about us. By the way, why did you get with me? Do you have a fantasy about being with two cousins," she asked sarcastically?

Surprised at what he was hearing, Adam explained why he got with her and that things weren't going any further. "Lisa is my girl and I'm not trying to date both of you. I met you, you looked attractive, and we got together." Wondering if she'd have a chance to get with Adam again, Tracy twist her hair around her fingers as she listened to him. Adam took several minutes to explain himself as Tracy sighed with frustration. Once he was done, she ended the call and angrily kicked her shoes across the room.

Every other day, Tracy came to his dorm to challenge his statement. It's Thursday night, and they have been having sex for so long that it seemed as if the days had joined together. Adam did it more for convenience than anything else. He had grown an interest in sleeping with Tracy, but it was merely because she was always there looking sexy. When they weren't engaged in intercourse, Adam and Tracy talked about all sorts of things.

He told her of his plans to be a physician, and talked about being married and having a family. The two of them would pause from talking about families, and would go through the procedures for making a family. Uncomfortable about Adam wearing a condom, Tracy grew to enjoy the 'careful' sex more. If there was a chance of her getting pregnant by Adam, the Lord knew that she would take it. However, it amazed Adam that he and Tracy were still getting together. Although he didn't initiate the sex, she always managed to make sure that he was satisfied after they had seen each other.

Having not heard from Adam in a few days, Tracy got into her car with Brenda and raced to Chicago. Prepared to stay for a week, Tracy and Brenda arrived in the city around 7:38pm. They arrived during a snow storm, so Tracy dropped Brenda off at her cousin's home, and she left headed for Lisa's. Once she found Lisa's home, she noticed that there was another car parked in the driveway. "She must have bought a BMW," Tracy whispered as she parked on the opposite side of the street. Getting out and walking to the front door, Lisa answered the knock and was surprised to find Tracy reaching out to hug her.

Embracing her, Lisa asked, "How are you and what are you doing in Chicago? This is really a surprise. Come in out of the snow." "I'm sorry to bust in on you like this, but I told you that I was coming to see you," Tracy said as she caught a glimpse of James. Lisa invited her inside and said, "James, this is my favorite cousin, Tracy. Tracy this is Adam's brother James." James stood up and stretched forth his hand to greet Tracy. Hearing the baby crying from a distance, Lisa left the room to tend to him.

Tracy sat next to James and he asked, "How was the traffic coming here from Michigan?" "It was snowing when we left, but it got worse as we got closer to Chicago," Tracy said as she looked around the home. James took a drink from his beer and asked, "Did someone come with you or are you alone?" Clearing her throat, Tracy replied, "My cousin Brenda came with me. I dropped her off at her other cousin house." "Well, how would you like to get together tonight and see the town," James asked as he placed his cell phone inside his blazer pocket? Anxiously, Tracy said, "Sure, that would be fine. Are there any places nearby?" "We'll come up with something," James remarked.

'This woman is more attractive than Lisa. She has a cute face, a pretty smile and a terrific body. I'm definitely taking her some place that she'd enjoy,' he thought while glancing at her. With each movement she made, James licked his lips as he noticed how Tracy's jeans were fitting her. As she slowly walked through the home, James cleared his throat as he sat speechless. However, once Tracy realized that he was watching her, she quickly took a seat next to him. Although, James preferred to see her walking around, because she looked so sexy as her breast stood upright.

Tracy sat for a few moments and then quickly stood up and began her second tour through the home, admiring how Lisa decorated it. As James was looking in Tracy's direction, Lisa came into the living room with Andre, and said, "We need to talk!" Tracy stood quietly in another room and listened to James and Lisa's conversation. "We've got to stop what we've been doing...tonight. Tracy's not dumb and I don't think it looks good for my baby's uncle to be sitting here. What if that was Adam at the door? He knows what's going on between us and I don't like that. So, let's just be platonic friends. The sex was great, but this is too close for comfort," Lisa said as she fed Andre his bottle.

Having heard their conversation, Tracy thought, 'That's why Adam didn't mind sleeping with me. His brother is having sex with Lisa. I wonder how he found out? Two can play at this game.' "This is a beautiful home," Tracy said as she joined James and Lisa in the living room. "Can I hold the baby," she asked? Lisa handed Andre to Tracy as James stood up and said, "I just wanted to show you my new car, so now Tracy and I have to be leaving. I'm taking her out for dinner and dancing. " Lisa took the baby and replied, "That's nice! One day you're going to have to come by and take Andre and I for a ride," she said with a smile.

"Is that your car parked out front," Tracy asked excitedly? James took her by the hand and said, "Get your jacket and I'll take you for a ride." Tracy kissed the baby, and she and James left for the evening. "Let's make some snow men, Tracy," James said playfully as he went outside and put his hand in the snow. Lisa watched as they got into the car drove away. Closing the front door she said, "Maybe Tracy can keep him entertained while we wait for your daddy." As she was walking away from the door, the doorbell rang. When she opened it, Adam was stomping the snow from his shoes. "Surprise," he said before entering the home.

With Andre in her arms, Lisa gave Adam a kiss. "I wasn't expecting you until tomorrow," Lisa said happily. Taking Andre into his arms, Adam palmed Lisa's butt cheek as he gave her a more passionate kiss. Home to enjoy the holidays, Adam made no mention of the past. What was done, was over and he was ready to move on. In Adam's mind, he had gotten revenge against Lisa and James. "Is there something in the kitchen to eat," he asked? Lisa said "No," and proceeded to look for a coupon to order a carry-out for the two of them.

"Tracy's here, but she's gone out with James," Lisa said. Adam never took his eyes from the baby as he nodded his head. He couldn't believe that Tracy was actually in Chicago, but he knew that if she was with James, the fling between him and Lisa would be quickly cooled off. "When did she arrive," he asked inquisitively? "She arrived about a half-an-hour before you. James wanted to take her out, so she left. He has a new car and he's dying to take someone for a ride," Lisa said cheerfully. "Was James here when she arrived," he asked? Nervously, Lisa replied, "Yeah, but he only came by to show me his new car. Is there something wrong with that?" Adam kissed

Lisa on the forehead and said, "You're my lady and this is my son, so things couldn't be better." Lisa grinned as she was pleased to hear Adam refer to her as his lady, instead of his friend.

Once the carry-out arrived, Lisa fed it to Adam as he held the baby. "It feels good to celebrate Christmas with my man and my son. Last year, we had no idea that things would work out like this. I was pregnant last year, but I didn't know that this would have been the outcome. This is not what we had planned when we met, or is it," Lisa asked? Adam laughed and with no reply to her statement, he looked on. "Is everything okay, baby," Lisa asked? Smiling, Adam replied, "Things couldn't be any better."

Lisa fed Adam the last of his meal before taking the baby to dress and change him for bed. As she left the bedroom, Adam undressed and got into the shower. As he was lathering his body, Lisa got into the shower with him. With the water glistening on their skin, Lisa and Adam held each other as they kissed. "Your body feels so good against mine," Lisa said as she drew Adam's body closer to hers. Adam hoisted Lisa off of her feet and inserted his penis into her.

Feet off of the tub floor, he gave her long strokes as she bounced on him. "Oh, yeah, don't stop Adam," Lisa begged as she bounced up and down on his shaft. After a few more humps, Adam came inside of Lisa, as she kept bucking against him. "Why did you come inside of me," she asked with a grin? Adam didn't say anything as he stared into her eyes. He then said as he let her body down, "I couldn't hold it. Let's just hope that you don't get pregnant again." Lisa then playfully smacked Adam's shoulder as she agreed with him.

CHAPTER
TWENTY-THREE

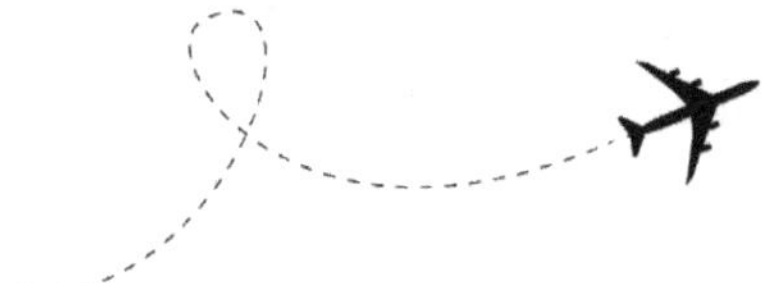

As James pulled into the underground garage, he and Tracy got out and ran for the underground hotel entrance. "Last one to the door has to give the other one a kiss," Tracy said playfully as she darted from the car. James ran behind her as he was eager to get her alone in his apartment. However, once in the elevator, they rode up to the 22nd floor and got off. Tracy followed James to his apartment, and stood with her arms around his waist as he opened the door. James turned the lights on and Tracy smacked his behind. "I can make you regret doing that," James said as he turned and took Tracy into his arms.

Staring into her eyes, James told Tracy to make herself at-home, and to help herself to anything she saw. Tracy continued looking in James eyes as she started helping him undress. "I see what I want," Tracy said as she tossed his jacket to the floor. James had never had a woman to undress him slowly, and it turned him on. "Be gentle, Tracy," he said as she unbuckled his pants. Grinning, Tracy asked, "Do you really want me to be gentle with you, James?" Smiling, James shook his head.

Standing before her in the nude, James watched as Tracy began to undress. James' erection grew harder as she slowly tossed her clothes next to his on the floor. "I think you want me. You're going to like the way I'm going to put it on you," Tracy said as she removed her panties. "I love a woman that wears sexy undergarments. The panties set everything off," James said as he held his baby maker. "If I had known that you were so attracted by panties, I would have brought some things from my personal stash."

"You can model for me another time. Right now I just want to hold you."

They left a pile of clothes at the front door as they made their way to the bedroom. Picking Tracy up as if they were crossing the thresh hold, James tossed her onto the king-sized bed. Spreading her legs, James jumped on the bed and landed face first between her legs. He began sucking and licking as Tracy kicked and bucked wildly. Removing his face from between her legs, James inserted his rod and started humping. Although tired, Tracy kept up with his strokes as they enjoyed having sex until just before break-of-day.

"I've never had anyone to go the distance with me. You are fantastic," James said as he wiped the sweat from his forehead. With the remainder of her energy, Tracy took James' manhood into her mouth and licked away their juices. He sighed with pleasure as she swallowed everything he had to offer. "Stop, Tracy! I can't take anymore," James said. "This has been great, but I have to call it quits. Let's get some sleep, and maybe have breakfast in the morning," he said while motioning for Tracy to lay next to him. Tracy laid in James' arm as his mind raced. 'Damn, this girl is too much. If I had her here with me, I would put these other women on hold. This is the kind of woman that I need to be with,' James thought to himself.

The next morning, James awakened to some good 'head' and more hot sex. Tracy was so hungry for him that she didn't want to see him rest until her needs were fulfilled. She wasn't worried about James' needs, because she knew that he was going to get-off. When they finished, Tracy and James sat on the sofa and drank a cup of coffee as the snow continued falling. The morning news played in the distance with the volume turned down low.

Sitting on the sofa wearing nothing, Tracy looked at James with a smile and asked, "Why isn't a successful guy like you married?" James thought about the question and said, "Marriage isn't for everyone, and I haven't found the right person. Women get with me because of my car, my looks or the fact that I'm a lawyer. I want to be known for more than that. It would be nice if people would accept me for me." Tracy took a sip of coffee and said flirtatiously, "I like you for whomever you are. I also like you for what you do," she said with a smile while staring at his limp penis. Following her eyes, he looked at his penis and laughed as Tracy opened and closed her legs. They sat quietly for a moment and James asked, "Why don't you pack your things and make the move to Chicago...you can stay with me." With a puzzled look on her face, Tracy stood up and walked to the window.

Thoughts raced through her head as she peered out of the panoramic view window. As she stood at the window, James admired the shape of her round rear end and Tracy's pop bottle curves. "Why don't you take a few days and think about my offer? I've never asked a woman to live with me, so it would be an honor if you said yes," James said sincerely. Stunned, Tracy didn't know what to say to his proposal. "If you're worried about employment, I know enough people in this city to help you find a good job. A job that pays well. Hell, I'm wealthy enough for the both us, if it were to come down to that. "Yeah, allow me to think about it, because we just met a few hours ago. This is sudden!"

Tracy sat her cup down, parted her butt cheeks and said, "Why don't you give me something to think about?" James leaped from the sofa and placed his hardware deep inside her gaping hole. Wetter than before, he started lunging-away at her. Tracy placed her hands on the window for balance as James dug into her womb. "I'm thinking, baby," she said repeatedly. The thought of having sex 22 stories in the sky with no one seeing them, made Tracy hotter than ever. Too tall to place her leg on his shoulder, Tracy placed her foot on the window ledge and gave James total access to her sopping vagina. As he slipped out of her, his sperm splattered onto the window ledge and carpet. With his penis in hand and his body shaking, James laid on the floor and shook as Tracy had turned him out.

Hearing his cell phone ring from a distance, James stood up and ran to the kitchen to answer it. While he checked his messages, Tracy sat on the window ledge and finished her coffee. Coming from the kitchen, James said, "My secretary called to remind me that I have a meeting at 11am. You're welcome to stay here, and I'll be back as soon as possible." "Do you have to leave now," Tracy asked? "It's a deal worth millions," James replied as he left to go and take a shower.

Left alone, the word million flashed in Tracy's mind. She had never been affiliated with anyone working for millions. As the water ran over James' body, Tracy climbed into the shower and began sucking his limp penis until it was erect. "No, you've got to stop or I'll never make this meeting," James said as he pushed her head away. Begging for him to let her continue, Tracy fell to her knee's as the warm water hit her face. Fondling James' groins, Tracy begged him to reconsider her making love to him again. As he washed the soap from his body, James said, "Baby, I promise to make it up to you when I return. You've got my honest word."

Stepping out of the shower, James began drying his body. "We'll finish this when I get back," James said as he walked out of the bathroom. Tracy climbed out of the shower and gave herself credit for trying to steal his attention. 'Well, at least I know that he'll be back,' Tracy thought as she followed behind him. "Are you leaving me alone in your apartment," Tracy asked? James didn't reply to her question as he had told her that she could remain there.

When she entered the bedroom, Tracy noticed that James was on the telephone. After his briefed conversation, he told Tracy to remain at the apartment until he returned from the office. "It's a bad day, so I'll probably be home around 2:30 or 3:00pm." James kissed Tracy, slipped on his suit jacket and left for work. As she closed the door behind him, Tracy grinned as she couldn't believe the tremendous offer that James was presenting to her. The thought of moving to Chicago excited her so much that Tracy ran naked through the apartment. Yelling as loud as she could, Tracy leaped around the apartment like a child on Christmas day.

CHAPTER
TWENTY-FOUR

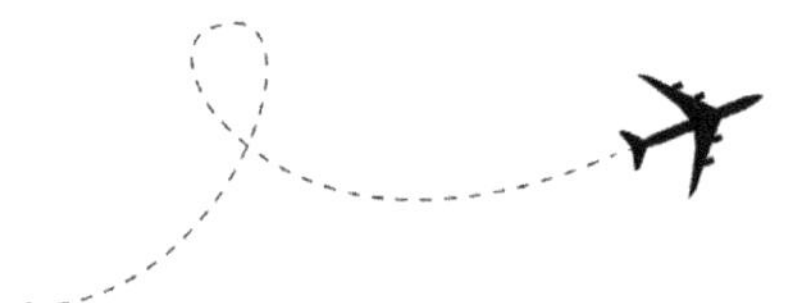

Taking Andre from his crib, Adam and Lisa were ready to leave home to do their Christmas shopping. 'I never knew that I would be doing this so early in my life,' Adam thought as he wrapped Andre in a blanket. Lisa was styling her hair as Adam and Andre were waiting for her. "Get used to it, son, because they are all slow. Even the fast ones are slow. We'll probably be setting here for another thirty minutes before she's ready," Adam said jokingly, as he attempted to educate Andre on a woman's punctuality. Lisa didn't bother paying them any attention as she grinned.

Tired of waiting, Adam went to the car and blew the horn, signaling for Lisa to come out of the house. Still in front of the mirror, Lisa was finishing her last curl when she heard the horn blow. Throwing different items into her purse as she raced through the house, Lisa grabbed her keys from the kitchen counter and ran outside to the truck. Once outside, she did the most incredible thing and fell into the snow. Once he realized that she wasn't hurt, Adam laughed playfully as Lisa began making snow angels and laughing loudly.

"We had no idea that it was going to take this long for you to get ready. Are you sure that you have everything, because I'm about to pull off," Adam asked as he put the car in gear? As he drove away, they began talking about what they were going to purchase, and what they wanted to do for the rest of the evening. "Have you decided what you were going to buy for your parents," Adam asked? "I believe your dad wants a new radar detector," Adam said, trying to remember what he needed to purchase for his parents. "Did my dad mention to you that he wanted a new radar," Lisa asked. "Well, he mentioned that he had gone out to price a new one the day we met," Adam replied. Sighing, Lisa said, "I can't wait to learn my way around this city," as she looked out of the window.

As Adam pulled into the parking structure of the shopping center, he said, "It shouldn't take long for you to learn your way around, because everything is so simple. The best thing to do is get lost and then find your way back to your starting point." Tracy placed a hat on her head, glanced at Adam and said, "Get the baby, Adam, while I try not to fall again." He parked the car and removed Andre's carrying chair as he slept. Lisa took the stroller from the trunk and they proceeded to walk into the mall.

On the worst winter day that Lisa had spent in Chicago, she was surprised to see so many people shopping. "It seems as if people stayed home from work to do last-minute holiday shopping," Lisa said as she placed Andre safely into his stroller. As they walked, Adam felt right at home because, he this was the shopping mall where he spent his weekends. However, it would have surprised Adam more if he had run into someone he knew.

A pair of shoes caught Lisa's attention, as Adam ran into an old male friend who he didn't want to see. While he and his friend talked, Lisa walked into the shoe store to browse around. "I'm surprised to see you with a baby. You are the last person that I would expect to have a baby. After all, you didn't have anyone by your side while we were in high school," his friend said as he was slowly walking away. "Don't be too surprised, because his mom is a Michigan 'dime piece' partner," Adam replied as his friend stared at him. "Damn, Adam Harris, the ladies man," were the last words spoken as they separated.

Adam went into 'Foot Locker' shoes, while Lisa window shopped. As he looked at the new shoe designs, Adam felt a tap on his shoulder. When he turned around, James was standing behind him. "I didn't know that you were home. How long have you been back," James asked cheerfully? "I arrived last night. Why are you here so early in the afternoon? Are you buying gifts for every girl you know or are you just browsing?" Laughing, James said, "Christmas is Friday, and I haven't decided on who deserves a gift and who doesn't." Grinning, Adam said, "You should stop walking around and buy something James for every girls who tolerates your arrogance." Laughing, James replied, "After meeting Tracy last night, I may have to push the other girls to the back of the line. That woman is awesome when it comes to sex. This may be the right one," Adam.

As they spoke, Lisa walked into 'Foot Locker' and stood next to Adam. "Hello, James," she said with the slightest bit of interest in him. James spoke to Lisa as he took short glances at her. 'She looks good,' James thought as he tried to be sociable. "How long are you guys going to be shopping," James asked as he reached for his cell phone? Placing a pair of shoes back onto the display stand, Adam said, "We'll be here long enough to figure out what everyone wants.

I heard that you and Tracy went out last night," Adam remarked in his attempt to distract Lisa's thoughts. "Did you guys have a nice time?" James laughed and said, "You know that she had a nice time with me. Hell, I believe in showing every woman a good time."

James glanced at Lisa with a smile and she turned her head away. 'This guy really knows how to spread his bull-shit,' Lisa thought as she fondled with her purse. "Let's go, Adam, because I don't want to be out here all afternoon." "Oh, by the way. I want to thank you Lisa for introducing me to your cousin, .she's fantastic," James said as Lisa turned to him and smiled. Nodding her head, she took Adam's hand and followed him further into the shopping mall.

Leaving his phone on top of the stroller, Adam went into another shoe store. The cell phone rang and Lisa picked it up and noticed Tracy's number on the display screen. "Why would Tracy be calling my man," she asked to herself? Lisa's first thought was that something must be going on that she doesn't know about. Jumping to conclusions, her thoughts raced as she couldn't believe what she had just witnessed.

When Adam came out of the shoe store, Lisa asked, "Why would Tracy be calling you? Is there something that I need to know?" Adam looked around with a surprised look on his face. As his cell phone beeped, he picked it up and looked at the number. "Why is she calling you, Adam? Are you sleeping with her, Lisa asked in an angry tone?"

Adam knew that he was caught, so he said, "Tracy and I ran into each other at a party and we exchanged numbers. After exchanging numbers, we got together that one night." Lisa put her hands over her face in disgust and said, "I don't believe that you slept with my cousin! Emotionally hurt, a tear ran down Lisa's cheek. "I don't believe you slept with my cousin," Lisa repeated as she took the stroller and walked away! Adam stood speechless as he wondered how she could be upset. 'Lisa slept with my brother and I didn't act like this,' he thought.

Lisa and Adam finished their shopping and left the mall. While riding home, Lisa didn't say anything to Adam, whom was lip syncing. Lisa refused to talk to him as she looked out of the window. "I don't want to go home with this hostility between us," he said. Lisa sighed and replied, "It wasn't right for me to sleep with your brother, but you didn't have to go out and do the same." Adam laughed and said, "I didn't do the same, because I didn't sleep with your brother." Lisa did not find his joke very amusing as she stated, "Don't try to be funny, Adam. You slept with my cousin and that's just as bad. Two wrongs don't make a right!"

Adam took Lisa's hand and said, "We both made a mistake, so let's put it behind us and not do it again." 'Maybe I'm over reacting,' Lisa thought. "Okay, let's leave the past in the past. I won't sleep with your brother, and you had better not sleep with Tracy. She'll be returning to my place, and you'd better not have any physical contact with her. Is that a deal," she asked? Adam nodded his head and kissed her hand. "It's you and I, Lisa...forever," he said sincerely. When Adam stopped at a stop-light, Lisa leaned over and kissed him. "Let's not hurt each other anymore. I don't agree with you sleeping with other girls in Michigan, but it's easier to deal with if I don't know about it," Lisa said as she glanced in the back seat at Andre, who was sleeping.

When they arrived at her condo, Lisa took the baby from the back seat and went into the house. 'Why would this freak take a chance on calling me if she's giving it to my brother,' Adam wondered as he turned his cell phone off. He then got out of the car and followed Lisa into the house. "Call and order a pizza, Adam, because I've got a taste for something spicy," she yelled from Andre's bedroom. Adam ordered the pizza and they talked until it arrived. After they had eaten, Adam laid on the bed beside Lisa and slowly ran his tongue along her neck. Lisa wasn't up for a round of sex, so they fondled and kissed one another before lying down and watching a movie.

"If you're nice, I'll give you a little taste later on; after Andre's had a bath and put to bed," Lisa said as she smacked her behind. Adam didn't respond as he looked at her naked body. He told her to give him a little taste, because he wasn't up for the long wait. Teasing him, she rubbed her breast and refused to let Adam touch her. 'Baby, as bad a I want you, I have got to let my body rest. You arrived last night and went to work. Oooh, what a night it was!"

CHAPTER
TWENTY-FIVE

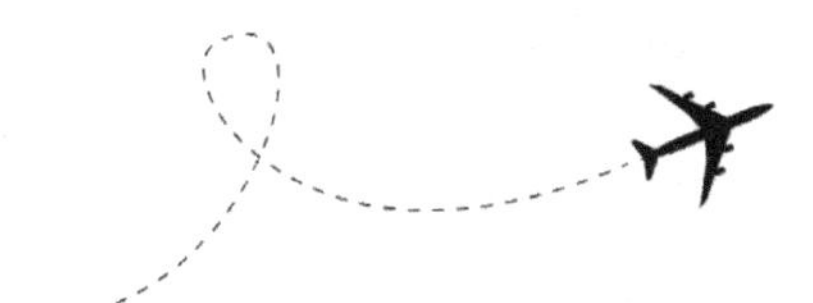

Tracy laid across the bed and drank a cup of tea while she waited for James to return from work. As she watched a 'Lifetime' movie, she got hot watching the characters making love. Sighing, Tracy heard the front door open and she leaped from the bed. James came through the door with several bags of gifts. When Tracy saw James, she ran and jumped into his arms. Kissing him, she said, "I've been waiting for you to come home. However, I wasn't aware that you were going to bring gifts with you." James kissed Tracy before he let her body down. Removing his trench coat, he said, "These gifts are for you. You can open them now, or you can wait until Christmas." James handed Tracy three bags and watched the expression on her face.

As she removed the items from the bags, Tracy's face lit up like a candle. "How can I ever thank you? These gifts are beautiful. I've got to go out and get something for you. Unless, you'd be satisfied with a little loving to warm you up," Tracy said as she tried on the leather jacket that he purchased. James said, "You've given me enough, and I'll settle for more of the same." Sauntering down the hall, James followed Tracy into the bedroom. "Do you want it now, or later," she asked playfully? Grinning, he replied, I'll wait until later, because my penis is sore from this morning's workout."

As James sat on the side of the bed and undressed, Tracy scanned through the cable channels. "My conference went well, and I've been wanting to tell you about it," James said as he threw his shoes into the closet. "I landed the deal, and after work I wanted to celebrate. When I left the office, I figured that the best way to celebrate was to go shopping for you. Some of the gifts are for my mom and dad, but it was more fun shopping for a lady like you. By the way, I ran into Adam and Lisa while I was at the mall. It seems as though they had the same idea in mind."

Tracy sat quietly as James continued discussing his day. She wondered if she should bring up the affair with her cousin or maybe wait and not say anything. Tracy chose not to say anything as she began massaging James' back. I want to thank you for the gifts, because I didn't expect to receive anything from someone whom I just met yesterday. As I think about it, I don't believe that giving you more sex would compensate for your kindness," Tracy said as she massaged his shoulders, also.

James turned to face Tracy and he asked, "Have you thought about my offer?" Tracy grinned and said, "I'll move to Chicago once I get some things taken care of. However, I'm a little worried, because I'm not established here. I don't have a job, nor a house to go to. There's so much that I have to do." James looked in her eyes and said, "Tell me how much time you need and I'll promise to be patient." I'm aware that moving out of state is a big step, but I'm willing to give you all of the support that you need. You just tell me what I can do."

Tracy hugged James and said, "Give me two months and I should have things squared away. Two months isn't a lot of time to develop a relationship, but if you're serious about being patient, then I'll be patient also," she said. "Baby, it's time for me to slow down and have a family, so of course I'm serious. I think there's a good reason why we met, and it wasn't for sex. An opportunity comes and it's best to jump at it when it's hot. A relationship is a lot of responsibility, but we can make it happen. What it's going to take is you and I getting use to each others ways, and habits," James said. Tracy kissed him and they fell onto the bed." "Understand that I'm not trying to rush you, Tracy. Sure, we've got to spend time together and get more familiar with one another, and I'm willing to take the risk."

To consummate the agreement, James climbed on top of Tracy as she inserted his penis into her wetness. Stroke–after–stroke, it wasn't long before Tracy and James were engrossed in screams of passion. They both begged for more as they made slow love to one another. Tracy got into every position that James desired, as he gave all of himself to her. With his pants at his ankles, James enjoyed his play time with Tracy. 'This is fantastic. Give me all of love muscle,' Tracy thought as she clawed his back.

Humping like a rabbit, James thought to himself, 'Oh, I want you so badly. Give me all of you.' Tracy and James came repeatedly, until there was no more that either one of them had to offer. The head of James' penis was bright red, and Tracy's vagina was wet and swollen. "Stay over on your side of the bed tonight," Tracy said playfully as she placed her hand between her legs.

Exhausted, James and Tracy went into the kitchen to prepare dinner. "Can you cook, because most men are inexperienced in the kitchen, Tracy asked? "I'm a chef in disguise. You can't be a bachelor and not know how to cook. Maybe I don't cook as often as some people, but I manage to keep my strength up. The last time I cooked a meal was last month. I had some guys from the office over for a meal and it turned out okay. We watched football and had a very good time," James said happily.

Taking the pot from his hand, Tracy said, "Well, if we're going to be living together, then you're gonna to have to get used to a woman doing the cooking. What I need is for you to tell me what you like and I'll have it ready when you come home." James smiled as he was moved by Tracy's take control nature. "Whatever you say, Miss Tracy. If you want to be the woman of the house, then help yourself. Just remember, I'm not trying to gain too much weight," he said jokingly.

Tracy finished cooking and sat next to James and fed him. He could see that Tracy enjoyed feeding him, because the look in her eyes gave her away. Once they had eaten, Tracy talked with Brenda for a while, before she and James got involved in a television movie. They laid in each others arm for hours as they weren't concerned about going anyplace or doing anything. Tracy and James watched two movies and shared a bag of pop corn.

"I like a woman that's also a good cook and one whom can pick out good movies to watch. It's been a while since I've sat down and actually enjoyed a movie. Usually, I watch all of the sports programs and sports highlight shows. One day I'm going to take you to the gym with me so that you can see me in action," James said as he ran his fingers through her hair. With a smirk on her face, Tracy softly said, "Baby, I would love to see you in action. I'm looking forward to sharing myself, and my life's interest with you. Sexy or not, I haven't had a lot of success with my relationship. However, I'm feeling optimistic about this opportunity to share my life with someone who's as caring as you are."

Overwhelmed by his kindness, Tracy felt like a helpless little girl as she laid in his arms. "I'm getting too attached to you, daddy," Tracy said as she softly kissed his abdomen. Smiling, James said, Our getting together was fate, because this is the first time since high school that I've been with someone without using a condom. However, if you get pregnant, I'm not going to allow you to work, so get rid of the thought. Looking in James' eyes, Tracy replied, "Who knows, James. Maybe we'll cross that bridge some day and make the most of it."

Tracy's eyes widened and she replied with a smile, "I never said anything about being pregnant or wanting to get pregnant. Now, if I discover that I'm pregnant, you will be the first one that I call. As far as working goes, I'm willing to let you be the bread winner in the house." Running her tongue across his nipple, Tracy thought, 'this is my kind of man. He wants to be the bread winner and the love-maker.

Grinning, Tracy said, I want to have nine children." Surprised, James replied, "I was hoping to have ten." All of a sudden, the kisses stopped and Tracy said, "I've got to think about that one." In an effort to call Tracy's bluff, James grinned as he glanced at her and the expression she wore. Glancing at one another, both them laughed. "We'd be worn out physically, mentally and sexually. Hey, let's just take it one child at a time...but there's no rush."

On Christmas morning, James and Tracy, who was wearing her new outfit, arrived at Lisa's condo just in time for breakfast. With smiles and greetings, Lisa invited them inside and offered them a cup of coffee or a cup of hot chocolate. Adam, who was preparing breakfast, set the table and they all sat down to eat. After Adam said grace and gave thanks, he asked, "So Tracy, are you enjoying Chicago? Is James showing you all of the hot-spots?"

Snickering, she looked at James and replied, "James has been showing me the hot-spots. 'Beginning with the one between my legs,' she thought with a grin. Looking sexy in her robe, James glanced at Lisa and licked his lips. "Your cousin is going to move to Chicago so that we can be together," James said as he cut his pancakes. Shocked, Lisa asked, "Is that what you want to do? Tracy remarked, "It's going to take some getting use too, but I think I'm going to like living with James. He promised to be supportive and that's all I need. There aren't many men who are willing to be supportive to someone they've just met. Who knows, maybe we'll get married some day."

"Are you saying that you're ready to settle down, James," Adam asked as he fed Andre his bottle? "It's about time for me to settle down, and besides, there's no better person to settle down with. Tracy is going to become the lady of my house. Do I have your blessings, Adam," James asked as Adam looked unsure about the arrangement? Smiling, "Adam agreed to the idea. You have my blessings, dear brother." Squeezing Tracy's hand, Lisa said, "Hey, I'm happy for you, cousin! Congratulations."

After breakfast, Tracy gathered her things from the truck and returned to the dining room. "Didn't you say that you had some other stops to make, James," Tracy asked as she was beginning to feel uncomfortable? As James got up from the table, Tracy went down the hall to the restroom, and ran into Adam, who was putting Andre to bed for his nap. "Look, Adam, I hope that you and I can remain friends. After all, I may become part of the family," Tracy said. Unaware that James was standing nearby, Adam replied, "I'm happy for you and I wish you and James the best. By the way, is he aware that you and I slept together?" Before Tracy could answer the question, James came around the corner and said, "She'll be sleeping with me from now on. Whatever you two were up too, stops right here and right now."

Lisa came around the corner and noticed everyone standing together. "What's going on? Did I miss something," she asked curiously? James sighed and said, "I slept with your girl and you slept with Tracy, so let's stop the games starting right now. We've all made mistakes, so let's move on with our lives." Startled, Tracy and Lisa looked at each other. "I'm aware that you slept with Adam, and I still can't believe it. You're my cousin and I never thought that you would go behind my back and sleep with my man," Lisa replied. Tracy hunched her shoulder and said, "These things happen sometimes, but it wasn't done intentionally. He and I ran into each other and one thing lead to another. I'm sorry for doing it and I can promise you that it won't happen again." Tracy and Lisa embraced each other while James and Adam shook hands in agreement and understanding.

At the end of the day, Lisa and Adam returned home without Andre. "I'm glad your mom decided to keep Andre. Now, you and I can really celebrate," Lisa said with a hint of mischief in her voice. Adam grinned and smacked her butt as they went into the house. Lisa threw her coat onto the sofa and Adam took her in his arms. "Baby, I'm sorry for what I did and I'm glad that it's out in the open among the four of us," Adam said as he looked in her eyes.

With her arms around his waist, Lisa looked in his eye and said, "Adam, I don't want you to hurt me anymore. I know that you're a man who enjoys being with other women, but please don't hurt me again. What would really make me happy, would be to be in love with you and have a strong family. It may sound like a dream, but I would love to be the mother of your children. I'll give you all of the children that you want." Adam and Lisa began kissing each other as they made their way to the bedroom. Walking with her in his arms, Lisa put all of her tongue into his hot, wet mouth. Adam did the same as they looked as if they were trying to tickle each others tonsils.

Once they were undressed, Lisa pushed Adam onto the bed and mounted him. Up and down, she grind her thighs into him as she took everything he had to offer. Adam moaned as she rode him with her eyes closed. The cream from her vagina oozed down his shaft and moistened the crack of his butt cheeks. When she started to climax, Lisa leaped so high that Adam was under the impression that she wanted to fly. Adam's body writhed underneath hers as she dug her nails into his chest, begging for him not to stop. Lisa rolled off of Adam and laid on her back.

Wiping the sweat from his brow, Adam pulled her to the edge of the bed and pushed her thighs back onto her chest. Slowly, he drove his penis into her. "Baby, you feel better than silk," Adam said as he plunged into her juices. Lisa's slow twist and wet turns made the sex feel good to Adam. "Merry Christmas, baby. I told you that Mrs. Claus had some good stuff for you," Lisa said with her eyes closed and her legs spread wide. They continued making love for thirty minutes or so, before they fell asleep in each others arm.

CHAPTER
TWENTY-SIX

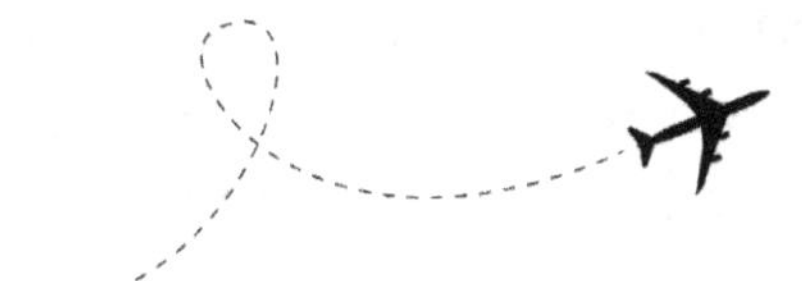

James and Tracy walked into his dark apartment and before he could turn on the lights, Tracy pushed James to the floor. She began undressing him. Removing his jacket, and shirt, James stood up and unbuckled his belt as Tracy unfastened his pants. The last thing he heard was the sound his zipper made when she pulled it down. Tracy put her mouth on his package so fast that all he could do was fall against the wall.

With his pants at his knee's, James lost his balance and fell to the floor. While on his back, Tracy sucked his throbbing man hood. With only the moonlight glaring through the panoramic window, James tried his best to get Tracy out of her clothes, but she made it difficult. The more he fought to get her undressed, the more she fought to hold him down.

Once Tracy stopped applying oral pressure to his penis, she started to undress. Removing her jacket, jeans, shirt and panties, Tracy got down on all fours. James knelt behind her and inserted his rock hard shaft and began his ride of victory. Stroke-after-stroke, the carpet burned his knee's. With each stroke it felt like James' skin was being burned off. Both their knee's were hot and sore, but neither one of them wanted to stop. 'This is the freakiest sex I've had since I moved into this place,' James thought as Tracy banged her butt cheeks against him. When she began to climax, Tracy arched her back and let out a moan that James had never heard before.

Placing his hands on her waist, James' strokes

became faster. 'This last stroke is going to throw me over the edge,' James thought as he released his wad into her. As they gasped for air, James laid on top of Tracy's back while his limp prick jumped around inside of her. Bodies covered in sweat, they got up and made their way to the bedroom. "Let me get some rest and I'll give you some more," James said as he staggered into the bedroom. "That session made my knee's weak," he said while falling onto the bed. Tracy, tired, held her head high and walked over to the window to open the blinds. "I want a little moonlight in the room," she said while sauntering to the bathroom.

Giving herself a breast exam, Tracy stood in the mirror and looked at her figure. Pushing her stomach out as far as possible, she tried to imagine herself expecting. 'Girl, what have you done? What are you about to do? I just promised this man that I would move to Chicago and live with him. I've used what my mother gave me and now I'm trapped. James wouldn't understand if I backed out of this deal. He's attractive, wealthy, educated and appears to know what he wants out of life. We're the same age, but he's got an advantage over me. This man promises to share everything that he has, and it's what he's shared so far that has me worried,' Tracy thought as she rubbed her stomach. "Lord, you know what's going on," Tracy said as she left the bathroom.

"James, are you feeling okay," she asked? When James didn't respond, she thought that he didn't hear her, and seconds later, he began to snore. Tracy took a blanket from the closet and covered him with it and laid down. As she played with the television remote, she rubbed her stomach almost as if she wished that she was pregnant. "Lord, you know," Tracy said as she looked toward heaven. The thought of her being pregnant with this man's baby excited Tracy, as she stared at his naked body.

CHAPTER
TWENTY-SEVEN

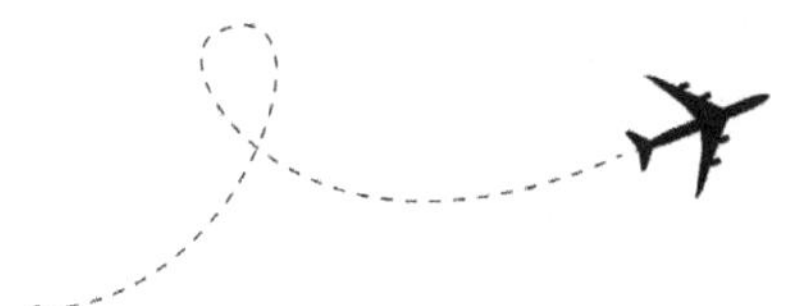

As the new year approached, Adam and Lisa drew closer together. Although she didn't see him as much as she wanted too, he made sure to be at home at a reasonable hour. Adam was helping his dad at the office to gain experience at being in a hospital environment. Instead of giving him a salary, Adam agreed that the experience would be enough. While Adam was at the hospital, Lisa played mommy. The clothes were folded, dinner was on the stove, and the baby was asleep. It became routine for her as she patiently waited for Adam to arrive.

When he came through the door, excited to see him, Lisa would run to Adam and plant a wet kiss on his lips. Adam enjoyed the attention because it reminded him of the moments that he's seen his parents share. However, when Andre was awake, Adam and Lisa would lie in bed and hold him. Giving soft kisses to one another, they enjoyed each others company, in the presence of their son. It was a moment they imagined, but not knowing it would occur like this. Still settling into her new position in the research department, Lisa was overjoyed to be receiving so much support from everyone.

On New Years' eve, Lisa invited James and Tracy over for dinner and spades. James and Tracy arrived early, which gave Adam enough time to finish preparing the meal. Everything was catered, but the host had to set it out for the guest. Andre was spending the night with Adam's parents, which gave everyone the chance to enjoy a quiet evening together. Before starting the card game, the couples sat and watched a movie that James chose. The movie was a comedy that everyone was enjoying.

"Do you have some appetizers or pop corn," James asked? Adam ran to the kitchen and returned with a tray of finger foods. The tray consisted of ham rolls, cheese, crackers, and several dipping sauces. "If you guys would like some more pop corn, I'll pop, I'll pop more," Adam remarked as he set the tray down. One trip to the kitchen, turned into several trips to the kitchen. Adam was forgetting everything he intended to get. "Slow down, baby. It's going to be okay," Lisa said teasingly.

After the movie and several hands of cards, Adam poured drinks for everyone as the new year approached. When the clock chimed 12am, everyone gave a toast, and the couples kissed and fondled each other. "Happy New Years everybody," James said as he raised his glass. They listened to old rhythm and blues classics for hours, before they broke up the gathering. After getting their jackets from the closet, Adam and Lisa walked James and Tracy to the front door. "James and I had a good time Lisa," Tracy said while giving Lisa a hug and a kiss on the cheek. Adam and James gave handshakes and wished each other a safe night.

While Adam closed the front door, Lisa turned out the lights. "Come on, Mr. Harris, we have work to do," Lisa said as she motioned for him to follow her. Adam followed Lisa into the bathroom and she said, "I didn't mean for you to follow me in here." Adam helped get Lisa out of her shorts and then she sat on the edge of the sink. Taking his shaft in her hand, Lisa offered guidance into her passion tunnel. With her legs spread wide, Adam applied slow, long, strokes to her. Filled with passion, Lisa bucked against him. "Give me all of your New Years love," she said while throwing her head back.

Adam increased his strokes until she came. "Don't take it out of me," Lisa whispered as she grind into him. Adam placed his hands on her butt cheeks and lifted Lisa off of the sink. As he held her, Adam more applied more strokes. Lisa bounced up and down on his rigid tool. He then put his hands underneath her calves and made faster strokes. Lisa's body gyrated as she tried to take all of him inside of her womb. Suddenly, they came together, making loud moans. Dripping wet, Lisa's butt cheeks felt softer than ever as Adam squeezed them. Lisa forced her tongue into Adam's mouth and kissed him passionately, as he held her body against his.

Once Lisa was out of Adam's arms, he smacked her butt while she walked away. Having had one drink too many, Lisa was ready for more as she laid with her legs spread. Adam couldn't resist as her leaped on top of her. Lisa played with her clit as he stroked her. "Stroke that kitty cat, Adam," Lisa said as she placed her hands on his shoulders. When she felt Adam was about to come, she smacked his butt. Adam gave her longer, harder thrust and then unleashed his load. Shaking vigorously, Lisa placed her hands on his waist and held on.

Pulling his penis away from Lisa's crotch, a wad of her secretions oozed out. He knew that from the way she was panting, that Lisa had come also. Sore from all of the excitement, Lisa closed her legs and rolled onto her side. "We'll finish this later," she said as Adam laid behind her. Lisa then informed him that she was taking birth control pills, and that the raw sex felt so much better than the plastic penetration. Shocked, Adam smiled and hunched his shoulders and said nothing. Too exhausted to give him more, Lisa asked Adam to lie down and hold her until she fell asleep. Anxiously, Adam held Lisa close, as her good-looking body felt warm next to his. With her sweaty butt cheeks up against him, Adam eagerly anticipated their next performance.

Meanwhile, James and Tracy fell onto the bed and began kissing. They kissed like two sweethearts who hadn't seen each other in months. Tracy grind on his bag of tricks as she worked to get James out of his shirt. Removing his shirt, James helped Tracy remove her sweater and bra. When her breast fell out, he immediately placed one in his mouth. While James sucked her breast, Tracy fumbled to get his belt undone, so that she could remove his pants. James released Tracy's breast and began unfastening his pants. Kneeling over him, Tracy took off her pants. As his soldier stood straight, Tracy climbed on top of him. James grabbed her butt and started giving her short strokes. "Stop teasing me," Tracy said as she began bucking. Lowering her body on top of his, James parted her butt cheeks and gave her repeated strokes. "That's my spot, baby. Please, give me all that you have to give? Let's make this New Year's day special," Tracy whispered in a seductive tone as her lowered body bounced up and down. Bucking like a wild woman, Tracy and James came together. The sheets were soaked with sweat and vaginal secretions, but neither of them seemed to mind.

James awakened later that morning receiving a 'head' job. Tracy had showered, and with her wet body poised over James, she went to work on his member. "Good morning," James said as he stroked her mouth. Tracy stopped before he could ejaculate. Jumping from the bed, she ran to the kitchen and returned with James' breakfast on a tray. "Surprise, I knew you'd have an appetite for something," she said with a big smile. Shaking his head in disbelief, James said, "I'm going to enjoy having you around." Wanting to try something new, Tracy continued giving James "head" while he ate. The "head" felt so good that he occasionally got choked on the food and beverage. Feeling freaky, Tracy sucked him until his plate was cleaned. "I hope you enjoyed your breakfast," she said with a grin.

James sighed and nodded his head. "Everything was lovely," he replied. James then rolled onto his side, "Wake me in a few hours, Tracy," he said after yawning. Tracy returned the tray to the kitchen, turned on the television and climbed into bed. She wanted to go another round, but Tracy also wanted to be considerate of his needs. After all, James had several drinks to celebrate New Years, and he probably had a slight hangover.

CHAPTER
TWENTY-EIGHT

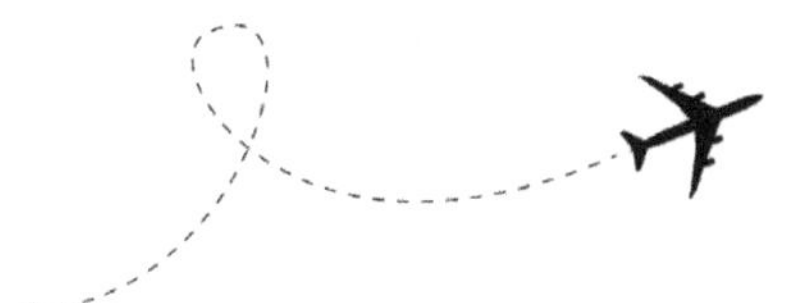

Lisa awakened Adam early that Sunday morning and gave him a round of sex. Afterwards, they drove to his parents home and picked up Andre and returned to the condo. Adam and Lisa took turns cuddling him and making funny faces. The sight of Adam interacting with Andre brought a smile to Lisa's face. 'I shouldn't complain about anything, because Adam is a terrific father. I just love the way he plays with his son. Thank God that I was able to give him a healthy child. It's going to be so nice when we can be a family all of the time. If I had listened to my parents, I would have probably had a baby for Lester Dawson, the high school nerd,' she thought.

"Well, it's almost time for you to be leaving. Are you going to be okay all by yourself, or do you need to stay another night? Adam handed Andre to Lisa and said, "I've got Mr. Dillon for a class tomorrow and I don't want to miss it. Besides, I've got some things that I want to go over before tomorrow's class begins." Without commenting, Lisa watched as Adam continued gathering his things. Although she didn't want him to leave, Lisa watched Adam as she thought about the hot sex that they shared.

Taking his luggage from the hallway, Adam tossed them into the family room. Taking a seat next to Lisa, he gave her a long kiss and he gave Andre a big hug. Once he put his jacket on, Adam packed his bags into his truck and sped away. Hours down the road, an unfamiliar phone number appeared on Adam's cell phone. Adam answered the phone only to realize that it was Stacy. "Happy New Year," she said in a loud voice! Adam returned the greeting and asked, "What made you call me after all of this time?" "I just got your number from Eric," she replied.

Stacy and Adam talked until he returned to the dorm. "I'm at the dorm, so can I call you back. Wait, I've got a better idea. Why don't you and I get together next Saturday," he asked? Stacy quickly agreed to meet with Adam, and they ended their conversation. Anxious to get unpacked, Adam hurried his bags off to his room. He then unpacked, showered, and laid across the bed. As he was reading the latest edition of his G Q magazine, there was a knock at the door.

When he answered the door, Adam found Kelly standing there with a bottle of champagne and wearing sun glasses. "Happy New Year," she shouted! Adam invited her inside and she gave him a big hug. "I've missed talking to you," Kelly said as Adam lifted her off of the floor. "I missed talking to you also," he said before releasing her. Kelly kicked off her shoes and said, "I was hoping that you and I could have a holiday toast. This bottle came from my sisters house. If she knew that I had it, she would probably kill me."

Adam handed Kelly a glass and asked, "Why are you wearing shades?" Kelly removed the glasses, revealing a black eye. She then took the bottle and poured some wine for herself. "It's a long story, but my boyfriend went through my purse and found the abortion receipt. I should have taken it out, but I wasn't thinking. Craig had been drinking and he found the receipt, and beat me up. I've been thinking about filing charges. However, if I file charges, he'll get thrown out of the military, then there's going to be trouble."

I brought the wine to put us in the mood, because these past weeks have been rough." They sat on the edge of the bed and took a sip from their glasses. "I'll take care of you," Adam said. Looking at her face made him feel bad for Kelly, because she's such a nice person. Although he didn't want to get involved, Adam wished that there was something that he could do for her. As Kelly sat with a smile on her face, Adam proceeded to apologize for the mess that she was in, because it was partially his fault. It takes two people to make a baby, and Adam believed that he should have been more careful. Adam thought that if he had said 'No' to Kelly, then this never would have happened.

After two glasses of wine, Adam was digging into Kelly's body. He gave it to her just the way she liked it. Fast, slow, and a combination of strokes always got Kelly off. With her flat stomach and round butt cheeks, Kelly twisted and turned until Adam made her beg him to stop. Wrapped in his arms, Kelly grind her butt against him while telling her story. Adam listened attentively as his penis poked Kelly in her back. Turning toward Adam, Kelly placed her leg over his and offered to give Adam a little of her love. Placing their sweaty bodies close together, Adam gave her slow strokes as Kelly sighed heavily. Excited, they both came faster than expected.

"I know that you have some, but I brought you two boxes of condoms. Now you don't have any reason to chicken out when I want some from you," Kelly said as she put on her panties. Adam watched closely as she got dressed. "Damn, Kelly's more attractive than I thought she was," Adam whispered to himself. "I'm so sore that I may not be back until the weekend or one day next week," Kelly said jokingly. Adam leaped from the bed and began getting dressed. "Just give me a call when you're ready," he replied. Kelly then apologized for not calling, while she put her jacket and sun glasses on.

Taking her by the hand, Adam walked Kelly to her car. It was a slow walk, because the snow was coming down fast and it was getting deeper. "Have you given any thought about you and I becoming a couple," Kelly asked as they got closer to her car.? "I enjoy having you around, but I haven't decided on whether or not you and I should become a couple," Adam remarked as Kelly searched for her keys. Kelly then unlocked the door and said, "Well, I hope that God hears my prayer and help you to make a decision." Kelly gave Adam a peck on the lips and got into her car and drove away.

Adam turned and walked into the dormitory. 'This female is really bugging me about becoming her man. Judging from the look of her eye, Kelly should try to take care of the guy she's dating. He's beating her up and she wants me to lick her wounds,' he thought. Adam then ran into some other residents in the building and briefly discussed his holiday with them. Once they broke up they're gathering, Adam went to his bedroom and washed Kelly's juices off of himself.

The next morning, Adam rose early and left for the library to study. He made good use of his study time by managing to look over everything. A few chapters were read, notes were taken, pending assignments were completed, and he hurried to class. Adam's professor was named Mr. Dillon, and from their first meeting, Adam knew that it was going to be a rocky experience. Mr. Dillon was a short, red neck sort of guy with a pudgy stomach. He wore his pants around his belly and often ran his hand across his bald head. Students and faculty often said that he needed a toupee. He sometimes wore different kinds, and they were usually salt/pepper to match his beard.

Their first meeting was rough and Adam was more than eager for the class to end. During the break, a student wearing jeans, a sweater and wedge heeled Timber Land boots, approached Adam. "Boy, you and Mr. Dillon are off to a bad start," she said with a smile. Adam smirked and replied, "I heard this old guy always had some hang-up with a student. This time, I guess I'm the bait," Adam said as he glanced at the young woman. 'She's got to be at least twenty-eight or twenty-nine,' Adam thought as he quickly looked her up and down. "My name is Tina, what's yours?" Adam cleared his throat and said, My names Adam.

"Hey, are you getting anything out of this," he asked, referring to the lecture? "It's going over my head," she said. I need this class to graduate and it's giving me trouble. This is only the first night, so I hope things get better. Mr. Dillon wants us to read those chapters and prepare for a short essay quiz.

What I need right now is a tutor," Tina said with a look of concern on her face. "I'm just the man you're looking for," Adam replied with a smile. "Are you serious? Can you tutor me in time for next week's quiz," she asked excitedly? "Come to dorm room M-36 on Friday and we'll work it out," Adam said as they entered the classroom.

After class, Tina followed Adam through the school. "Can I walk to the dorms with you so that I'll know where I'm going," Tina asked as she stared up at Adam? Adam lead Tina to his room, where she immediately took a seat on the bed and began looking through his collection of magazines. "It's too soon to get a study room, so I figured we would study here in my room. However, I must let you know that I take my time seriously. If we're going to have regularly scheduled tutoring sessions, then you'll have to sign up with the tutoring center. What we will focus on are your weak points and take it from there." Tina had become so comfortable that she didn't hear much of what Adam said. "What time should I be here on Friday?" "My class ends at 2:30, so try to be here by 4pm," he said.

Those next three-and-a-half days were hectic for Adam. The assignments weren't overwhelming, but getting use to the new instructors was a headache. Adam found himself arguing with some and debating with others. He's now preparing to leave his Friday afternoon class and the time wasn't passing fast enough. "Why doesn't this lady just let us go," Adam whispered to the girl sitting next to him? Adam then glanced at her notebook and noticed that her name was Denise. The girl smiled and whispered, "That's my name!" Adam returned the smile and wrote her name on a piece of paper. Denise whispered her phone number as he wrote it down. "Am I disturbing your concentration, Mr. Harris," the professor yelled? "No Mrs. Sim's." Adam and Denise grinned.

Adam returned to the dorm and found Tina setting in the lobby. Before she noticed him, he left the building and came through another entrance. As he walked through the corridor, Tina was standing with her back to Adam. "This girl looks good from the back," he whispered to himself. Quietly stepping up to her, Adam asked, "Are you ready to get started?" Nervously, Tina jumped as she was caught by surprise. They walked to his room together after stopping to get some beverage from the vending machine.

Tina walked inside the room as Adam held the door. "Come in and make yourself comfortable," he said in his sexy voice. Adam turned on his latest jazz CD, and stood behind Tina. Gently, he removed her coat as she was impressed by how neat the room looked. "Most guys have trashy bedrooms, but this is nice. What's the flavor of that candle," Tina asked as she inhaled the aromatic scent? "That's mahogany scented," Adam replied as he laid out her books on the desk. Tina had come to his room to study, but she was open for other suggestions.

Adam and Tina studied for four hours, taking short breaks in between. "I told you that I took my time seriously. Did you think that I was kidding," he asked jokingly? Tina's forehead rested on the desk as she could not believe how exhausted her body felt. "I can't take any more, Adam. My brain feels like it wants to explode. As a matter of fact, I don't want to see or talk about nothing that pertains to the human body," Tina said as she ran her fingers through her hair. Adam laughed as he stretched. This was just the first night, but it gets better. Tina stood up and fell onto the bed. 'I can't believe she fell on my workbench,' Adam thought as he completed his stretches.

"Is it okay if I lay here for a minute? My brain is on an overload. If I'm not ready for this quiz, then I won't ever be ready," Tina said as she sighed. Adam said, "Yeah, it's okay. He then sat on the edge of the bed while Tina kicked off her shoes. I wish my boyfriend was studying to be a doctor," she said. "What is your boyfriend studying? Is this his last year also?" Tina shook her head and said, "My boyfriend doesn't even want me to be in school. I believe he feels threatened because he doesn't have the option of attending school. He stole a car when he was young and he also got caught with drugs a few years ago. I believe he spent more than a year in jail".

From that moment, Tina talked for more than an hour. She told Adam about her family, friends, jobs and anything else that she could remember. What caught Adams' attention was when Tina began gyrating. "Is everything okay," he asked inquisitively? Laughing, Tina continued gyrating. "I'm horny," she replied. "Well, maybe you should do something about that," Adam remarked. "Will you help me do something about it," Tina asked? Adam cleared his throat and asked, "What about your boyfriend? Isn't it his job to satisfy your needs?" Tina laughed and said, "Forget about him. Besides, I just want you to knock off the edge. Do you think you could give me a little?"

"I'm not responsible for what happens afterward," Adam said jokingly. He then removed his sweat pants and underwear while kicking off his gym shoes. Tina peeled her jeans off and tossed them in the corner with her sweater. As she ran her hands along the insides of her thighs, Adam put on a condom. Tina spread her legs wide and Adam climbed into her. "Oh, I like it like this," she said. Tina's moans grew louder as Adam plunged into her womb.

With her legs on his shoulders, Tina dug her nails into his forearm. Adam grit his teeth as it felt as if she were drawing blood from his arm. The harder Tina dug her nails into his skin, the harder Adam's strokes became. Tina then bit her lip as she held in her moans and cries. When Adam gave her his final strokes, Tina let out a loud yell. "Be quiet," Adam whispered. Sliding on her juices, Adam slowed his strokes. "Stay right there, so that I can feel your thing jump around inside of me," Tina whispered as she placed her hands on his thighs. "I hope this doesn't interfere with our tutoring sessions, because having you as a tutor is going to work out for me," she said between grunts. As Adam hovered over Tina, he gave her a couple of strokes and withdrew his goods.

Adam and Tina took turns washing up. When

Adam was done, he slipped on his sweat pants while Tina put her shoes on. "Remember to go to the tutoring center. Tell them that we've spoken and that it would be okay to put you down as a regular. Don't worry about paying me, because the program pays my salary." Tina put on her jacket and kissed Adam on his cheek. "Thanks for helping me out. You knocked the edge off and I feel like a new person. I'll make arrangements to meet with you next week or I'll just wait and see you in class on Monday," Tina said as she stood at the door. Adam took his keys from the table and walked Tina to the front entrance. "I'll see you later," Adam said as he held the door for her.

Adam returned to his bedroom and fell onto the recliner. 'Every woman I meet wants to give me the sex. No one could have told me that it was going to be this simple. I began with Lisa, and now there's Kelly, Tina and Stacey. By the way, I'm supposed to pick-up Stacey tomorrow,' Adam thought as he pulled his pants off.

After falling onto the bed, Adam's cell phone rang, and was surprised to hear Lisa's voice; they talked for a half-an-hour. He confessed how he felt about her since spending the holiday with her and Andre. Lisa bubbled with joy as she sat at her office desk listening to Adam's confessions of having had a wonderful holiday. They talked about getting together as soon as possible, because Lisa was in the mood for some romance. Once they were finished talking, Adam placed the phone next to his pillow and went to sleep.

The next morning, Adam awakened to the sound of the phone ringing. Looking at the caller I.D., he tried to recognize the phone number. When he answered it, Stacey was on the other end asking what time he was planning to pick her up. The clock read 10am, and Adam knew that he wasn't going back to sleep. He then got out of bed, showered and left to pick-up Stacey. Once he was on the highway, the trip seemed longer than usual. After making his way through the Saturday morning traffic, he arrived at her apartment at 12:23pm. Stacey was waiting at the door, and when he pulled into the parking structure, she ran and leaped into the car. "Hi, Chi-Town," she said before kissing him.

Stacey talked until they reached Ann Arbor. She peered out of the window as she was amazed by the towns appearance. "Are we going to your dorm," she asked? Keeping his eyes on the road, Adam replied, "No, I've got another place for us to spend the day." They rode around until Adam came to the condo division. He pulled the car into the garage and they both got out. "How can you afford a place like this? Are you rich or something? Tell your parents to lend me a few thousand dollars," Stacey said jokingly. Adam laughed as he invited Stacey into the house. "Make yourself comfortable while I make brunch. Oh, and take your shoes off before you walk through the house," he remarked from the kitchen.

While he prepared brunch, Stacey sat on the sofa and nursed a glass of orange juice. "I really like your place, Adam. Although, I was expecting to go to your dorm room," she said while scanning through a magazine. At that point, Adam began placing the breakfast plates onto the table. Stacey closed the magazine and walked into the dining room. Before she or Adam sat down, she placed her arms around Adam and gave him a wet kiss. "I hope you feel up to helping me work this food off," Stacey said as she placed her hand on Adam's crotch. "Well, we'll just have to see about that," Adam replied as he pulled the chair out for Stacey.

Stacey made flirtatious gestures at Adam as she chewed her food. Finishing before Adam, Stacey began removing her clothes. Adam nearly choked on his food when he saw her gyrating in front of him. However, he continued eating while enjoying the show. With a banana in her mouth, Stacey acted as if she was giving 'head.' As his penis tried to burst its way through his pants, Adam tried his best to ignore her.

Adam cleared the table and lead Stacey to the bedroom. One glance at the king-sized bed made her mouth drop. "Damn, this is a huge bed. You need me to stay with you and keep this thing warm." Stacey laid her naked body across the bed while Adam removed his clothing. Crawling toward her, Stacey spread her legs and reached for him. He began to gently suck her nipples while she squirmed underneath him.

Holding her breast together, Adam sucked both nipples as her moans grew louder. Adam then ran his tongue down her stomach, stopping at her navel. When he placed his tongue in her navel, waves of lust ran through Stacey's body. "Ooh, I want you so bad,

Adam," Stacey whispered as she wrapped her legs around his waist. He then pushed Stacey's knee's toward her chest and glided into her wet hole.
Slowly, Adam worked his penis inside of her. "Ooh, that's my spot, Chi-Town," Stacey said as she writhed beneath his body. Suddenly, their eye's met and Adam began giving Stacey the strokes that she wanted. Biting his lower lip, Adam drove deeper into her sopping wet love tunnel. Stacey was so wet and soft that it felt as if he was stroking doctors' cotton. Stacey's juices glistened Adam's abdomen when she came. Screaming for more, he gave all that he had to give. Holding her feet at his chest, Adam banged away as Stacey kept begging for him not to stop. "Take this dick," Adam said as he released his wad into his condom.

Adam quickly removed the condom and Stacey began jerking him off. "Let all of it come out, Adam," Stacey said as she squeezed the head. Adam pushed her hand away and placed his arm around her. Lying on her back, Adam moved his hand up and down her body. Stacey moaned as she enjoyed his touch. 'This girl is good,' Adam thought with a smile on his face. She then turned to face Adam and began kissing his sweaty chest. "Damn, I like what you do to me, Chi-Town. If you keep this up, you may become my baby's daddy."

"Do you want to have kids, Stacey asked? "Not interested," Adam replied while he laid with his eyes closed. "Why are we talking about children? Turn the television on while I order a pizza. What do you want on the pizza," Adam asked as he reached for his cell phone? "Whatever you get will be fine with me," Stacey said as she stared at Adam's muscular frame. "Baby, You've got a nice body. Can I have some more of you," Stacey asked as she kissed Adam's neck? "I'll take care of you," Adam replied as he dialed the restaurant's phone number.

Once the pizza arrived, Stacey and Adam laid in bed and watched a horror movie. After talking with her, he realized that she wasn't a dummy. Stacey talked about her dreams and the goals that she's set for herself. She wasn't exactly Adam's type, but he thought she'd do. After all, it's only a sex thing. Stacey was interested in Adam, but she wasn't sure how to approach him. In her mind, Adam is a gorgeous guy with a great body, smart and sexually talented. However, landing him was her biggest challenge.

When they talked, she tried to impress Adam with her speech. Choosing her words correctly, it was obvious that she had some form of education. "How are your classes," Adam asked with a mouth filled with pizza? "The second semester is going okay, so far. But, I'll be glad to see winter break come," she replied. "Also, what time would you like to return home," he asked. Stacey laughed and said, "Have me home by 10am because I have to be at work by 1pm." This was exactly what Adam didn't want to hear, because he was hoping to relax before school resumed on Monday. Placing his hand over his face, Adam finished his pizza and began fondling Stacey. They had sex for the remainder of the evening. After the pizza was finished and the other one had been started on, they laid down with their stomachs full.

For every pound they gained, they burned it off with steamy sex. Stacey had come so many times that she felt overwhelmed by Adam's presence. With every chance she got, Stacey was gently touching and feeling on him. It was almost compulsive. She rubbed his body when they were having sex and she rubbed him more when they were done.

"Could you see yourself dating someone like me," Stacey asked as Adam gasped for air? His chest heaving up and down, Adam acted as if he didn't hear the question. Stacey repeated the question and Adam told her that she looked nice. "Why don't you and I start dating? We've known each other since you moved to Michigan, so what could be better. To be truthful, I could leave now, but I'd miss you too much. You're a great guy to talk with and you're smart. The sex is awesome and the climaxes are sensational. Distance would be our only challenge, but we've got to trust each other," she said sincerely. Adam cleared his throat and told Stacey that he would think about it.

Depending on who awoke first, Stacey and Adam had sex several times in the morning hours. He may have gotten out of bed at 2am to use the bathroom, but if it awakened her, they would have sex. This joining together occurred several times that night. When Stacey awakened that morning, her vagina was sore from all of the friction. Stacey shook Adam until he awakened and began to get dressed. Sleepily, Stacey put her clothes on and went into the living room. Adam joined her and they left for her apartment. The trip was as simple as overnight delivery. Adam drove her to the front entrance, gave her a hug and kiss on the cheek, and hurried back to Ann Arbor.

On this cold morning, the sun was up and the wind was blowing. Adam pulled his truck into the garage and went into the house. He tidied up as he walked throughout the house, before getting into the shower. Adam took a long shower, and when he was done, he began changing the sheets. Sprinkling powder on the mattress, Adam changed the linen and vacuumed the floors. It took long for Adam to complete this task as he listened to the sports highlights. After drinking two glasses of milk, Adam went into the bedroom and got into bed. "Let me set this television timer," Adam whispered as he glanced at the T.V. screen. He watched television for twenty minutes and fell asleep.

Adam was later awakened by Kelly, whom was calling because she wanted to come and visit him. Adam told her that this was a bad time and that he would call her back. Kelly accepted the answer, but she was curious. She wondered if Adam was busy sleeping with someone else. As thoughts ran through her mind, Kelly became upset.

Kelly's imagination was getting the best of her and she didn't realize it. 'I know he's not sleeping with someone else. That thing he has belongs to me. Maybe I should take a drive over to the dormitory,' she thought. Kelly then remembered that she and Adam weren't going together. "I need to stop tripping, because I don't know what he's up to. Knowing Adam, he's probably studying or giving someone tutoring time," Kelly said as she stared at her reflection in the mirror.

Adam awakened at 8:30pm after having a full day of rest. Twenty minutes went by before he turned on the television. 'I got to slow things down a little. It feels like I've been having sex a lot since I moved away from Chicago. Thank God that my grade point average is high, and getting higher. Although I'm getting a lot of sex, I don't believe that I need this much. I've got to reaffirm my goals before I sleep with half the school. On top of all of that, I've got Kelly and Stacey asking me to date them. They're both attractive in their own way, but I don't want to date them," Adam thought as he scanned through the channels. Scaring him, the cell phone began ringing. Instead of answering the call, Adam tossed the phone onto the night stand. "I'm going back to sleep," Adam said as he laid the remote down and pulled the sheets over his head.

When Adam awakened that next morning, he arrived at the library earlier than usual. By the time he finished a cup of cocoa, the librarian was opening the front door. As usual, Adam remained in the library until his class began. He studied all of his up coming material and took short breaks. During the lunch break, Adam dined with some faculty members. Hours after the lunch, Adam returned to the school and continued studying. The class started at 7pm and Adam was eager to get it over with. He gathered all of his belongings and hurried to class. As he was setting down, Tina crept into the room and sat next to Adam. "Hi," she said cheerfully. Surprised, Adam nodded his head and smiled as he removed the text book from his bag.

Throughout the class period, Tina wrote notes pertaining to the lecture, and some containing sexual messages. Mr. Dillon's lecture was more interesting than last week's discussion. Toward the end of the class, Mr. Dillon had everyone to remove all supplies from their desk. "Once everyone is settled, I will pass out today's quiz. If you guys read the chapter, then there shouldn't be any problems answering the question," Mr. Dillon said as he stood before the class. "I didn't read the entire chapter," Tina whispered to Adam.

Not much of a talker in class, Adam ignored Tina. Responding to her statements with a smirk or a smile, he shook his head. 'I hope she doesn't ask me for any answers,' Adam thought as he stared at the chalkboard. "Can we get together after class? We don't have to do anything, just have a drink or something," Tina asked as Mr. Dillon passed out the quiz. Adam did not answer her question.

Adam finished the quiz before Tina. "Meet me in the library when you're done," he whispered to Tina, who had three essay questions to complete. The library was filled with students. Everyone was working on a project that was probably due before winter break. Recognizing some familiar faces, Adam took a seat at a table that was being shared by four young ladies. Two of the girls lived on campus and two were commuters. "Do you mind if I sit here for a while," he asked with a smile? Eager for a guy to sit with them, they all invited Adam to have a seat. Once he sat down, each girl flirted with him in her own way. They told him that he was cute, muscular, smelled good, along with a host of other compliments. Although he enjoyed the compliments, Adam saw Tina coming through the door and he left the table. "Excuse me, but I'm meeting someone from my group here in the library. I hope that we can get together again," Adam said as he pushed his chair underneath the table. As he was walking by, a hand grabbed the sleeve of his jacket. Heather, who didn't live on campus, placed her phone number in his hand and said, "Call me when you get a chance." Adam smiled as the three girls teased Heather.

Heather was a short haired brunet who commuted to the campus from Livonia. It had been mentioned that a girl named Heather paid to live on campus. When her classes were overwhelming, she would often pay–by–the–day to sleep in one of the vacant rooms. However, when there were no vacant rooms, she would pay someone to let her spend the night in their room. What Adam admired most about Heather was that she was attractive, had a gorgeous tan, and a pretty smile.

Adam met Tina at the door before she could come into the library. "Let's take a ride to McDonald's," Adam said as he approached Tina. She quickly followed him, trying to keep up. "Can you slow down so that I can walk with you," Tina shouted as Adam walked ahead of her? "I'm sorry for leaving you, but my thoughts are racing. I have my mind on a Big Mac and a vanilla shake," he said with a smile. As they approached the building exit, Tina placed her hand inside of Adams.'

'Where is she going with this,' he thought as they walked across the parking lot? "What am I thinking about," Adam asked himself in disbelief? "Where are you parked," Adam asked as he glanced at her? Tina lead Adam toward the other side of the parking lot where she hoped to find her car parked. "I thought you knew where you were leading me," she asked sarcastically. Adam grinned as he kept walking along the side of her. "I'm not leading you. You're suppose to be leading me," Adam replied.

"Why doesn't a nice looking guy like you have a girl friend? Are you saving yourself for the right woman? If you are, then I'm the one. Don't give me an answer now, but once my boyfriend and I are through, I would like to get with you. The sex was great, and I've been thinking about it in detail," Tina said as she dipped her french fries in ketchup. "I like the way your small frame felt when you were in my arms. Maybe we'll do it again in the near future. Unless, you decide to save your relationship and turn me down," Adam said coyly as he drank his milk shake.

Tina took a bite of her sandwich and replied, "There's nothing to save, because I'm not dumb. I've got to build a future for myself. I'm nearly thirty years old and I can't afford to waste time. You're younger than I am, but there is something about you that I like. Oh, in case you were wondering, this is not the 'dick' talking. If Demi Moore can have a young man, then so can I. All you have to do is keep doing what you do," she said in a sassy tone. Adam laughed as he wiped his hands and gathered his trash. "Well, I'm ready to get back to the dorms if you're done," Adam said as he placed his sweatshirt hood over his head. Tina finished her fries and rose with Adam.

Once they were inside of her car, Tina leaned toward Adam and gave him a kiss. Adam wasn't expecting the kiss, so he was hesitant to reciprocate. After a few moments, Adam quickened the kiss and pulled away. Mesmerized, Tina stared at Adam as if he had given her the best kiss that she had ever had. Starting the engine and putting the car into gear, Tina placed her hand on Adam's thigh as she drove away. Adam made the best of the trip as she rubbed his inner thigh and his crotch.

Wanting to tease her, Adam unfolded his trouser snake from within his boxers and let it hang out. Tina took it in her hand and jerked on it like a stick shift. Rubbing gently, she made circular strokes around the head. Adam's moans grew louder, as he knew that it turned her on. "Go ahead and shoot your stuff on my dash board," Tina said aggressively as she kept pulling it. Suddenly, Adam opened his eyes and they were seconds away from the dormitory. He pushed her hand away and said, "We'll finish this later, because I'm about to get out of the car." Tina was so excited that she didn't want him to leave. "Can I come in for a few minutes? We can finish what we started," Tina said as if she was pleading with him. Adam told her to give him a call, as he got out of the car.

Tina watched Adam as he walked up the snow-covered side walk. "Damn, I like that brother," she whispered to herself. Placing her hand between her legs, Tina quickly rubbed her crotch and said, "Ooh, you make me hot." Once he was out of sight, Tina drove away from the dormitory facility. 'Should I keep messing around with Terence or should I just call everything off? Terence doesn't want a woman making more money than he does, and he's got other outside women. I must be crazy to keep hanging onto him. He's fathered two babies since we've been together, and he's been arrested twice for probation violation. How much more am I willing to put up with, because I don't see a future in this? Adam may be young, but he's ambitious and I can work with that. The sex is much better than you-know-who's. I'm going to get closer and find out what he's really into,' Tina thought as she raced toward the expressway.

Adam, who minutes later, went to his room and found a short note stuck on his door. Kelly had left a note asking Adam to call her. He went into the room, tossed his jacket onto the chair and leaped onto the bed. Before he could turn on the television, there was a knock at the door. Although he didn't want to be bothered, Adam made his way to the door. "It's your favorite friend," Kelly shouted. Adam opened the door and she looked at him with her hazel eyes. "Can I please spend the night, because I have an early class? I want to spend the night because it's going to take a while for me to get home. Also, the weather man said that we should expect more snow flurries," Kelly said as she spoke continuously.

"Come on in," Adam said as he stretched forth his hand to greet her. "Thank you so much, Adam," Kelly said cheerfully as she kissed him on the cheek. Adam smacked her butt cheeks as she entered the room. "Why did you smack my behind," she asked cheerfully? "Because you kissed my cheek," Adam said arrogantly as he leaped onto the bed. "Get comfortable and watch a movie with me. Press the start button on the microwave and we can share some pop corn," he said.

Happy to be in his presence, Kelly would have stood on her head to make Adam happy. While the popcorn popped, Kelly removed her clothes. Standing before Adam dressed in a white bra and matching thong, Kelly tossed her clothes onto the chair and took the pop corn from the microwave. "Can you pass me one of those miniature orange juice bottles from the shelf," Adam asked as the movie critics began? Kelly took two juices from the shelf and climbed onto the bed. "Are you going to sleep in your sweat pants," she asked? Smiling, Adam began removing his pants and underwear. Kelly took a glance at Adam's slightly erect penis and asked, "Did I choose the wrong time to spend the night with you?" Adam grinned and took the popcorn from Kelly's hand. "Don't let this monster frighten you," he said.

Teased by the sight of his nude body, Kelly leaned forward to take something from the television stand. Leaning forward gave Adam a clear view of her butt, with the thin string poised between the crack of her cheeks. Stretching forth his arm, Adam gently caressed Kelly's baby soft rear end. Wanting to be touched by Adam, Kelly enjoyed every touch and squeeze. "Can't you behave yourself," she asked playfully? As he continued rubbing her backside, Adam replied, "I only wanted to touch something warm and soft." Remaining on all fours, Kelly made her butt cheek's clap as he stared at her. Kelly then laid down next to Adam, as she paid more attention to his erect penis than she did the movie.

The time on the clock was 10:46pm, and it was nearing Kelly's bedtime. She ran her hand across Adam's masculine chest and asked, "Can I get a taste before I go to sleep?" While Kelly removed her thong and bra, Adam turned off the television, put on a condom, and reached for Kelly. Once his hand touched her warm body, Adam rolled on top of her and she put his penis into her womb. Adam wasn't in the mood for sex, so he gave her a combination of slow strokes. Kelly grabbed Adam's butt and forced him to give her more. "Come on, Adam, and give it to me," Kelly cried as she ran her hand across his back.

One-by-one, Adam began applying harder thrust. With her legs wrapped around his waist, Kelly humped her body against his. She wanted to receive the full capacity of each stroke. They continued for a half-an-hour, before Kelly climaxed. Digging her nails into his shoulders, Kelly placed her mouth into the pillow and began screaming. "I'm about to come," Adam said as he thrust into her wet hole. "Come on, Adam," Kelly said as she writhed wildly beneath him. Pushing his wang as far as it would go, Adam released his load. Into the condom. As he remained on top of her, she ran her fingers across his sweaty back as they both sighed softly. "I don't want you to stop, but I've got to get some sleep. If you get up before I do, then it would be nice for you to wake me up with something special." Adam didn't say a word as he kept grinding his limp penis into her. Kelly was so wet that Adam had to force himself to get off of her. "Let's get some sleep and we'll see what happens in the morning."

The next morning, Adam and Kelly awakened at the same time. "I can't believe it's morning," Kelly said as she climbed on top of Adam. Straddling his waist, Kelly worked his penis into her hole. As he laid still, she began riding him like a wild woman. Wanting to get all of Adam inside of her, Kelly bounced hard on his rigid tool. Adam squeezed her breast as she kept riding. Within minutes, Kelly arched her back and released her load. Moaning and sighing, Kelly kept riding as she tried to bring Adam to a climax. Adam didn't have to climax, but he enjoyed her warm body so much that he didn't say anything as he continued applying long strokes.

Kelly climbed off of Adam and said, "Good morning, my chocolate baby." Adam said 'good morning,' and turned to his side as he watched Kelly get dressed. "So, what's up for you," Adam asked as she yawned. While washing her crotch, Kelly said, "I've got to meet my group in the library and then I've got to take a quiz in Biology class." Adam watched the clock as Kelly hurried to get dressed. She put her jacket on, grabbed her book bag and kissed

Adam goodbye. "I'll call you later this week," Kelly said as she left the room. Sighing deeply, Adam put the sheet over his head and went to sleep.

CHAPTER

TWENTY-NINE

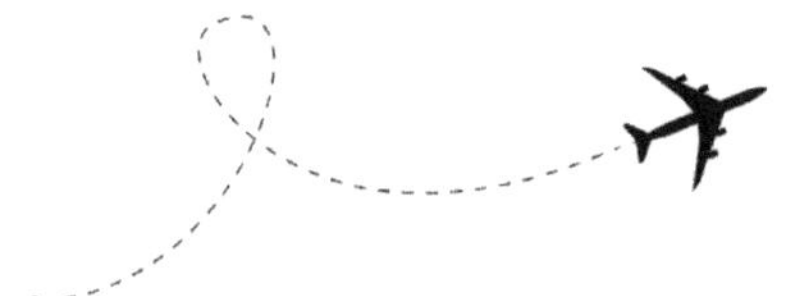

The remainder of Adam's two years were not as academically challenging as the first two years. He managed to stay on top of his studies, while his relationship with various girls changed. Many of the girls wanted more than he could offer. After spending time with Adam, they wanted relationships, and commitments from him. Aside from the sex escapades, Adam managed to maintain his single status and complete the requirements for graduation. The closer he got to graduation, the more girls came to him with lustrous offers. Some wanted to buy his affection, while others tried to capture him with their charm.

Kelly was still coming around, but more than before. As the relationship with her boyfriend went through its trials, she managed to cry on Adam's broad shoulders. Adam had considered ending their sex relationship, but Kelly turned out to be one of the best at what she did. From season to season, she and Adam managed to work up a sweat. However, having an idea of what Adam was to become, Kelly was hoping to go along for the ride. He's on his way to grad. school while Kelly is settling with a degree in nursing. The nursing profession wasn't a bad idea for Kelly, but she knew that the career differences between her and Adam would clash.

Only two months away from graduation, Adam received an intern position at the university hospital. He was to work alongside one of the top female gynecologist. If it wasn't for the help of his old instructor, Mr. Dillon, the position wouldn't have been attained. Mr. Dillon had spoken to Adam on several occasions about getting him inside the hospital doors, and after a lot of consideration, Dr. Sharon Sullivan accepted his intern proposal.

Dr. Sullivan wanted Adam to begin his internship two weeks before the fall semester was to begin. Once he received the news, Adam danced around his dorm room like a little child. "Thank you, Lord, for letting me get accepted into the intern program," Adam shouted as he raised his head toward heaven. Excited, Adam decided to wait until after graduation to tell everyone the good news. Although the desire to tell someone was eating away at him, he swore not to mention it, because it would be the highlight of his graduation celebration. He was aware that Lisa would want to know, but then she would probably tell everyone else and spoil the surprise.

Dressed in a pair of gray slacks, dark shirt, and dress shoes, Adam went to the university hospital to meet Dr. Sullivan. Part of Dr. Sullivan's requirement was for Adam to meet with her immediately after receiving his letter of acceptance into the intern program. Confidently, Adam sat outside of Dr. Sullivan's office as he waited to be seen. "Dr. Sullivan will be with you shortly," the receptionist said as she reached for the telephone receiver. 'I hope Dr. Sullivan is as nice as Mr. Dillon said she was,' Adam thought as he fingered through the office collection of medical journals.

"Dr. Sullivan will see you now," the receptionist remarked as she held the door for him. Adam stood up, took his briefcase from the chair and followed the receptionist to Dr. Sullivan's office. "Is the office always this quiet," Adam asked as he looked at the paintings that lined the corridor? "Dr. Sullivan is usually out of the office on Wednesday's, but she made an exception today," the receptionist said as she let the door close behind them. "By the way, what is your name," Adam asked as he stepped into the office. "My name is Joan," she replied with a smile before closing the door behind her.

"Please, take a seat, Adam," a soft voice called out. As he approached the chair to sit down, Dr. Sullivan slowly turned away from the window and placed her cell phone on the desk. Extending her hand, she said, "I'm pleased to finally meet you, Adam Harris." Your name is going to sound good going across the P.A. system at the hospital. "Dr. Harris, you're needed in the emergency room," Dr. Sullivan teased as she shook his hand. Surprised by her beauty, he and Dr. Sullivan made eye contact. "Make yourself comfortable, Adam, so we can get more familiar with one another. Please excuse my desk, but as you can see, I've got a lot going on," the doctor said as she reclined in her desk chair.

Adam talked with Dr. Sullivan for an hour-and-a-half, before leaving her office. The doctor explained what she expected from an intern, while Adam discussed what he was hoping to attain. Based on this first meeting, both of them was sure that they were going to have a successful partnership. It would be months before he could begin his practice, but Adam remained eager to start. "If you change your mind and decide to let me begin before the beginning of the semester, then please give me a call," Adam said as he stood at the exit door shaking Dr. Sullivan's hand. Finding Adam attractive, the doctor stared intensely at him while he said his final words. "If you have any questions about anything, feel free to call my office and leave a message. I'm usually busy, but I will take the time to return your call," the doctor said as she closed the door behind him.

Excitedly, Adam ran to his car, as he felt the desire to celebrate. 'This semester is practically over and I've got a position at the hospital. Dr. Sullivan isn't bad looking for a woman in her 40's. Although, Mr. Dillon didn't tell me that she was tall. I envisioned a short woman with a snobbish attitude. However, if things were different between us, I could see myself wrapped in her long arms and being caressed by her long fingers. I think we're going to make a perfect team, once I start working with her. What she should do is consider letting me share her office space, because I like the way she has it decorated,' Adam thought at he drove to the dormitory.

Suddenly, he noticed a car that he hadn't seen in over a year. The car belonged to Tina, and once he saw the license plates, Adam was positive that it was she who was waiting outside for him. He parked several rows behind her, and watched as Tina held her cell phone to her ear. "This is the end of the school semester and these women are still sweating me," Adam said as he peered through her back window. Taking in a deep breath, Adam got out of the car and approached Tina's car, walking slowly. "Maybe I can walk past her without being noticed," Adam said as he drew closer to her car.

As Adam attempted to walk past the car, Tina noticed him and called out. "Adam! I've been waiting for you to arrive." "Let me call you later, she said before ending the call. "Come here and give me a hug or something. How have you been doing, and what have you been doing?

The last time we saw each other was great, because we had so much fun. Are you ready for graduation," Tina asked as she got out of the car and embraced Adam in the parking lot?

Adam returned the embrace, as he held her tightly. "Damn, you feel good in my arms," he said with a devilish grin. "It has been a long time since we've seen each other, but it is a pleasant surprise. What are you about to get into," Adam asked as he looked Tina up and down? Closing her car door, Tina asked, "Is there some place where we can go and talk, or are you busy?"

Adam took Tina by the hand and they walked to the school cafeteria. "How are your classes going, because you became a mystery to everyone in our class? We thought you dropped the class or maybe even dropped out of school," Adam said as they walked down the corridor toward the cafeteria. Tina didn't know exactly what to say, so she held her head down and mumbled something indistinctly. "What did you just say," Adam asked as he looked down at her? Tina raised her head to look at Adam and said,

"Things happen, and that's the best way that I can explain it."

When they arrived at the cafeteria, dorm students and faculty members had occupied every table and chair in the room. "Do you want anything to eat or drink," he asked? Tina took an apple and an orange from the counter and said, "This will be enough for me." Adam ordered his meal and he and Tina left for his dorm room. "I'm so hungry that I can eat everything on this tray and you too," Adam said as he stopped to take a glance at Tina's behind. Tossing her orange into the air and catching it, Tina replied, "I didn't know that you believed in going down on a girl." Adam smiled and didn't say anything as they approached the elevator.

Once they were on the elevator, Adam remarked, "I've tried it, but it's not something that I would like to make a habit of doing." Tina grinned and said, "Maybe I can help you change your mind. If you want to make my kitty-cat purr, then it's okay with me. I've only had it done once or twice, but I do remember how good it felt." As they stepped off of the elevator, Adam contemplated whether or not he should take her up on the potential offer that presented itself. Although, when they arrived at his room, the mood changed as he was surprised to find an envelope taped to his door. Balancing the food tray, Adam used his free hand to remove the envelope. "It must be from the other girl that you've been sleeping with," Tina said sarcastically.

When they entered the room, Adam sat the

tray down and kicked off his shoes. Tina walked past Adam with an attitude and dropped down on the sofa. Suspiciously, Adam looked at Tina and wondered what was wrong. "Ah, is there a problem that you would like discuss? You're acting as if you have an attitude. I hope that seeing this card isn't going to bring the beast out in you," Adam said as he picked up his tray and sat down. Angrily, Tina said, "It bothers me to think about you being with someone else. We haven't seen each other in a long time, but I wasn't expecting to see you on these terms. What you should do is tell the other girl that you can't see her anymore." Grinning, Adam thought, 'This woman must be out of her mind.'

"I passed all of my online classes, and I'm about to graduate. If you're interested in me, then we can start things off right. However, if you're not ready to be with me, then just say so and I'll understand," Tina said as she sat with her arms folded. Adam never took his eyes from the television as he felt the hostile vibes coming from Tina. "Well, don't you have anything to say or were you ignoring me, Adam," she asked?

Adam wiped his mouth with his napkin and said, "You must have me mixed up with someone else. This is our first time seeing each other in a long time, and I can't believe that you have the nerve to come in here demanding anything. I've been getting with different girls since I came to this university and I'm not about to stop. Yes, I know who sent me this card and I don't think it should matter to you, because she was here before you were. Now, if you don't like the way I'm living, then you can leave and not come back. There is always someone waiting in the wings. To be honest, I've been with more girls on this campus than you can imagine, so what's your point," Adam said as he stared intensely at Tina with a smirk on his face.

Tina unfolded her arms and said, "I don't believe that you have the nerve to sit here and tell me some crazy nonsense like this. The only reason why I got with you is because I was lonely and needed some sex. As far as I'm concerned, you can keep on doing it with these young, silly females, because I'm not pressed for you." Adam laughed and asked, "Then why were you waiting for me outside? Are you going to tell me that after all of this time, you've just become lonely? Maybe you're going to say that you felt guilty for leaving me here without anyone to sleep with."

Tina didn't know what else to say as she sat next to him picking at her fingernails. She was stunned by the way he spoke to her, and she just couldn't believe that it was happening. Tina then stared at the television screen as she tried to think of some way to get back at him. "Why don't you leave, Tina, because I've got to call and check on my son," Adam said as he walked the tray over to his desk and sat it down? Tina sat with a surprised look on her face. "I can't believe that this guy had a child while I was away," she whispered to herself. "I didn't know that you had a son, Adam. Why didn't you tell me you had a son, or was it a secret? If I knew that you had a son, then maybe I would have stayed away," Tina said harshly.

Adam leaped onto the bed and said, "It doesn't matter, Tina. You just revealed to me that you have a problem with me having friends and I can't deal with that. I'm about to graduate shortly, and I'm ready to cut-loose all of my ties to this undergrad status. That includes the classes, the professors and the girls. I've gotten enough sex in four years to last me a year. In regards to my son, he will be three years old this summer and I'm not concerned about how anyone feels about it. You or no one else can stop me from being me, and that is a father with plenty of outside companionship."

Tina grinned and shook her head as she leaned forward and placed her forehead in the palms of her hands. "I can't believe this mess. Would it make a difference if I told you that I quit my boyfriend just to be with you," she asked as a tear ran down her cheek? Adam shook his head as he scanned the cable channels. "We haven't seen each other in a long time, and I don't want to believe that you actually thought that I was waiting for you. The way I see it, you should have stayed in touch with me and I could have persuaded you to stay with your man. I have a relationship with my son's mother and no one can compete with that. She's a good mother and one day we're going to be together like parents should be.

Don't think for a second that I'm trying to hurt you by telling you this, but I'm a man and I want to be honest. This card, nor the person who sent this card, should be an issue to you. There is a 100% chance that I won't open the card because I get them all of the time. I know what these cards say before I break the seal. If you came here to get laid, then you should have left your attitude outside of my door," Adam said as he glanced at Tina sitting with her head down.

Tina lifted her head and grinned. "You certainly know how to drive a woman crazy," she said while getting up from the sofa to remove her shirt. Adam watched as Tina peeled off her clothes. "I'm sorry for the way I've acted, but I didn't wait for you this long just to leave here without getting what I came for. Will you make love to me, or are you too upset to get-it-up," Tina asked as she tossed her panties at him? Dodging the panties, Adam paused for a moment and with a straight face, he climbed off of the bed and removed his clothes. Before he could place his condom on, Tina dropped to her knee's and placed his long penis into her warm mouth.

Slowly, she sucked the head as Adam stood with his eyes closed. He placed his hand on her head to help control the rhythm. Occasionally, Tina would glance up at Adam, because the look on his face made her love hole creamy. "I love the way you look when I'm sucking this monster," Tina said as she ran her tongue along his chocolate shaft. After minutes of sucking, Adam said, "Get on your knee's and give it to me like the freak that you are." Tina stood up and replied, "It's about time you realized that I was a freak."

While Tina knelt before Adam, he worked to put his condom on. "Your masculine body makes me so hot," Tina said as she ran her fingers across her swollen labia. Adam made sure the condom was secured before he stood behind her and placed the head of his penis at Tina's vaginal opening. "You're gonna have to work it in, because it's been a while since I've had sex," Tina said as she raised her rear end higher. Adam began to stab her hole with the head of his prick until she let him in. "Oh, give it to me, Adam," Tina cried as he stretched her gaping hole.

Five minutes into their session, Tina bounced her behind on his prick like there was no tomorrow. "Give me all of that good stuff," Tina repeated as Adam hit her hot spot. Adam closed his eyes and placed his hand on her butt as Tina gave him all that she had to give. "Keep giving it to me until you come," he said as Tina increased her pace. "Oh, you're so big that I don't want to come. It feels so good," Tina cried as she tried to refrain from climaxing.

As her paced increased, Adam began thrusting his penis deep inside of Tina. "You old women like passionate sex, just like the young women," Adam said as he thrust into her with everything he had to give. Suddenly, Adam whispered, "I'm about to come," as Tina banged her booty against his pelvis. "Come with me, Adam," she cried as they came together. Adam kept stroking as his spunk filled the condom.

Afterwards, Tina laid in Adam's arms as they caught their breath. "Did you mean everything you said about having a son, Adam," Tina asked as she ran her finger across his nipples? "I meant every word,"

Adam said as he increased the television volume. "I still have a relationship with my son's mother and we hope to be together some day. Although, I still have a few girls that I get with regularly. After all, I'm young and I want to get some of this freaking out of the way before I totally commit myself to anyone." Tina sat quietly as she tried to absorb some of what Adam was telling her. "I quit my boyfriend last week and I was hoping that you were available for a relationship," Tina said as she took Adam's limp penis in her hand. Adam took a deep breath and said, "I didn't mean for you to see this card taped to my door, but I wasn't expecting to see it either. I get them so regularly that I stopped opening them. Many of these girls only get with me because they believe that I'm going to rescue them from the mess that their living in," Adam said as he pulled Tina close to him. "Is one of these girls the mother of your child," she asked in a curious tone? Adam shook his head and said, "My son lives with his mom, and she doesn't live in Michigan."

Quickly, he saw this as an opportunity to express that his son lived out of state, and that there was nothing that Tina needed to fear about them being together. Tina then sat up and straddled Adam. "If she's not here, then we're free to have fun, fun, fun, and more fun," she said jokingly. Adam nodded his head as he fondled her breast with one hand and squeezed her butt cheek with the other. "That's right, so put this monster back inside and let's get to it," Adam said as she hovered over him. In an instant, Adam's penis was buried inside of Tina as their sweaty aroma filled the room.

After their session, both Adam and Tina took short naps before she was to leave for the night. "Will I see you again? If you're going to say no, then don't say anything," Tina remarked as she put on her panties. Adam took her advice and didn't say a word. However, Tina got the hint, and instead of nagging him, she continued getting dressed. "Do you mind if I call you sometime, just to see how you're doing," Tina asked as she stood before Adam dressed in her panties and bra?

Adam couldn't resist the sight of her, so he got out of bed and took Tina in his arm. He held her close as his erect penis poked her in the stomach. "You should get that thing out of the way before I get the wrong idea and make you regret standing here," she said with a sinister grin. Adam began kissing her passionately, as Tina wrapped her arms around him. I want you to come and see me after graduation, Adam whispered as he placed his tongue in her ear. Softly, she sighed while enjoying the penetration.

Lifting Tina off of her feet, Adam laid her on the bed and quickly removed her panties. Wet from the last session, he slid his penis into her without a condom. Amazed at how good his flesh felt inside of her, Tina put her legs around his waist and pulled Adam close to her. "Freak me like you mean it," she said as he began applying quick thrust to her heated womb. Once they came, Adam's body fell on top of Tina's and they held each other.

While running his tongue along her neck, Tina

moaned as she ran her fingers along his sweaty back. After a few minutes had passed, Tina said, "Let me up, Adam, because it's getting late and I'm getting lazy. Besides, I've got to be at work early tomorrow." Adam got up off of Tina and she made her way to the sink to wash away the secreted juices shared between her and Adam. Although Adam was only making conversation with Tina, he wasn't sure if he actually wanted her to come around after graduation. The sex with her was pleasurable, but the time away had killed his true desire for her.

Tina stood at the foot of the bed and watched as Adam laid naked before her. Seeing him lying there like that made it even more difficult for her to leave. Tina desperately wanted to stay the night, but she didn't have a clue as to how that was going to be possible. At this point, she was more surprised that a young man like Adam had turned her out. 'I wish that I could put this man in my purse and take him everywhere with me,' Tina thought as she cleared her throat. "Aren't you going to walk me to my car," Tina asked as she never took her eyes off of Adam's limp third leg?

"You're an attractive man," she whispered to herself. Adam got out of bed and slipped on a pair of track pants and house slippers. "Have you passed out your graduation invitations," Adam asked as he put on his tee-shirt? Tina paused as she watched him put the tee-shirt on. "Ah, I've started inviting a few people, but I'm going to need some more invitations. Have you started sending out your invitations," Tina asked as she stood patiently at the door? Adam never gave her an answer as he searched for his keys.

Tina did her best to stay calm as she witnessed several girls trying to get Adam's attention as they walked to her car. "Hey Adam, when you get the time, why don't you come over and play a few hands," a female voice called out as he and Tina made their way upstairs. "Do your fans ever go to sleep, or do they sit outside of your door all night? My emotions must be getting the best of me, because I can't take all of the attention that you're getting. We don't have any papers on each other, but it's during times like this that I wish we did," Tina remarked as they made their way to the front entrance.

Puzzled by her last statement, Adam asked, "Why do you think that things would be different if you had papers on me? I'm my own man and I need a woman with a high self-esteem in my life. There is no need to be jealous, because I'm going to do what I do, and you're going to do what you do. Hell, if we were married, you'd probably hate me because I refuse to ask my wife permission to do simple things like playing cards," Adam said as they walked toward the parking lot.

'This guy has been speaking his mind all afternoon,' Tina thought as she listened to Adam's remarks. "I'll be around to see you after graduation, Adam, and I hope that things will be different. Tell your women that when they see my car parked in the parking structure. that I'm here and I want all of your attention. If you have a problem telling them what's up between you and me, then I can help get the point across," she said. Adam found Tina's remarks humorous, and he began laughing hysterically. "You need to slow down, because all we have is a sexual fling taking place. You're free to be with whomever you want to be with and I'm free to do the same. If anyone asks, just tell them that we are friends or study partners, because you don't control this 'monster.' I don't have any rings on my fingers or in my nose, so that means that I can come and go as I please," Adam said as they approached her car.

Tina searched for her keys, and while Adam stood next to her, she asked, "Am I being too pushy, or do I just make you nervous?" Adam scratched his head and said, "Just be who you are, because I'm not moved by anything you say or do. You try to be pushy and jealous, but if that's your nature, then I'll have to learn how to relate to you. However, you need to realize that we have a sex thing and that tripping about who has interest in me doesn't bring us any closer to each other. I'm on my way to grad. school and I'm not concerned about who's interested in me, nor why they're interested. Once I get my classes to flowing, it will be an up hill climb from there." Tina found her keys and Adam took them out of her hand.

Stepping aside, Tina moved out of the way as Adam unlocked the door and opened it for her. Tina smiled and before getting into the car, she placed her hand behind Adam's head and gave him a long, passionate kiss. "When I'm around you, I don't want to leave your presence," Tina whispered as she looked into his eyes. Jokingly, Adam said, "You wouldn't know what to do if you had me all to yourself. You'd probably try to talk me into getting you pregnant so that I can hang around all of the time." Tina grinned as she got into the car. "Why don't you let me have you for a while and you can see for yourself exactly what I would do with you," Tina remarked as she closed her door? Walking away, Adam jokingly said, "You'd probably hurt a young guy like myself." Adam then turned and slowly walked backwards as he watched Tina drive out of the parking lot and onto the street. Just as he turned around and walked toward the front entrance, the girl whom had called out to Adam was waiting for him on the stairs.

As he approached the dormitory, Adam wondered what this girl was waiting for. The girl is a sophomore named Jennifer Conner, and her dad was the CEO of a multi-million dollar Forbes' 500 company. Because Jennifer was deaf in one ear, she majored in sign language and had plans of becoming a teacher. Jennifer was attractive to say the least, but Adam was leery about getting with her. He didn't think she was beneath him because of her disability, but he was skeptical as to how she would react if he put the 'depth' on her. Many of her female and male associates said that she was interested in black guys, but Adam had never seen her connected with anyone. However, something inside of him was saying that tonight was his night to find out what she was really about.

"Didn't you just invite me to play a few hands of cards," Adam asked as he stood on the landing? Sitting with her arms crossed, as if she was cool, Jennifer said, "I changed my mind about playing cards. I'm feeling home sick, and I'm ready for this semester to end. Was that your girlfriend that I saw you walking with?" With both hands in his pockets, Adam shook his head as he glanced toward the sky. "Why don't you sit down and talk to me for a while," Jennifer said as she looked up at Adam?

Dressed in a hooded sweater, Adam put the hood over his head and sat next to Jennifer. Clearing her throat, Jennifer asked, "So, how are your classes going?" Adam hunched his shoulders and said, "Senior Seminar is the only class that I have, and it meets twice a week, so things are going okay." Jennifer turned her cell phone off and said, "The rumor is that you're one of the brightest guys on campus. How does it feel to be one of the schools top tutors?" "It's okay, I guess. Although, I'm glad that my tutoring sessions have come to an end, because I need the break," he said.

After talking for thirty minutes, Jennifer asked if he'd mind setting inside out of the cool spring air. Adam agreed, and once they were inside, Jennifer suggested that they go to his dorm room and hang out for an hour-or-so. They then walked to his room, where she went inside and took a seat on the Futon sofa. "I really like your room. Is your bed always unmade," she asked jokingly? Adam laughed and replied, "I make it up in the mornings, but today was one of my lazy days." He was trying to conceal the fact that he and Tina had just gotten out of bed. "There's a rumor around the dormitory that you have slept with several girls on campus. But, what I want to know is why you've never given me a chance to sleep with you," Jennifer asked curiously?

Adam grinned as he tried to ignore the question. After a few minutes of silence, he said, "I didn't know that you were interested in sleeping with me. If I had known, then maybe we could have gotten together on a few occasions. However, the rumor is that you come from a wealthy background, so I assumed that a girl like you wouldn't be interested in a guy like me." Trying to entice him, Jennifer asked, "Is it too late for you and I to get together, or would you rather sit here and talk?" Adam removed his shirt and said, "It's not too late, but I have to warn you that I'm not responsible for how things may turn out between us." "I'll take my chances," Jennifer said as she removed her shoes. While she began to remove her shorts and panties, Adam took off his track pants and tossed them to the floor. Naked underneath his track pants, Jennifer was shocked when she saw his enormous penis hanging.

"Boy, you have a nice, large penis." She then sat on the sofa as Adam stepped close to her. Jennifer took his penis and placed it in her mouth. Adam was overwhelmed at how well she gave a blow job. Her mouth was wet, and with each stroke he moaned softly. When she was done, Jennifer stood up and walked over to the bed and laid down.

Horny, she spread her firm thighs, giving him a clear view of what she had to offer. Adam took a condom from the desk drawer and opened it. Before he could put it on, Jennifer asked, "Is this going to hurt? I've never been with anyone as large as you."

Without saying a word, Adam climbed on top of Jennifer as she helped him find her wet opening. Once inside, Adam began stroking her as if he was stroking a virgin. "Jennifer, your hole is tight," Adam said as he worked his way inside.

Placing a pillow over her head, Adam thrust deep into Jennifer's womb as she screamed into the pillow. The wetter she became, the more strokes he began applying. Excited, Jennifer thrust her pelvis toward Adam to receive his long strokes. The sex lasted ten or twelve minutes before they came. Although, Adam noticed that Jennifer had come at least twice since they began. Arching his back, Adam came in the condom as his body collapsed on top of hers. Drenched in her juices, Adam gave her slow thrust as their sweat covered them.

Slowly writhing beneath him, Jennifer asked, "Can I spend the night here in your room? I want you to give me some more before I go to class tomorrow." "It's okay with me," Adam said as he increased the pace of his thrust. Inch-after-inch, Jennifer took all of Adam as the time crept by. It wasn't long before they realized that they had been having sex for over an hour. Tired and satisfied, Adam withdrew his pipe and they rested in each others arms.

Before drifting off to sleep, Adam had to agree that for a wealthy, deaf girl with a hearing aide, Jennifer gave a good performance. Several times during the morning hours, they found themselves enraptured in quickies that heightened the sexual experience. Jennifer couldn't seem to get enough, as she initiated the early morning sex. Once the sun rose, Adam received another blow job before diving into her guts and bringing her to another climax. Jennifer couldn't believe the experience as she wished that they could have gotten together months ago.

As her wake up time approached, Jennifer laid in Adam's arms as she was in no hurry to leave his room. "I think you'd better leave before you miss your morning class," Adam said as she ran her fingers along his thigh. As Jennifer savored the moment, she took a deep breath and got out of bed. By now, she was angry because she had to leave this stud and go to class. "If I wasn't having a final exam this morning, I would probably persuade you to stay in bed with me for the rest of the day," Jennifer said as she put her shoes on.

Adam yawned as he got out of bed to let Jennifer out of his room. Standing behind her as she stood at the door, Jennifer turned around and gave Adam a peck on the lips. "Thanks for a beautiful night! Maybe we can get together again before graduation," Jennifer said as she ran her fingers along his shaft. Adam didn't say a word as he opened the door and watched Jennifer's tanned body walk down the dimly lit corridor. Once she was off the unit, Adam shut the door and returned to bed.

CHAPTER

THIRTY

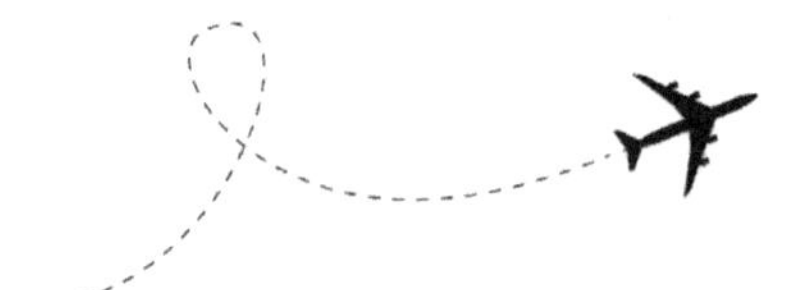

Two days away from graduation, and Adam was more excited than the weeks before. This was the day that he was to pick-up Lisa and Andre from the airport, and he was already running late. Kelly had come by the night before and she didn't leave until the day in-question. Adam quickly dressed and rushed off to the airport. Luckily, Lisa's plane was late, which gave him more time to get himself together mentally. He hadn't been with Lisa in a month, so Adam was cautious not to refer to her by another girls name while they were together. "Last night was a good night," Adam said to himself as he got out of his truck and approached to terminal entrance.

Fearing that he may have to wait, Adam was surprised when he saw Lisa standing at the terminal entrance with Andre in her arms. "Good morning, Lisa," Adam said as he gave her a kiss. Adam then took the sleeping Andre in his arm, while he carried Lisa's duffel bag on his shoulders. "How was your flight," Adam asked as Lisa walked close to him? "The flight was nice, but I hope the sex is even better, Lisa said as she pinched his butt cheek.

Adam grinned as he walked Lisa to the parking garage. He then placed Andre in his car seat while Lisa climbed into the passenger seat. While driving away from the terminal, Lisa put her hand on Adam's thigh to signal that she was ready to make love. "I can't wait to get you home, baby. It's been a month since you and I were together and I'm about to explode." Adam placed his hand on Lisa's thigh as waves of ecstacy passed through her body.

Lisa then unfastened her shorts and said, "Put your finger in me for a few minutes. I want you to feel what you're about to get into." Adam teased Lisa by refusing to put his finger in her hot hole. Attempting to entice him, Lisa put her hand inside her panties, and placed her index finger in her mouth as she rubbed her breast. "I'm going to make you want me so badly that you may have to pull off the road and suck my tit or something," she said.

When they made it to the condo, Adam quickly took Andre out of his car seat and followed Lisa into the house. While he put Andre in his crib, Lisa went into the bedroom and began undressing. Adam came into the room and she asked him not to say a word. "Just take your clothes off so you can satisfy my needs." Speechless, Adam took his clothes off and got in bed. With his penis as hard as a roll of quarters, Lisa took control of the situation. She prompted Adam to get into as many odd positions as possible, as she couldn't seem to get enough of him.

Suddenly, after an hour of hot sex, Andre started crying. Adam was about to come, when Lisa asked him to stop long enough for her to check on the baby. Lisa then left the room and returned with Andre in her arms. "Here's your daddy," she said while handing Andre to Adam. It was as if the sex went out the window as Adam put his attention into caring for Andre. The day seemed to pass by as Adam played with the baby and Lisa slept.

Once the baby drank a bottle of juice and went back to sleep, Adam awakened Lisa in a familiar manner. He thrust his penis into Lisa as she laid beside him with her legs spread. As the strokes got good to her, Lisa put her arms around Adam and urged him to keep stroking. "Oh baby, I've been waiting for this," Lisa whispered as she sucked his neck. After they came, Adam and Lisa went to sleep.

Adam was later awakened by the phone, but instead of answering it, he turned it off and pulled Lisa close to him. The feel of her warm body was all Adam needed to put him back to sleep. Unconsciously, Lisa pushed her buttocks against Adam and it was all she needed to do to get him aroused. As the morning sun beat through the blinds, they found themselves in a horizontal position. Highly aroused, Lisa screamed as if someone was hurting her. "Don't stop," she cried as Adam brought her to a climax.

Lisa thrust her pelvis upward as Adam gave slow thrust. "I can't wait for you to come home, baby," she whispered as he glided on her juices. Just as Adam was about to ejaculate, Lisa got up off of him and he shot his sperm on the sheets. Lisa rubbed her clit as she watched Adam's body tremble. "It blows your mind, baby. I can help you come like that, again," Lisa said as she ran her tongue along the head of his penis.

Sensitive to the touch, Adam's mind raced each time Lisa touched the tip of his head. Stop "Lisa," he said while pushing Lisa away. With his hand clasped over Lisa's hand, which was holding his sword of justice, they both shook his shaft vigorously. "Oh, that felt so good. I knew that you would give me what I've been missing. We'll have to do that again," Adam said as he pulled Lisa down onto his chest and gave her a wet kiss.

The next day, Adam enjoyed Lisa's presence as she assisted him in preparing for his big day. Like high school lovers, he and Lisa spent time walking through the shopping plaza, and taking in shows with Andre. The night before graduation day was just as wild as the first day that Lisa arrived to Michigan. They sent Andre to his grandparents and they had sex throughout the house. Hours went by before they finally called it quits.

With the bed drenched in bodily secretions, they laid still...too exhausted to change the sheets. "I meant what I said about you coming home to be with Andre and I, Adam. The more I see you, the more I want to see you. Coming home every other week is driving me crazy, because I hate to see you leave. Do you understand what I'm telling you," Lisa asked as she laid in his arm? Adam compassionately replied, "We'll be together once I get this business taken care of. I'm picking up information very quickly, and who is to say how long it will take me to pass the state medical exam. It's obvious that I'm on a roll, so just roll with me. The Lord is by my side and I can't lose." The next morning, Adam and Lisa rose early for a quick session. It seemed to have made their day go smoother, as things seemed to fall into place. They helped each other dress and found time to share a glass of orange juice and a bagel. "I don't want to stay for the entire program, so once I've taken my walk across the stage, watch for my cue. My parents will be waiting for you out front, so you'll need to look for them when we arrive. I'm going inside the auditorium, because we've got to line up. However, I will be looking for you amongst others," he said flirtatiously. Lisa then leaned toward Adam and placed a kiss on his lips.

When they arrived at the auditorium, they nervously made their way through the crowd. It was such a joyous occasion as friendly faces covered the grounds. Graduates took pictures while they waited for the ceremony to begin, and children played nearby. There were so many people attending the ceremony that Adam had a difficult time locating his family. Suddenly, he saw his father, and taking Lisa by the hand, they made their way toward him. "Dad," he called out as the casually dressed gentleman turned around. After a few embraces and some portraits, Adam left to join the graduating class. Honored as a valedictorian, Adam proudly sat on stage with the other graduates and faculty members.

Aside from the boring speakers, the event didn't last very long. Because of a misunderstanding in communication, Adam managed to stay for the entire ceremony. Anxious to leave, he found it difficult to get anyone's attention. Lisa had taught some of the students, which really helped to enhance her excitement. Although, she was more moved by the fact that she made a difference in their lives, and in Adam's life. Once the final speech was made, everyone threw their hats into the sky. Confetti filled the room as hoards of people shouted.

Quickly, Adam got out of his seat and rushed toward the exit. Hovering over others, Adam took pictures with some and gave out hugs. Always smiling, students and parents gravitated toward him. It was as if Adam was a walking magnet. It was while walking through the crowd that he and Tina spotted each other. The look on their face was very obvious. It was a look of secrecy and attraction.

"Congratulation," Adam said as he gave Tina a hug. Tina returned the hug and before she could speak, Lisa and Andre were standing next to Adam. Unashamed of who he was, Adam took Andre in his arms and introduced Tina and Lisa. "You have a handsome son, Adam. What's his name," Tina asked as she reached for Andre's hand? "His name is Andre. This is my little road dog," Adam said playfully. Unable to talk for long, Tina walked away and joined her family and friends.

After Adam gathered around for family photos', everyone joined together for a celebration dinner. There were eight in the party, so accommodations were made to seat everyone comfortably. Once everyone had eaten, Adam stood and said, "I would like to have everyone's attention. I just wanted to announce to you guys at this time that I've been accepted into an intern program. The program doesn't begin until August, but I've already met with the department head of gynecology."

Everyone applauded as they gave Adam a ton of praises. Lisa sat with her mouth hanging opened as she fed Andre his bottle. "Why didn't you tell me that you got accepted? You just wanted to keep this surprise to yourself until today. I'm so happy for you," Lisa said cheerfully, as she gave Adam a peck on the lips. At that moment, Adam's father approached him with his hand drawn. Giving Adam a firm handshake, his dad whispered, "I'm proud of you, Adam, so keep up the good work." Adam stood up, smiled and gave his father a big hug. "Thanks, dad. Hearing you say that means a lot to me."

Once his parents were back in their hotel room, and Adam and Lisa was home, he received a phone call. Adam answered the phone, only to find his brother on the opposite end. "Hey, Adam, I was only calling to congratulate you," James said in his drunken voice. Adam talked with James for five or ten minutes before getting off of the phone. While he talked with James, Lisa put Andre to bed and dressed in a lingerie that would certainly get his attention.

When Adam entered the room, the aroma therapy candle scent nearly took his breath away. "The room smells nice," Adam said as he noticed Lisa lying in a sexy pose. "Stand still and allow me to undress you. I think it's the least that I can do for the future doctor. Something inside of me got excited and I lit up like a light bulb when I saw you walking across that stage," Lisa said as she removed Adam shirt and unbuckled his pants. Adam looked at Lisa with a smile on his face as he watched her undress him. Once he was naked, Lisa laid down and spread her legs and said, "I'm not ready to have another child, but I want you to give it to me as if we were making another one. Make me feel like that woman you want me to be," Lisa said as she sat up in bed.

Slowly, and gently, Adam got into bed and ran his hand along Lisa's firm thighs. "You feel good. Every time I touch you; you feel good. Feel better than you did when we first got together," Adam whispered as he gently ran his tongue over her nipple. Lisa sighed as Adam slowly parted her thighs. "This is something that you haven't done in a long time," Lisa remarked as she pushed Adam's head down between her moist thighs. Playfully, he quickly moved his tongue over her protruding clitoris.

With each flicker from his tongue, a chill ran down Lisa's spine. "I'm all yours, Adam. Take me any way that you want me," she whispered between her soft moans and sighs. Getting up from his crouched position, Adam turned on the radio and went back to what he was doing. As the music played softly, he took his time licking her in the softest place. Lisa's juices covered his face as Adam worked to bring her to a climax. "I don't want to come, baby," Lisa said as she writhed before him. Inserting one, then two fingers into her wet hole, Adam continued licking her love button. Lisa held out for as long as she could before she placed her face into the pillow and yelled. As she rubbed her breast, Lisa removed the lingerie while she kept moaning and reaching for Adam's head.

Overwhelmed by the feeling of ecstacy, Lisa quickly pushed Adam's head away from its present place. "Baby, you've got to stop for a minute," Lisa said as her chest heaved up and down. Under regular circumstances, I would go to sleep and leave you setting here," she said jokingly as Adam climbed between her legs. "Baby, I think you had better use a condom, because I'm not ready to have another child running around, nor did I bring my birth control pills. Besides, Andre is a hand full." Adam quickly stopped what he was doing and put on a condom. "Now, where were we," Adam asked as he placed the penis head up against her swollen lips?

As Adam worked his way inside of her wetness, Lisa opened her legs wide, to receive all of him. With a quick push, he was inside. Lisa's vagina was so warm that it felt as if it was burning the skin off of his penis. However, she was very tight, and getting inside of her was as pleasurable as lying between her moist thighs. They both had their backs arched as he gave, and she took. Lisa raised her legs high and wrapped her arms around Adam's neck. "Ride it, daddy," Lisa said as Adam hit her hot spot. "Is that where you want it? Does it feel okay to you, or should I give you more," Adam asked as pellets of sweat covered his forehead?

Before either one of them climaxed, Lisa rolled Adam onto his back and straddled his waist. Forcefully, she climbed down on his rigid shaft, and bounced up and down as Adam applied his strokes. With each stroke, Lisa let out a loud moan or a soft sigh. She came repeatedly, as Adam was drained of all his sperm. Still wanting more of him inside of her, Lisa kept Adam up for another hour-and-a-half before ending their session.

When Lisa awakened on Sunday morning, she rose to the smell of fresh bacon and sausages. When she got out of the bed, Lisa went into the living room and watched from the distance, as Adam ate along side Andre. 'I can't wait for the three of us to be together as a family. He's so attractive sitting there with his son. Adam Harris, the future physician and full time director of gynecology. Lisa Harris, wife of renown gynecologists, Adam Harris,' she thought while staring at the two of them playing and eating. "Hey, what's my man doing with my son? Is daddy feeding the little man," Lisa asked jokingly as she placed her hand on Adam's shoulder? "Good morning. I heard the baby making noise, so I got out of bed and fixed breakfast for the two of you. Do you have an appetite," Adam asked as he wiped the stain on Andre's shirt?

Dressed in a robe, Lisa slowly walked toward the kitchen as she tried to entice Adam with her beauty. "You're walking like someone who wants to get in trouble. Didn't you get enough pleasure last night," he asked in a devilish tone? Lisa grinned as she took a coffee mug from the cabinet. "I never get enough. I just take a break," she said playfully. Adam laughed as he continued playing with Andre. "Did you hear that son? She said that she never gets enough of your dad. Do you think that I should take her statement to another level," he asked as he threw Andre into the air? "Don't do that Adam, because it makes me nervous to see him thrown into the air. Besides, he might throw-up on you," Lisa said as she shook her head in disbelief.

Once she poured her coffee, Lisa walked over to the table and sat down. Playfully, she and Adam teased Andre and tickled his feet. "You can go and play with your toys," Adam said as he placed Andre on the floor. "Hi, baby," Adam remarked as he leaned forward to give Lisa a kiss. "Are you going to take care of me before I leave this afternoon," Lisa asked as she sipped her coffee? Adam stood up and asked, "Don't you know the answer to that question? You are going to be so relaxed when you leave that you're going to fall asleep as soon as the plane lifts off." "Once Andre takes his nap, you and I are going to have a long talk," Adam said as he did humping motions at the back of his chair. Grinning, Lisa replied, "We'll see if you can do a repeat of last night, Mr. Harris." He then went into Andre's room and began watching television with him.

While he and Lisa waited for Andre to fall asleep, they managed to finish packing the suitcases for the return trip to Chicago. Just as Lisa gathered the last piece of clothing, she peeked in Andre's room and noticed that he was sleeping. Lisa put a shirt in the luggage and went into the bedroom, where Adam was watching sports highlights. Immediately, Lisa began taking off her clothes as she said, "Your son is asleep, so it's time for you to stand up to your promise."

Without taking his eyes off of the television screen, Adam removed his shorts and underwear. "Give it to me," Adam said as Lisa climbed into bed. "Put a condom on, Adam. I told you that I wasn't ready to have another kid. We're only going to pretend that we're making another one. You know, just go through the motions." Adam put on a condom and the show began. Lying on her back with one leg raised, Adam thrust his manhood into her wet vagina. "How wet can you get it," Adam asked as he gave her long strokes? "How wet does your cock want it, Adam," Lisa asked as she took his thrust?

With her eyes closed, Lisa's body shook as she reached her climax. As her juices rushed out, the sight of his glistening penis made Adam as horny-as-ever. Feeling like he was about to lose control and release his wad, Adam humped faster as Lisa begged him not to stop. Once they came, Lisa tried to drain all of the sperm from Adam's balls. When she was sure that he was dry, she climbed off of his penis and began sucking the head of it. Adam squirmed across the bed as the feeling of her tongue brought him to another climax.

After a restful sleep, Lisa was awakened by the telephone ringing. She talked for a few minutes and then hang-up the receiver. "Adam, I need you to get up because your parents said that they'll be ready to leave shortly. They want us to meet them at their hotel in an hour." Quickly, Adam got out of bed and went into the bathroom. "Don't start the shower without me," Lisa called out as she went into the living room.

Adam didn't pay Lisa any attention, as he turned on the shower. Playfully, Lisa got into the shower and said, "Sometimes you can be so hard headed." Adam began washing her body, and later, she washed his. "Ooh, I'm going to miss you so much," Lisa remarked as she washed his rigid penis. "I'll be home to take care of you in a couple of weeks," he replied as she squeezed her butt cheeks together. "Two weeks is too long. I want you to come with us today," Lisa said with a straight face.

Her statement changed the mood and Adam got out of the shower. Throwing the wash towel into the sink, Lisa followed Adam into the bedroom. "Why can't you come with us? You're out of school and the time is definitely right. What are you going to do if you stay here for the entire summer," she asked with frustration in her voice? Adam didn't say a word as he continued drying off.

The drive to the hotel seemed to have taken forever, as Adam would not say anything to Lisa. "Adam Harris, you are going to give me some kind of answer before I get out of this car," she said in an angry tone. Never taking his eye's off the road, Adam said, "I have a life here in Michigan and I'm not going to leave for a couple of weeks. Something told me that you were going to try to persuade me to come home. Well, I'm not leaving right now."

Lisa believed that he was going to stay in Michigan because he had other women's needs to take care of. "I didn't want to believe it, but you're staying here because you have another woman to see," Lisa said as she looked out of the passengers window. Continuously, she told Adam how she felt and what she believed was the reason for him not leaving. As they pulled the car into the hotel parking lot, Adam sighed and got out of the car. Opening the trunk and taking their luggage out, he replied, "You can believe anything you choose too. I'm not going to Chicago, now, and that's my final word." Taking Andre in her arms, Lisa stormed into the hotel, where she found Adam's parents waiting in the lobby.

When Adam walked into the hotel carrying the duffel bags, his mom walked up to him and asked if everything was okay between him and Lisa. Adam dropped the bags and shrugged his shoulders. "She's upset, but it will pass. We've been arguing about why I'm not going back to Chicago with her and Andre." Gail put her finger over her lips. "I don't want to hear any more."

Adam then received a hug and a firm hand shake from his dad as they exchanged words. He then said good-byes to his brother and sister, before everyone left for the airport. When he got to Lisa, Adam gave her a hug and said, "I hope you have a good flight," as he pinched Andre's cheek. "I'll see you in a couple of weeks, son." Adam then picked up the duffel bags and carried them out to the limousine. "You guys get to travel to the airport in style," he said. After they said their final good-bye's, Adam returned to his truck and drove away.

'This woman must be crazy to think that I'm going back to Chicago, when I've gotten myself established here. I just graduated and I haven't had a chance to finish celebrating. Going home is the last thing on my mind. What will be good right now is a hot meal and a good movie. Once I eat something,

I'll be able to get some sleep and just chill out. Lisa acts as if she doesn't understand what it's like to be tired after a semester. Hell, I might go to sleep and not wake up for a couple of days,' Adam thought. "My body may not know how to act once it gets a full nights rest," Adam said as he drove along the crowded street.

It appeared that after the graduation, there were more people on the road, and it only heightened Adam's interest in wanting to get home. As he made his way to the condo, his cell phone rang several times before he answered it. That's probably Lisa calling, to apologize for being silly," Adam said as he reached for the phone. When he looked at the display screen, he noticed that it was a call from Stacey. In a cheerful voice, Adam answered the phone and he and Stacey talked until he arrived at the condo. The conversation put a twinkle in his eye's as he and Stacey planned to get together and celebrate his graduation. "Everything is going back to normal," Adam said as he got out of the car. Before he was able to enter the home, another call came through, and then another. Adam appreciated the attention, but he saw this as an opportunity to do his thing, get educated and have an okay summer.

CHAPTER
THIRTY-ONE

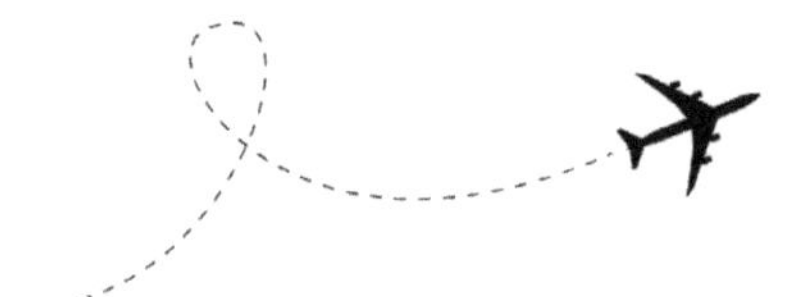

Adam's summer went exactly as planned. He and Lisa made up and broke up several times over the summer, while he continued putting miles on his car, driving to and from Chicago. Once he moved out of the dormitory and into the condo, the sex continued to roll in. He was no longer sleeping with the same girls, as other women were giving him tons of attention. Whenever he wasn't bothered with Lisa, there was always someone there to keep him warm over the summer months. At this point, Adam viewed himself as a well-rounded student. The school was shut down for the summer, but class was still in session.

Excited about attending grad. school, Adam eagerly anticipated on seeing the two weeks remaining, to fly by. It was not only a time to start his classes, but his intern program was also set to start within two weeks. To his surprise, Adam received a phone call late one Friday night from Dr. Sullivan. Excited about hearing her voice, he listened attentively as she invited him to spend the day at her home.

He accepted the invitation and they concluded their fifteen minute conversation. "Yes, I would be happy to come to your home," Adam shouted as he cheerfully skipped through the house! 'I wonder if I should take something with me, like a case of coolers or a nice wine,' he thought after opening the refrigerator. "I'll just play it by ear," Adam whispered as he closed the refrigerator and blew a kiss at the picture of Andre that was setting nearby.

Once he spoke with Dr. Sullivan that bright and sunny morning, Adam got dressed and ventured off to her home. Wearing a large smile and catching the sights, he listened to the radio as he thought happy thoughts and stared out of the window. Checking the addresses on the homes, Adam pulled into the driveway of the home that Dr. Sullivan described to him. "Damn, she's got a nice looking place," Adam said as he caught a glimpse of the horses next door. Turning off the engine and opening a pack of gum, Adam placed a piece in his mouth and got out of the truck.

"Come inside," a voice called out. Amazed at the scenery, he looked at everything within sight. Gliding past the outdoor furniture, Adam walked through the sliding door that lead into the kitchen. "Did you have any problems finding the house? A lot of my friends and co-workers complain that it's difficult to find, especially at night," Dr. Sullivan said as she prepared a chef salad.

Stepping up to the kitchen counter, Adam replied, "The directions were clear and the ride was pleasant. This area has a country setting, at least until you get into this subdivision. I was surprised at how quickly the scenery changed. Have you been living here for a long time," he asked with a smile as she handed him a glass of fresh lemonade? "I've been in this home for thirteen years. My ex-husband and I purchased it before he and I separated. So, my kids went off to college, and I've been here alone since they left. When they're home, my son stays here with me, and my daughter visits. Usually when she's here, she stays with her boyfriend or one of her girlfriends. You're welcome to look around while I finish preparing lunch," she said in a cheerful voice.

"This lemonade is good, Adam said as he looked at the pictures that lined her living room wall and mantle. When he came to the picture of a tanned young lady with long sandy colored hair, Adam found it difficult to take his attention off of the photo. 'Damn, she's cute-as-hell,' Adam thought as he searched for family resemblance. "Is this girl dressed in the graduation robe your daughter," he asked, hoping that she would say no? With a glass of lemonade in hand, Dr. Sullivan entered the room and stood next to Adam.

"That's my daughter, Stephanie, who's currently attending Arizona State University. This is her second year, and she likes it, so far. Sometimes she's so unpredictable that it's unbelievable," Dr. Sullivan remarked as she began to point at a photo of two twin males. "These are my son's, Jordan and Jonathan, whom are both attending Purdue University on athletic scholarships. This is their first year, and I hope that it goes well for them, " she said. Adam then took a seat on the sofa as he watched Dr. Sullivan place the photos back where they belonged. The sofa cushions were so soft that his entire body sank into the material. "These cushions are softer than a baby's butt," Adam whispered to himself.

Standing 5'11, Dr. Sullivan sat down next to Adam. "I did the outdoor grilling this morning, so there's not anything left to prepare. Would you like to go into the basement and watch a movie or a sports program," the doctor asked as she watched Adam drink his lemonade? Adam sat the empty glass down, and said, "We can do whatever you choose, because I'm your guest. However, a good movie would be okay right about now. Do you have any pets, Dr. Sullivan," he asked as she stood up? Picking up Adam's glass from the table, she took it into the kitchen. "I don't care much for animals, because when they die it takes a lot out of you. By the way, call me Sharon."

The good doctor had a terrific figure, and Adam couldn't resist admiring it as she walked around in of the kitchen. Her round butt moved in a rhythm that enticed the young intern. "My Lord," he whispered to himself as he stared at her hips moving from right-to left. "Come with me, Adam," Sharon called out as she opened a door off of the kitchen. "My entertainment center is in the basement," Sharon said as Adam followed her with a fresh glass of lemonade.

Once he was in the basement, Adam was amazed at how nicely it was decorated. There was a 65' inch flat screen television in the corner of the room, accented by matching recliners and surround sound speakers. In the center of the room, there was a cherry colored sofa that highlighted the throw rug that covered a portion of the floor. On the opposite side of the room, there was a bar that was stocked with all sorts of drinks. "Your basement is fantastic. Do you throw many parties," he asked as Sharon sat in one of the recliners? "I don't come down her often," she replied while turning on the television.

Adam then walked over and took a seat in the recliner, opposite Dr. Sullivan's. "This is where my kids hang out when they're home. The most that I'll do down here is dust the furniture or vacuum the floor. Hey, why don't you kick your shoes off and get comfortable," Sharon said as she ran her fingers through her shoulder length hair. Not saying anything to one-another, Adam slowly looked through Sharon's list of movies.

When he came across one that would be interesting, he put it into the DVD player. "Let's watch 'Once Upon a Time in Mexico,' because I've never watched it in its entirety," he said. Dr. Sullivan took a sip from her glass and said, "I'm an open-minded German woman, so whatever you choose is okay with me. Although, I was just thinking that you and I are going to get along well. You're smart, and that's exactly the kind of person I need working by my side. Mr. Dillon may not have told you, but I don't usually work with interns," Sharon said as she read the movie credits. "Thank you for accepting me into the program," Adam said as he looked over at Sharon.

Hours went by, and although engrossed in their second movie, Sharon cleared away the dishes and dimmed the basement lights. "I hope you don't mind my turning down the lights. Once I eat something, I'm no good. All I want to do is get into something comfortable and lie down. By the way, Adam, do you have a girlfriend? Whether you do or not, you'd better watch your back around the hospital, because those nurses are searching high and low for a black man," Dr. Sullivan said as a warning to Adam. Adam grinned and thought to himself, 'I'm not worried about those nurses.'

"Are any of those nurses German like yourself," Adam asked as he placed his glass of lemonade down? Dr. Sullivan picked her glass up from the floor and asked, "Does it matter what origin they are? Do you have any prejudices about German women or white women in general?" "I heard that German women were freaky when it came to black men. However, If any of them are German, then I'm interested. I need someone who can turn me out. You know, give it to me so well that I begin walking backwards down the street with a flashlight, looking for them in the day time," he said jokingly.

Dr. Sullivan laughed hysterically and asked, "Do you think I'm a freak, Adam? Maybe my husband divorced me because he couldn't keep up. What do you think?" With a look of curiosity on his face, he asked, "Were you married to a black man, or was he of some other race?" Clearing her throat, Sharon explained to Adam that he was a high yellow black man with a fondness for women, especially white women.

Near the end of the second movie, Dr. Sullivan sat on the sofa with Adam and poured her life out to him. She talked about her ex-husband and why she hasn't dated in more than three years. Adam heard stories about her children and what lead to the break up of her and Carl. "Carl and I divorced because he was in-love with his secretary," she said. She's thirty-some years younger than I, and pregnant with their second child."

"Apparently, she became pregnant with the first child while we were going through our divorce. Our kids have begun to accept the fact that we're not together, but they're not too crazy about his wife. After-all, Tiffany is only a few years younger than my daughter. I've asked Carl several times about how that makes him feel, and all he does is sigh and change the subject.

We've been divorced for four years and I haven't had sex since our last time together. I thought that by having sex with him, our marriage would be restored, but it didn't work. What hurt me the most is the fact that we were married for twenty seven years, and I lost him to a younger woman. However, I don't feel bad about it, because she recently told me that he's now dating someone who's four years younger than she is," Dr. Sullivan said as she lay on the sofa with her feet resting on Adam's legs.

"Would you like a drink, Adam, or do you drink? If you do, then help yourself to anything that's on the bar," Sharon said. Adam felt the physical attraction between him and Dr. Sullivan, but he didn't want to make any hasty decisions. Lifting her feet off of his legs, Adam stood up and she said, "I'll have whatever you have." While Sharon changed the movie in the DVD player, Adam walked over to the bar and began preparing their drinks. "I like Seagram and orange juice," Adam said. Dr. Sullivan never heard a word that Adam had said as she was lost in her own world. With her rear end pointed in his direction, Adam made several glances at it while he sighed. 'This woman has a bad body,' Adam thought as he placed ice cubes in their glasses. "Tell me if this is too strong," Adam said as he approached her. Slowly rising from her kneeling position, Sharon caught Adam staring at her rear end. 'Damn, this young man is so attractive. I bet a young buck like that is good in bed,' Dr. Sullivan thought as she took her drink from his strong hand. "Here's a toast to a pleasant evening," Sharon said as they tapped their glasses together. "Ting," was the sound the glasses made before they took a sip.

"Do you prefer young women or older women," Dr. Sullivan asked as they took their seats on the sofa? Shocked by the question, Adam cleared his throat and remarked, "I hope your drink isn't too strong." After taking a sip from her glass, Sharon replied, "After talking about Carl, you can give me as many strong drinks as I can stand. However, this drink is potent. Now, are you going to answer my question, or should I assume that you like young German girls, with firm bodies."

Adam laughed and asked, "Why does the woman have to be German? A woman is a woman no matter what age she is, or origin." Dr. Sullivan finished her drink in one gulp and said, "I thought you had a thing for German women, or is it the rumors about German women that has you so excited?" Taking the glass from her hand and asking if she wanted a refill, Adam took both glasses and walked over to the bar.

"I dated a German girl during my freshman year, and she was wild. Every time we got together, it was an unforgettable moment. Although, we weren't meant to be together, because I wasn't ready for a relationship, and she was involved with a guy in the military. All she wanted to do was have sex, because like yourself, she wasn't getting any satisfaction," Adam stated as he approached Sharon with a fresh drink. Dr. Sullivan's eye's danced as she watched Adam slowly approach her. With her eyes focused on his crotch, she took the drink from his hand.

Sharon and Adam drank four glasses of Seagram and orange juice together before they realized that they were tipsy, and in the mood. "You're welcome to spend the night, because after drinking these many drinks, no one should be allowed to drive. Speaking for myself, I haven't had these many drinks since Carl and I separated." Although their speech was slurred, they managed to get their point across.

Despite how tipsy they were, Adam and Sharon managed to hold their liquor as they continued talking, and pouring more drinks. Sitting on the sofa with her legs spread, Sharon took deep breaths to clear her mind. Walking over to the DVD player to remove the movie they were watching, Dr. Sullivan asked, "Would you mind if we watch this movie in my bedroom? I'm tipsy, but not enough to want to go to sleep in the basement." Adam sighed and told Sharon that it would be okay with him.

Turning off the television, she told Adam to take the liquor and orange juice from the bar and bring it to the bedroom. Adam took the liquor and placed it under his arm while he held the bottle of orange juice, and glasses. Following Sharon upstairs, he had the pleasure of watching her behind move poetically as they made their way from the basement. "You've got a nice butt, Dr. Sullivan," Adam said as he followed closely. Looking back at him, she asked, "Are you making a pass at me or is that your liquor talking, Mr. Harris?" Closing the door behind him, Adam remarked, "I'm just giving you a compliment, doctor."

Leading him into the bedroom, she told Adam to make himself comfortable while she took a shower. "If you like, you're welcome to take a shower after I'm done," she said, hoping that he would agree to her suggestion. Adam poured their drinks and left out the ice. "Thanks, Sharon. Maybe I'll take you up on your offer." As the doctor went into the bathroom, Adam scanned through the cable channels. Minutes later, Dr. Sullivan called Adam into the bathroom and asked him to wash her back.

Obliged to do it, Adam removed his socks and went into the steamy bathroom. When he opened the shower door, he stared at her tanned rear end as she handed him a sponge. 'This woman's body is unbelievable. I've got to touch her butt at least once,' he thought while lathering her back with shower gel. Sighing as if she enjoyed his touch, Sharon asked, "Are you going to answer my question, Adam?" He thought for a minute about her question and said, "I like women regardless of their age. If they're legal and have their head on right, then we can get together. But, I must admit that there are some very attractive women here in Michigan." While running the sponge across her butt, Dr. Sullivan glanced over her shoulder at Adam, who then handed the sponge back to her.

Dr. Sullivan came out of the shower with a towel wrapped around her waist and said, "The shower is all yours! If you need something to slip into, then just let me know. I don't want you to be embarrassed setting here next to me." Adam got up from the bed and went into the steamy bathroom and removed his clothes. Taking a wash cloth into his hand, he got into the shower and began lathering his body.

Before he finished showering, Sharon went into the bathroom and asked, "Would you like for me to wash your back?" Without saying a word, Adam pushed the shower door open and handed her his wash towel. Dr. Sullivan washed his muscular back, while she stared at his tight, chocolate, rear-end. Overwhelmed by his appearance, she gave the wash cloth to Adam and hurried out of the bathroom, feeling as if she was spinning out of control.

Minutes later, Adam came out of the bathroom with a towel wrapped around his waist. He then noticed Dr. Sullivan lying on the bed in a short night gown. It didn't reveal much, but just seeing her voluptuous thighs was all he needed to get aroused. "Get your drink and have a seat next to me," she said flirtatiously. Approaching the ice bucket, Adam put ice into his drink and took a seat on the bed. Setting with the lights dimmed, Sharon sat in a way that gave Adam a better view of her thighs, calves, and hairy crotch. "Do you want children someday, Adam?" Stirring the drink with his pinky finger, Adam replied that he wanted more kids someday. "I have a son who lives with his mom in Chicago, and right now, he's more than a hand full."

Setting her glass on the night stand, Dr. Sullivan asked, "When was the last time you saw each other?" "Are you talking about my son and me, or are you talking about his mom?" Sharon told him that she was referring to him and his son. Adam then told her that he goes home to visit his son at least twice a month. Making their conversation short, Sharon finished her drink and opened Adam's towel to release his chocolate treasure.

Taking it in hand, Sharon ran her hand along his shaft and made circular motions around the head. "This feels so damn good! You need to leave this with me," she said jokingly. "Would you know what to do with it," he asked? "After all, it's been a long time since you've held a real one. You probably forgot what a nice one taste like," he whispered as she kept stroking him with her hand.

While Adam stared at the television, Dr. Sullivan leaned toward him and put his penis in her mouth. "Do you like the way it taste," Adam asked while moaning softly? "This black pipe tastes good. I wish I had something like this laying beside me every night. Just lay back and enjoy this," Sharon said softly as she soaked his penis with her saliva. Adam thrust his penis in her mouth as she brought him close to a climax.

Wanting to return the favor, Adam pushed her away and got between her legs. Sucking on her breast, and then her stomach, he gently placed his tongue on her love button. Her long legs spread wide, Adam licked and sucked on her clit. Sharon came so quickly that it surprised both of them. Removing her gown, she begged Adam to give her what she wanted.

He then got out of bed and went to the bathroom to get a condom from his pocket. When he returned, Sharon explained to him that she couldn't get pregnant, and that using a condom wasn't necessary. Adam tossed the condom onto the floor and resumed his position. The head of his penis was so large that Dr. Sullivan let out a deep moan as he worked his way inside. "Give me that good love, Adam," Dr. Sullivan said as her hole opened up to receive him. Daddy's going to take care of you, Adam whispered as he began to apply deep, slow strokes.

Dr. Sullivan spread her legs as far as possible, as she gave him all that she had. What started out as a few strokes, lasted all night. Dr. Sullivan had not had sex in such a long time that she would not let Adam rest for a moment. Like a bucking bull, she bounced on him until the sun rose. It surprised both of them, because he was sure that she would have enough by now. "I'm going to break this monster off in your hole," Adam said as he came for the last time.

Chest heaving up and down like someone who had just run a race, Sharon put her hand over her eyes as the room had begun to spin. "I'm not sure if it was the drink or my inner desire that made me behave like that. However, I must say that I had a good time and now I've got to get some sleep," Sharon said as she turned to her side. His fat snake facing her round butt, Adam lifted her leg and entered her foo foo from the rear. "Just one more shot before we call it quits," Adam whispered as she anticipated the last ride.

Already wet, Adam slid into her hole and began pumping slowly/rhythmically. Overwhelmed with lust, he and Sharon managed to come at the same time. The noises they made were so passionate that they weren't able to make another sound. Removing his penis and placing his arm around her waist, they drifted off to sleep.

When Adam rose that evening around 4:08pm, he noticed that Sharon was not in bed. Before he could call her name, he heard a set of keys fall onto a hard surface. Dr. Sullivan then entered the room and sat on the side of the bed. She began undressing as she did not know that Adam was awake. "Take your panties off and come here," Adam whispered, startling Sharon. "I thought you were asleep. If you want me to take my panties off, then give me a few minutes to brush my teeth and freshen up," Sharon said as she finished undressing. Dr. Sullivan went into the bathroom and when she returned, Adam was lying on his back, while his penis gave rise to the sheets, creating a tee-pee effect.

As she climbed into bed, pulled the sheets back and took a seat on his rigid love pole, Dr. Sullivan gently rode Adam until her hole was open and ready for action. Taking her hair into her hands and arching her back, Sharon's thighs bucked against Adam as she rode him; as if it was her first time, or her last time being with him. "Oh, your prick hurts. Give me more of it, Adam. Ride this aged pussy," Sharon cried as she glistened every inch of his member. Her juices flowed so heavily that it soaked the sheets beneath him.

Pulling her down on top of his chest, Adam clutched her butt cheeks and gave her good, steady strokes. When her wet tongue wasn't in his ear, she cried out for more. "Take all of me," Dr. Sullivan said as she came. "Oh, baby, just let me get some rest and we can finish where we left off," she whispered in his ear. Adam didn't pay her any attention as he took her for two more laps. Within an hour-and-a-half, Dr. Sullivan came so many times that she lost count. Unable to say another word, she rolled off of Adam and immediately fell asleep.

CHAPTER
THIRTY-TWO

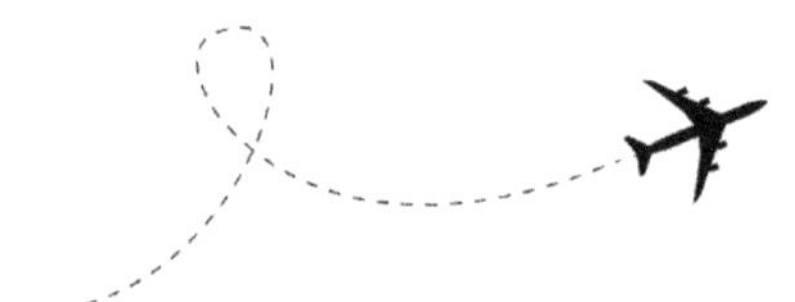

Once his internship began, Adam gave his all to his studies and to his new supervisor/instructor. When he wasn't assisting Dr. Sullivan in the pre-natal unit, or triage, Adam was busy studying and trying to take care of Dr. Sullivan's sexual needs. During the two weeks that lead up to the beginning of the school semester, he and Dr. Sullivan had sex like rabbits as she could not get enough. While at the hospital, they remained professional, but when the time was right, he had Dr. Sullivan screaming like some of her patients. When they were around other faculty members, they behave professionally, but many would have been surprised to know that they were going home together.

At this stage of the game, not only were they going home together, but he had received a key to the house. Sharon told Adam that she wanted to see him after work, and that he needed his own key. Many days she would come home from working overtime and find Adam walking through the house wearing a stiff one. The sight of him being there made the doctor happy, because she knew the outcome of seeing him.

Their relationship lasted for months, and neither of them gave away their secret. Adam found Sharon attractive, and the trinkets were nice also. Unlike the young girls, Sharon knew the types of gifts that Adam would appreciate. She gave gifts like an adult woman, while others gave gifts like high school girls experiencing their first orgasm. However, Adam never let anything taking place between them get in the way of his studies or his work at the hospital.

"How would you like to get together this weekend for a picnic? It's supposed to be the last nice weather weekend that we're going to have," Dr. Sullivan said to Adam before he punched out for the day. "That would be nice," Adam said as he removed his scrubs. "I'll let you know when and where by this Thursday, but no later than Friday," Sharon said as she left to shower after a delivery. "Oh, by the way, bring something that you know I'm going to like," Sharon said as she pointed toward her crotch. Adam grinned as he continued removing his soiled clothes.

Once the weekend arrived, Adam was invited to meet Sharon at her home, which sat off of the water. When he arrived, she greeted him at the back door with a picnic basket in hand. "Have you decided where we're going to have the picnic," he asked as he held the door for her? Giving him a quick kiss, she replied, "It's a surprise, so don't ask any questions. Besides, you just make sure that you have something special for me.

"While you're waiting for me to finish packing, you can get into the truck and get comfortable," Sharon said as she went back into the house. 'This woman is something else,' Adam thought as he climbed into the front seat of her Ford Explorer. Seconds after getting comfortable, Sharon locked the house up and got into the driver's seat. "Let's have some fun, Mr. Harris. After the long week that we've had, I think we deserve to have a quiet evening alone on the last nice day of the year. Did you manage to get any studying done this week," Dr. Sullivan asked as she placed her hand on his thigh? "Oh, I've got to stay on top of my studies," Adam said in a confident tone. However, once he made that statement, Sharon turned up the radio volume as they drove along not saying a word to one another.

Surprisingly, Dr. Sullivan drove through the front gate of a local marina and parked her car as Adam looked on in amazement. "Are you going to tell me that you have a boat," Adam asked as he looked at all of the yachts and speedboats present? There were hoards of people standing around the docks socializing and detailing their cruisers. "Help me get the things from in-back, and we can begin our day," she said as Adam stood outside of the truck wearing a pair of sun glasses, looking cool. 'This woman has it going on. Having Dr. Sullivan for a boss gives me a positive edge, because if I wasn't dark, people would probably think I'm her son,' Adam thought as he looked at the firm bodies standing nearby.

Dr. Sullivan handed Adam the picnic basket and closed the hatch. "Let's take a walk," Sharon said as she made her way toward a mass of people. "Which one of these is yours," Adam asked excitedly? Sharon never said a word as she walked ahead of Adam. Feeling as young as he looked, she tried her best to stay ahead of the competition that was eye balling her love interest. Although, many of the on lookers didn't have a body that looked half as good as hers.

"How much further do we have to walk," Adam asked as Sharon turned toward the dock where her boat was setting? "Watch your step, because it can be a little slippery," she said as they climbed onto the

44' Sea Ray Express. Dr. Sullivan opened the door leading to the lower level and invited Adam to come down and join her. "My husband and I purchased this before we divorced and the judge granted it to me in the settlement. Carl was upset about the judges decision, but that's life," Sharon said as she placed her purse on the table.

Dr. Sullivan then took the picnic basket from Adam and gave him a long, passionate kiss. "I've been planning this for weeks. You just don't know how you make me feel inside. When we're at work, I look at you and I want to rip your clothes off and just hold you close to me," Sharon remarked as she tightened her grip around Adam's neck. 'I've heard of big hugs, but this one is choking me to death,' Adam thought as he placed his arms around her waist. "Now, go up-top and enjoy the sun. This is such a beautiful day. Don't you think this is a beautiful day, Adam," Dr. Sullivan asked as she removed her pants, revealing a bikini bottom, and a halter top, covered by a tee-shirt? Adam ran his hands across his head and said, "It's a gorgeous day, and If you lead the way, then I'll follow."

Thanks to their early start, Adam and Sharon were able to spend the entire afternoon at sea. She drove the cruiser into the middle of the ocean and that's where they remained for the evening. They sat on the deck and talked for hours. When they weren't talking on deck, Dr. Sullivan was giving him blow-jobs on deck. "This is amazing," was the only phrase that ran through Adam' mind as he enjoyed the motherly attention. When it came time for them to eat, Adam looked forward to a meal, because he needed it to replenish his strength. Although, after the meal, Sharon expected more from him.

The motion in the ocean, became a true statement as they screwed over every inch of the boat. These fuck-buddies began having sex inside of the cabin and when the sun went down, they had sex on the outer deck. The deck was small, but they managed to accomplish their goal. For hours, Adam gave Dr. Sullivan everything he could possibly give her. He turned her in every position he could come up with, and he didn't give her a chance to scream for help. "I'm going to shut this woman's mouth once and for all,' Adam whispered as he dug deep into the crevice of her dormant womb.

When they were done, Sharon had been through so much that it hurt when she tried to pee. It was at that point that she knew that she had received enough good loving to last her a while. "Do you want some more of this," Adam shouted as he held his erect member in his hand?! With a sound of nervousness in her voice, Sharon said, "I'll take my cell phone and call the Coast Guard for help if you come near me with that thing. You did your job so well that it hurts me to use the bathroom. I think I need to take a break from you for a couple of days. If I keep messing with that thing, I'll go in to work tomorrow walking like someone whose rode a horse over the weekend. Don't call me, I'll call you, Sharon said as she sat with her hand between her legs.

Adam turned on the overhead cabin light and

searched for his clothes, that were underneath her clothes. "I should have told you to stop after you sucked my clit and took me for three rounds," Sharon remarked as she sat shaking her head. "Sometimes you've got to know when to stop," Adam said with a grin as he put his tee-shirt on.

Dr. Sullivan moved slowly as she struggled to grasp the fact that this young man had worn her out sexually. "I'm too old for this," Sharon said as she began to put her clothes on. Sitting with her panties in her hand, Dr. Sullivan's legs were too numb for her to lift them and put her panties on. Adam grinned as he watched the old girl get herself together. "Hey, it's just what the doctor ordered."

CHAPTER
THIRTY-THREE

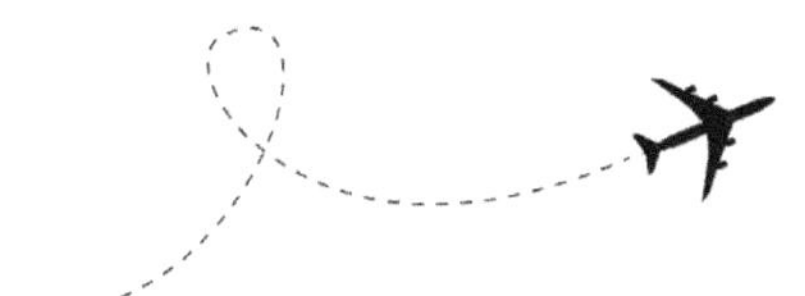

The three years of residency went by quickly, as Adam tried to break off his relationship with Dr. Sullivan several times. Although he managed to keep Lisa satisfied, Dr. Sullivan became possessive as she feared that she would lose her lover. Whether at work or at home, Sharon put pressure on Adam, as she tried to persuade him to remain in Michigan. "We can be secret lovers for the rest of our lives," is what she said to Adam on many occasions. As his graduation commencement grew closer, Adam did his best to give Dr. Sullivan all of the sex that he had give. However, he and Lisa continued making arrangements/plans to be together as a family.

When he arrived at the hospital, Adam found Dr. Sullivan waiting for him in her office. With an unpleasant look on her face, she invited Adam to sit down. "Your commencement is Saturday, and I've been giving our relationship a lot of thought," she said. "What I've discovered is that I'm in love with you, and it doesn't seem to make a difference to you. If it mattered, then you would strongly consider remaining here at the hospital. I understand that you have a long-standing relationship with your son's mother, and I respect that."

Getting up from her chair, Dr. Sullivan approached Adam, slowly. "I need an answer from you by Friday, because I'm an emotional wreck. You came into my life and I feel as if I've taken advantage of you, and I'm sorry for doing that." Adam sat quietly as he listened to her. Sharon then gave Adam a kiss and took two steps back. Adam placed his fingers over his mouth and said, "I'll be leaving this intern/

residency position on Thursday, and I'll have my answer by then." Adam then stood up and gave Dr. Sullivan a warm embrace before leaving the room.

As the next three days went by, Adam managed to avoid Dr. Sullivan as he kept their relationship professional. They maintained a good working relationship, but it eventually came to an end. Once Adam realized that Lisa had arrived from Chicago, he returned Dr. Sullivan's house key and informed her that their fling was finished. Hurt, Dr. Sullivan ran from her office with tears in her eye's.

Shrugging his shoulders, Adam placed his badge on her desk and walked away. Never turning around, Adam ran out to his truck, and he hurried to the airport. Due to a mistake in flights, he had to travel to Metropolitan Airport to meet her. Adam didn't enjoy the trip, but it did allow the time to think about some things, before he and Lisa got together.

Confused about where he was, Adam drove around for thirty minutes. After speaking with security guards regarding flight arrivals, he finally located Lisa and Andre at the luggage pick up. Seeing Adam coming through the door, Andre pulled away from Lisa and ran to meet his dad. Arms open, Adam picked up his son and walked over to meet Lisa. After speaking to one another, they kissed each other and made their way to the parking structure. "You've finally done it, Adam," Lisa said as they walked toward the garage entrance. Adam didn't say a word as he looked in her eye's and smiled.

During their trip to Ann Arbor, they talked like two strangers as they discussed the latest events. They were both talkative individuals, but Lisa held the title in this match. After getting something to eat, and purchasing a movie, they returned to the condo where everything went back to normal. Adam knew that Dr. Sullivan had his address and phone number, but he hoped that she would not do anything drastic. After all, she was a hurt woman, who probably felt as if she had nothing else to lose.

Lisa and Adam put Andre to bed and the love making began. It had been one month since they had been together, and every stroke was on time. When they weren't watching the entertaining movie, the movie was watching them. Sweat poured down his chest as Lisa's body gyrated hysterically. Adam had her legs spread as he stood between them, banging away at her passion tunnel.

Lisa screamed for so long that she became hoarse. To help save her voice, Adam put a pillow over her head to muffle the screams. Happy to see each other, they made love until Lisa told Adam that she had enough. Lying on his back, covered in sweat and juices, Adam's heart beat fast as he worked to catch his breath. "I love it when you come home," Adam told Lisa as she struggled to stand on her weak legs. Together, they laughed and fell asleep before the movie ended.

When Saturday morning arrived, Adam and Andre got dressed as Lisa took her shower. Suddenly, Adam's cell phone rang and he answered it. To his surprise, Dr. Sullivan gave Adam her best wishes and said that she would see him at the commencement. For a moment, Adam felt like a heel for turning Dr. Sullivan down the way that he did. However, he shook the feeling off, and once dressed, he and Lisa left for the auditorium. Adam smiled a huge smile as he looked at the faces of his friends, family, parents and loved ones. Outside of the auditorium, he and his family took pictures, as hundreds of others gathered nearby. "Give me a good luck kiss, Lisa," Adam said as he joined the graduating class.

The graduation lasted longer than many expected it too, as everyone became impatient. Young and old, people began walking through the auditorium as the speaker kept talking. Asleep in the crowd, Adam wasn't aware of anything that was said or done, by the speaker. However, once the last words were spoken, Adam's eye's quickly opened. Shaking his head and wiping his eyes, Adam sat upright as he waited for his name to be called. Lisa and Andre sat on the edge of their seats as they eagerly anticipated on hearing Adam's name being called out of three hundred and twenty students.

Once they called his name, Adam stood up, walked to the stage, accepted his degree and ran away shouting. Excited to finally be considered a doctor, he sat amongst the others with a huge grin on his face and a look of relief in his eyes. Just then, his eye's met Dr. Sullivan's, and with a smile, they winked their eye's at each other and enjoyed the remainder of the ceremony.

Adam felt as if they were never going to say the last name as he looked in the balcony at Lisa and Andre. This moment produced one of the greatest feelings that Adam had ever experienced. He was surrounded by hundreds of friends, faculty and family, and it brought joy to his heart. Seeing the smiling faces was only half of the commencement, as he waited for the chance to say his final goodbyes. After the last name was finally called, everyone threw their hats into the sky, but Adam held onto his.

In hoards, people rushed toward the exit doors. The scene reminded Adam of the last commencement, but this time it was different. As he smiled and took pictures with many others, he suddenly dropped down on one knee in front of Lisa/family. Standing with her hand over her mouth, she listened as Adam spoke softly. "The student is now a grown man, and as a man, I would like for you to be my wife." Adam then placed a platinum and diamond engagement ring on Lisa's finger. Giving him a huge embrace, she said yes, as well wishers began clapping.

THE END!

www.ingramcontent.com/pod-product-compliance
Lightning Source LLC
Chambersburg PA
CBHW070721010826
48977CB00006B/124